UNNATURAL JUSTICE

By Su Ridley

Kenton Publishing

Published by KENTON PUBLISHING
The Granary,
Hatham Green Lane,
Stansted
SEVENOAKS
Kent, TN15 7PL
+44 (0) 1474 853669

www.suridley.com

First published in Great Britain in 2004 by
KENTON PUBLISHING

Cataloguing in Publication Data is available from the British Library

ISBN   0 9546223 0 8 (C format)

Typeset in Palatino by Ark Creative, Norwich

Printed and bound in Great Britain by
Mackays of Chatham plc, Chatham, Kent

To my husband Mike
whose constant support
has never wavered.

ACKNOWLEDGEMENTS:

I would like to thank and acknowledge the grateful support of all those who helped with this book:

Pat & Terry Martin; Ian Morton; Sheron Boyle and Detective Chief Superintendent Bob Taylor (retired); Damian Wilson; Leon Crisp; Ken Gibson; Eric & Margaret Chambers; Jan Mudge; Caron Rodgerson; Debbie Rendall; Eileen Swanson; James Lee; Dr Chris Blackburn; Pip Blackburn; David & Molly Williams; Ann Brooker; Steve & Jackie Whitby; Christopher Bell; Diane Richardson; Irene & Bob Sait; Mark & Tricia Eyles-Thomas; Roger Gray; Nigel Bowden; Philip Eccles; Sue Blackhall; Ken Connor; Maggie Howie and Paulene Blazdell-Williams.

Special thanks to Melissa Mudge for her research and secretarial skills, for which she was far too overqualified. And to my daughter Brigitte for designing the book jacket and for listening.

While all the characters in this story are fictitious, the hotels and restaurants do exist. I thoroughly recommend them…

Su Ridley, February 2004

UNNATURAL JUSTICE

Who thinks the law
has anything to do with justice?
It's what we have
because we can't have justice.

William McIlvanney

PROLOGUE

New Haven, Connecticut, 1950

'WHEN you came into this world just two weeks ago, I couldn't have been more happy. You were born into the greatest democracy on Earth - a place you could be proud to grow up in. Now, son, I'm not so sure. Today, I learned one of the hardest lessons of my life, that when privilege and wealth speak, the law is deaf. Money and power will always defeat natural justice.

'I never expected my life as a cop to be easy but as I watched that poor girl sobbing into her mother's shoulder, so hard her blouse was wringing wet, my heart nearly broke in two.

'Then, at last, she gave up the name of the boy who had raped her in the grounds of Yale University. I say boy. He wasn't a boy he was a man, just a few years younger than me. At last we had his name. There were other victims, too. It was my partner who made the connection between the two brutal rapes and the death of a third girl.

'He was your typical, rich college type. Everything privilege and his class had given him. When we told him he was under arrest for rape, he didn't bat an eyelid, didn't flash fear at all. God he was arrogant. When we got him back to the station, he didn't even deny what he'd done. He just said, "Prove it". He kept telling us the girls were willing, but he hadn't seen the look of utter devastation in her eyes, the emptiness. I knew she wasn't willing.

'Within ten minutes of hauling this utter bastard to the station for questioning, his father, who is the state Governor, and his uncle, who's a high-powered lawyer as well as being the mayor

1

of our proud town, both weighed in.

'Politics and power were too much for justice to stand a chance. The Chief of Police was threatened with losing his job if the charges weren't dropped. We watched the killer walk out of the station and there was nothing we could do about it. I need this job son. I've got you and your mom to support.

'We were ordered to destroy the case file - the lives of three decent ordinary girls and their loving families were destroyed with it. I won't forget, ever, but I won't allow him to destroy our lives too.

'Goodnight, sleep tight.'

He gently leaned over and kissed his son on the forehead.

CHAPTER ONE

Cambridge, England, Sunday May 5

HE WAS WAITING on the river bank. He'd deliberately arrived early. His nerves tingled with the thrill of anticipation. He reached inside his pocket again. His fingers stroked the smooth, cool glass of the phial that encased the clear blue liquid.

The first home-made batch of Blue Heaven had been too strong. He thought of Jennifer. She had been at the party, so many witnesses yet not one of them had seen anything. Sex with her had been quick, too quick. He remembered the pleasure he'd felt when he found out she was in a coma. The pleasure had been even more intense when he had visited her in hospital, seeing her lying there. Her mother had even thanked him for being there. The second batch he had used on Claire had been perfect. His thirst for power was unquenched. Now he was going to try a third time. This girl would die.

He had been watching Hayley Bannerman for over a month. He knew where she went, who her friends were, what she drank. She thought she was so clever but he would show her who was in control. He had planned the day meticulously. He knew she would be with them.

As he stood there, clutching the glass phial in his pocket, a feeling of power surged through his body. He was beginning to get an erection. His beautiful erection, his powerful erection.

The sound of laughter jolted him from his daydream. They were walking towards him, smiling, unsuspecting. She was with them just as he'd planned. Light cotton trousers and a tight white top showed off her firm young body. He closed his eyes and held his face up towards the warmth of the sun, absorbing every moment, imprinting the images on his brain. She wouldn't remember much about this beautiful Sunday. He did not want to forget a thing.

Scudamores have been hiring punts on the River Cam since 1910. They are as much a part of Cambridge as the colleges, libraries and churches that cram the narrow streets of this ancient university city. Half a dozen shallow, flat-bottomed boats lay in a neat line, nose to the bank, along the still river. Their names had been lovingly repainted for the beginning of the summer season. He did not panic that many of the punts were already out on the water. He had reserved three boats and paid for them in advance.

The Quayside was busy. Henry's Bar and Caffé Uno were doing a roaring trade. Tourists and students unable to find a table and chairs spilled out onto newly-mown lawns near the river. As he'd arranged, Hayley climbed into his punt, leaving the rest of the group to fill the two other boats. He pushed off the bank, skilfully using the ten-feet-long pole to guide the punt upstream.

Avoiding a family of swans patiently waiting to be fed by the nearby crowds, he eased the punt beneath a black iron bridge. He tapped the tip of the pole against the metal underside of the bridge.

'I always get a little nervous going under your bridges after hearing that nursery rhyme. Does this one look sturdy enough?' he asked breaking the silence.

Hayley giggled. 'That was London Bridge, and if I remember rightly, it was you Americans who bought it.'

'You could be right,' he laughed.

She lay across the bright blue cushions, lazily dipping her

hand in the cool water. He watched her carefully. There was no denying she was beautiful but he didn't like her. It wasn't her beauty he despised but her intelligence. His pulse thumped in the side of his neck. Today, he needed her.

Screams and laughter from the punts trailing behind made him turn suddenly. His friends. Today they were going to help him release the power he felt welling up inside.

A large crowd had gathered on the next bridge, to watch them go by. He spotted Claire among the throng. For a split second their eyes locked. Fear flashed across her face. An unexpected delight. He felt another surge of adrenaline as the image of Claire, submissive, powerless, flashed inside his brain. He didn't acknowledge her. His eyes were already on his next victim. Twice he had been interviewed by the police but his alibi was too tight for them to pin anything on him.

*

Henry's Bar was a student pub. The beer was cheap, the food good. The three boys slaked their thirst from the exertion of punting by downing pints at a table outside in the sunshine overlooking the river. The girls headed to the bathroom.

'So Hayley, how are you getting on with the American?' asked Megan, with a knowing wink. Megan Furby was the blonde-haired history student who'd let out a wild scream when Rob Smithson had tried to throw her overboard from the second punt. She had been Hayley's best friend since they teamed up in Fresher's Week, the get-together for newcomers to the college at the start of each academic year.

'Are we looking at the blossoming of another sordid Megan affair?' Hayley asked.

'Don't change the subject. You still haven't answered my question.'

Hayley leaned over the sink and peered into the mirror,

slowly adjusting her make-up.

'Well?' pleaded Megan.

'He wants me to call him Chuck. What more can I say?'

The girlfriends burst into laughter, then Hayley's smile faltered. She placed her lipstick on the sink and looked directly at Megan's reflection in the mirror.

'Actually, the guy gives me the creeps. I don't know what it is about him but he makes the hairs on the back of my neck stand on end,' said Hayley picking up her lipstick again. 'I thought I'd have one more drink and then go. Besides, I need to finish that last bit of course work so I can start Monday morning with a clear conscience.'

Megan gave a disapproving shake of her head, 'You girl, are getting old before your time.'

When they got back to the table, the American was missing. Hayley leaned over to Rob, 'Go on. Make my day. Tell me he's gone.'

'He thought you needed another drink. He's gone to get you one, specially.'

Rob emphasised the last word and gave a wink. Hayley grimaced. She was going to hit the next person who winked at her.

'I think I'll take this opportunity to make a quick exit,' said Hayley as she stood up and slung a bag over her shoulder. 'See you guys tomorrow.'

He was right behind her. As she turned to leave, he was only inches from her face. She took an involuntary step backwards. He'd been at the bar when he'd seen Hayley was about to leave. A wave of panic consumed him. She couldn't leave. That wasn't part of the plan. He couldn't let her take control. He felt the power slipping from him. He would not let that happen. The anger began to rise, his temples thudded.

Blocking her path, he thrust out a glass of Bloody Mary. 'At least stay for ten more minutes and finish your drink. You have to stay.' His walnut brown eyes bore into her. Her skin prickled as she felt his breath on her face.

'I'm sorry, I can't. I really have to get back and finish this blasted essay.'

Again she tried to make her way from the bar. Megan took hold of her arm, 'Come on, just one more drink. Ten more minutes and then I'll walk back with you. Pleeeease.'

Hayley shrugged, reluctantly put her handbag down and sat back in her seat. The American placed the drink in front of her. She gave him a weak smile of thanks and took a long, deep sip.

As he watched her drink the vodka and tomato juice laced with Worcestershire sauce, he felt his body relax. Panic slowly subsided but anger still burned like an ember inside him. How dare she jeopardise his plan? Who did she think she was, dictating how the day would turn out? The day was his again.

*

He'd got the mixture right. He'd added just enough Blue Heaven to the Bloody Mary to make her look drunk. He smiled, pleased at his own genius. She moaned as he and Megan gently laid her on the narrow divan bed in her tiny room in the Hall of Residence. He made sure Megan didn't see him disengage the Yale lock as the pair of them left the room, leaving Hayley alone. He needed an excuse to return. There wasn't much time before he'd have to administer the second dose of the drug to knock her unconscious.

'I'll catch up with you this evening. I've got some work to do in the library,' he said, gently closing the door.

As Megan walked back down the corridor to join the boys back at the pub, he looked at his watch. He'd fill in ten minutes and then go back to the room.

The library was packed with bleary-eyed students cramming

for final exams. The librarian would remember him. He made sure of that by dropping the small pile of books he was carrying to the table. Each minute ticked painfully by. He was in control of his destiny. No one could stop him now. His father and grandfather were too far away to meddle. His father was on business in France, his grandfather back at the family home in the United States.

He slipped away from the library, returned to her room and slowly opened the door. He froze for a moment. She had fallen onto her knees on the floor and was using the bed to drag herself up. He pulled her up and sat her on the bed. Hayley looked at him through glazed eyes. She couldn't focus. Her head swam.

'Thirsty,' she whispered. 'I'm thirsty.'

He took a mug from a shelf above the small hand basin in the corner of the room. He filled it with water, pulled the glass tube of Blue Heaven from his pocket. Pouring the sapphire liquid into the glass of water gave him his erection. He handed her the cup. He could see the liquid was the wrong colour, but Hayley was too thirsty and dazed to notice. She emptied the glass in one gulp.

For a brief second, Hayley focused. The American stood in front of her. She was falling. Salt. The water hadn't quenched her thirst. Darkness engulfed her.

Hayley lay unconscious on the bed as the American undid his flies. He removed her knickers. Power surged through him as he thrust his penis inside her. The feeling of powerlessness that had dogged his whole life always disappeared when he was with his girls. The forces that had ruled his entire life, dictated his every move couldn't touch him here.

The familiar bitter taste produced by adrenaline filled his mouth. He looked down at Hayley, her dark brown hair spread on the pillow but he saw the face of Jennifer, his first victim. His body shuddered with excitement as he recalled how he heard of Jennifer's death. The girl was dead because of him. That had been an unplanned and unexpected thrill. He wanted that high again - the high that came with death. His hands gripped around Hayley's throat, thumbs squeezing her windpipe.

A knock at the door. He released his grip on her neck. As his body froze in panic, he ejaculated.

'Hayley, are you all right? It's Megan.'

He didn't breathe, didn't move.

Megan's voice trembled as concern turned to fear, 'Hayley, I know you're in there. I'll go and get my key to your door. I'll only be a couple of minutes.'

West pulled up his trousers, a red mist clouded his vision. His day had been ruined by Megan's interference. She would pay for this. She would be next on his list.

He waited silently until he heard the footsteps disappear and left without even glancing at his victim.

CHAPTER TWO

Bandirma, Turkey, Sunday, May 5

THE TOWERING steel hull of the *Star Supreme* blocked out the daylight on the dockside. This windowless skyscraper was a floating multi-storey car park. It travelled the world transporting cars for a Japanese motor manufacturer. A fleet of brand-new cars streamed down a huge ramp, that extended 100 feet like a giant's arm, crooked at the elbow, from the rear of the ship down to the dockside.

Normally, a crew of twenty dockers would unload the ship at a rate of between ninety and one hundred cars an hour. A local union dispute had left the dockside crew short-handed.

So merchant seaman Will Davies, his cabin mate Demos Katsaris and two Italian cousins had been pulled off their duties onboard the *Star Supreme* to help. They were behind schedule. It had taken nearly four hours to drive two hundred and sixty new cars off, and now sixty second-hand cars were being loaded back on.

Will found himself behind the wheel of an old, box-shaped Mercedes which, like many of the cars destined for Africa, had long since seen better days. The Merc spewed out smoke as Will coaxed it slowly up the steep ramp. The teenager struggled with the heavy steering as the car lurched towards the tight left-hand bend. He had almost negotiated the near ninety-degree corner when he caught the chrome bumper on the crash barrier. As he tugged the wheel hard to the right to correct his mistake, the passenger side footplate scraped along the metal barrier. A high-pitched screech echoed across the ramp.

Will looked frantically around, although another couple of scratches would have been hard to spot on the already pock-marked body work. No one had seen him. He reversed slightly and managed to head the car in the right direction.

At the top of the ramp, Marco Alessandri, a fearsome Italian, controlled the flow of cars onto the eight decks each the size of a football pitch. He motioned Will to steer the black Mercedes on to Deck Four. Will panicked, fearing the Italian had seen him scrape the door. Will nervously wound down the window, bracing himself for the expected confrontation.

'Park it in here,' barked the Italian.

'I thought this one was going up with the rest.'

'Do as you're told. Park it in here...then clear off.'

As he parked the car, Will felt his muscles relax realising no one had seen the bump. He had originally been told to take the car to Deck Five, but he had always been wary of the Italian and his equally-violent cousin who was also on the crew. Will wasn't about to get into an argument over a beat-up old Mercedes that he didn't even own.

By the time he climbed out of the car, the Italian was nowhere to be seen. Will seized the chance to see how much damage he'd actually done. Paint had been peeled off almost half the driver's door. As he bent down to inspect the dent, he noticed a grey powder trickling from a gash in the bottom of the door. Unsure of what to do next, Will looked around suspiciously. He caught sight of the Italian striding towards him, clearly angered at being disobeyed.

'What are you doing?' he snarled. 'I thought I told you to get the hell out of here.'

'I was just going,' Will said, his voice shaking. He quickly walked away. He turned back for one quick glance as he headed towards the stairs. The Italian was crouching beside the dented door.

Later, safely in the tiny eight-feet by ten-feet cabin he shared with Demos Katsaris, Will began to tell his bunkmate about the accident. He stopped mid-sentence. Demos looked at him.

'It's nothing. Don't worry about it.'

CHAPTER THREE

JANE BLACKBURN reached down and turned the car radio up even louder. The M11 motorway was quiet for a Sunday evening. She smiled as she mused over the enjoyable weekend house party thrown by her old friend, Sally Goodman.

Sally had been there the night she had met John. She had been chief bridesmaid at their wedding. Sally had always been there to hold her together in the four years since John's death. Jane and Sally had the kind of relationship where they could pick up a conversation having not seen each other for months.

She glanced down at the speedometer. Surprised to see the needle nudging 100 miles an hour, she eased her foot off the accelerator. Nasty habit, she thought as the red Alfa Romeo 156 slowed down. Jane had bought the Alfa six years ago and a week later John had brought home a classic MGTA. Distractedly, she recalled the day John sheepishly pulled into the drive in the sixty-five-year-old sports car, trying to appear casual but expecting Jane to explode at the expense.

He needn't have worried. She instantly fell in love with the little car, just as John had. In the months after John's death, people had constantly tried to persuade her to sell the dark blue soft-top that had once been owned by a World War II pilot, but she'd resisted. The MG was part of him and she loved to take it out for long drives when she needed to get away, to think. Besides, she had always tried to follow her own maxim, "Do what you feel is right and not what others think is best."

Jane was too wrapped up in her thoughts to notice the

flashing blue lights in her rear view mirror. It wasn't until she heard a quick blast on the siren that she took her foot off the accelerator and pulled over to the hard shoulder.

'Blast,' she muttered as she watched one of the two traffic officers get out of the car. She reached across to her handbag, took out her driver's licence, then stepped out of the car. She'd once been told, 'First rule when you are pulled over by a traffic cop, don't let him look down at you.' She grinned at the irony of this advice as she watched the 6'3" officer striding towards her.

The policeman could feel the pulsating beat of the music as he approached the car. He watched as a woman in her late thirties climbed out of the driver's door. She was 5'5" with dark brown hair and fiery brown eyes. She was dressed in Burberry trousers with a pale-green roll-neck sweater, topped off with a silk scarf. As she leaned against the car, he could see she was ten to fifteen pounds overweight, but she was an attractive woman.

'Detective Inspector Blackburn,' he announced.

The officer didn't wait for a reply. 'If you had turned down the music, you'd have heard your phone ringing, ma'am. You need to call the station immediately.'

'What's going on?'

'I'm not sure. We were told you'd be travelling home on this road and were asked to keep an eye out for you.'

'Who's looking for me?', she asked

'Detective Sergeant Cheney, ma'am.'

'Thanks. I'll give him a call now.'

The officer watched Jane open the door, letting the music blare out even more loudly. He shook his head at her in mock exasperation.

'Oh, and if you could just keep the speed down a little ma'am. It's not going to help my career booking a DI.'

She smiled apologetically, 'Sorry Chris.'

The young officer grinned, 'Consider yourself officially warned.' He turned and walked back to his patrol car.

Jane climbed into the Alfa, turned down the music and picked up her phone lying face down on the passenger seat. Seven missed calls. What the hell was going on? She couldn't immediately think what the emergency would be. She knew it had to be important for her team to interrupt her on a rare weekend off.

Detective Sergeant Steve Cheney was one of her best and closest officers. She called the station.

A deep voice answered the phone. 'DS Cheney'

'Don't you have a family to go home to Steve?'

'That's rich coming from you, Jane,' he said.

'What have you got?'

'You're not going to like it. Rape. To be more precise, we think it's date rape. We've received a call from Addenbrooke's Hospital. A young girl, Hayley Bannerman, was brought in by her father. He's a GP. He suspected she'd been drugged, possibly molested. The girl has confirmed she was raped.'

'Has she been coherent enough to give us any details? Any names?'

'Charles West. A young American student at Cambridge University. She says it happened after they had drinks at a pub with friends. She can't remember too much about it, though.'

'Has West been brought in?'

'Melanie and Gary have gone to bring him in for questioning.'

Jane knew Steve too well. He would not have phoned unless there was more to the story.

'So what's the catch? Why the emergency?'

'Do you remember the girl found in a coma after a party at St John's College several months back?'

'You mean Jennifer Clarke. You know I like victims to have

15

names. Go on.'

'Er, yeah, Jennifer,' Cheney said. 'The forensic lab discovered traces of GHB, the date rape drug in blood samples taken not long after she was found unconscious. When this latest complaint came in, Melanie began checking the old files on that case again. Seems West was at the party where Jennifer collapsed. He was one of the guys that had been pulled in for questioning. Jennifer and Hayley were both at St John's, and it just so happens that West is at the same college.'

'Looks like our American may be worth talking to.'

'Welcome back!' Steve joked sarcastically.

Jane sighed. 'I've a feeling I'm going to need another weekend's holiday after this. I'll be in as soon as I can.'

Driving back to the station, Jane burned with anger as she recalled the long hours she and her officers had spent trying to track down rapists in the past. They were always the hardest and most emotionally draining cases, the anguish of the victims and their families, her frustration at so often finding herself powerless to do anything about the situation.

Rape crushed girls' lives. The agony of looking into their eyes as she explained there was virtually nothing she could do to help them. Only seven out of every hundred rape cases that go to court end in a conviction. The statistics in trials where date rape drugs have been used are even worse.

The relaxing weekend was already a distant memory. Jane swung left into Parkside and pulled into the police station car park. The uninspiring dark grey 1970s concrete facade did little to lift her mood. She swiped an electronic key card in the automatic lock and the door clicked open. She had always made a point of popping her head into the Duty Sergeant's small office just inside the front door to pick up any interesting station gossip.

'How's your new grandson?', Jane asked Sergeant Tim Roberts.

'Small, bald, cries a lot and constantly demands drink.'

Jane smiled. 'I can see the family resemblance. Anything interesting in today?'

'Nothing. Unless, of course, you want to investigate the student who was caught by his girlfriend cheating on her, so she threw all his clothes into one of those green charity clothes bins. You know the ones, next to the bottle banks. They've got Oxfam stamped on them.'

'Hardly a major crime.'

Roberts burst out laughing. 'You haven't heard the best bit. The stupid prat crawled in after them and while he was in there, the heat of the bin caused his body to swell and he couldn't get back out. His girlfriend just left him. It was three hours before anybody heard his cries for help and it took the fire brigade another three quarters of an hour to get there and cut him loose. He wants us to prosecute her for criminal damage.'

'Let me guess,' said Jane. 'He's a law student.'

The pair of them burst out laughing.

'Where is he now?'

'Somebody took him up to Accident and Emergency to have his wounds dressed.'

'Where do these people come from?' Jane wondered, shaking her head in amusement and disbelief.

Wearily, she climbed the stairs to her office. CID was on the second floor. Pushing open the double doors, she saw most of the twenty or so detectives' desks were empty. It always unnerved her when the office, usually heaving with activity, was quiet. Even in these days of e-mails, the notice boards were overflowing with messages. Gary Johnson's desk was still a tip, piled high with paperwork he always found an excuse not to finish. A depressing stockpile of case files scattered across the other desks. Except for Jill's of course. Her secretary had left her desk absolutely immaculate as always. Two photographs of her cat sat neatly facing her, while three small stuffed animals perched on top of her computer screen. As DI, Jane had a small office at the far end of the room. Its three glass walls gave her no privacy and made her feel like she was sitting in a goldfish bowl.

Steve Cheney sat at his desk just outside her door. He looked up as he heard her heels on the grey tile floor.

'Welcome back,' he said, cracking a broad smile. His parents, who had emigrated to the UK from the Caribbean in the 1950s, had instilled a work ethic in him that bordered on obsessive. He was 6'2" had the body of an athlete and didn't carry one extra pound, which made him envied by most of his male colleagues and desired by most of the females. The only thing that saved him from the men was his skill as an officer. His devotion to his pretty wife Anne had managed to keep the women in the office at bay.

'How's Hayley?' she asked.

'Still in hospital, the doctor treating her said she's shaken but the effects of the drug will wear off quickly. Her father has actually been pretty helpful, which makes a nice change. Her mother died of cancer four years ago, which probably explains why the father is a bit more supportive than many parents who find themselves in this situation.'

'Did the hospital say when she'll be able to come in to make a statement?'

'Kathryn Spencer, from the Force Sexual Offences Unit is with her now at the hospital. The police surgeon is there taking intimate samples and Scenes Of Crime are photographing bruises found on the girl's neck.'

Jane winced at the thought of what the young girl would be going through.

'The girl, Hayley, is still a bit dazed but she has managed to give us the basic details of the incident and has officially complained,' said Steve. 'She can't remember too much at the moment. DS Spencer will take a full statement from her tomorrow morning. She wants to give her the opportunity to go home and recover a bit first.'

'Do the doctors want to keep her in?'

'Yes, only overnight.'

'And Charles West?'

'Gary Johnson has just phoned to say he and Melanie Gibson will be back at the station with him in five minutes. They've already bagged up the clothes the kid was supposedly wearing at the time.'

'Good. I want you and Melanie to interview him when they bring him in. Sound him out, see if he'll talk. If nothing else, get a brief holding statement until Hayley can give us more details in the morning.'

'Gibson?' asked Steve.

'Yes, she's the one who made the possible connection between West and both victims, Hayley and Jennifer. Let her ask the questions.'

Detective Constable Melanie Gibson was young and attractive. She was extremely sharp and dedicated to the job. Jane knew from experience nothing was likely to incite a rapist more than being interviewed by a young woman officer. Men who crave power from dominating and humiliating women are suddenly vulnerable when they are at the mercy of a woman. That completely overwhelming sense of disempowerment had been the downfall of quite a few rapists Jane had dealt with in the past.

'I'm here now, so I think I'll watch for five minutes or so while you interview him,' Jane told Steve. 'Use Interview Room Four. I'll get Tim Roberts to turn on the video link so I can see the interview but, first, I need coffee.'

Interview Room Four was twelve feet square and windowless. A four-feet by two table rested against one wall. Only a large tape recorder and an ashtray broke up the dull grey plastic top. Melanie and Steve sat opposite the boy. In a room down the corridor, Jane watched West on a screen. She turned up the volume. Charles West was 6'1", broad-shouldered with dark-brown hair and brown eyes. He had a classic square jaw, almost movie star good looks.

Gibson tried to create an informal atmosphere by asking West if he would like some coffee. It was a ploy aimed at encouraging the suspect to talk. But the American quickly set the tone of the interview.

'This isn't a dinner date and none of us wants to be here, so let's just get on with it shall we?' West glanced dismissively at Melanie before turning his attention to Steve, assuming that the male officer was running the interview. 'Can we keep this short? Some of us have lives to lead.'

Melanie came straight to the point. 'Where were you earlier today, between 11am and 5pm?'

Jane watched West's confusion as Melanie began the questioning. Quite soon, she hoped, that confusion would turn to anger and resentment at having to answer to a young woman and his innocent act would slip.

'We were at Henry's Bar for lunch, where we always go on a Sunday.'

'We? Who's we?'

'Me and some of my friends from college.'

'Do you know a girl called Hayley Bannerman?'

'Yeah. She was at the pub with us. She got pretty drunk so Megan and I took her back to her dorm room and we left. Megan went back to the pub but I went to the library.'

'Did anybody see you at the library?'

Jane did not take her eyes off West. He slouched back in his chair, his hands in his pockets and his legs stretched out and crossed underneath the table, trying to give the impression that he had nothing more serious to discuss than an overdue parking ticket. Occasionally, half way through a sentence, he would pause slightly to carefully consider his answer making sure it all fitted into place. Occasionally he'd bite his bottom lip. Via the close-circuit camera, Jane could make out his hands repeatedly clenching in his pockets as the questions continued.

'Hayley Bannerman has alleged that, following the lunch at Henry's Bar, you entered her room and had sexual intercourse with her without her consent. She claims you raped her, Mr West.'

West slowly leaned forward and placed his arms on the table. His voice was steady and his eyes did not leave Melanie's face. West had told them his home was in Washington DC, but Jane was sure his accent was from New England.

'She must have got it wrong. I was at the library. You can ask the librarian. She saw me.'

The fist-clenching had gone. Either he had not raped Hayley or he had a supreme control over his own emotions, well beyond his nineteen years. It was clear they weren't going to get much more out of him for the moment. They would question him again after Hayley's interview tomorrow. A night in the cells might do this arrogant young man some good, thought Jane.

'Why don't we leave it there, Mr West,' Melanie said.

'What happens now?' he asked, the faintest of smiles crossing his face.

'We make one or two enquiries, check out your story and go from there. Give us the names of your friends and anyone who may have seen you in the library. If your story checks out then we'll let you go. Is there anyone you'd like us to contact to say you're here? A family member?'

The American turned on Gibson angrily.

'No!'

Steve turned to the camera and raised an eyebrow. Jane had noticed it too. The young man's anger was thinly masking another emotion, fear.

Jane stood out in the hallway with Melanie and Steve while they waited for a uniformed PC to take the American to the cells.

'Interesting. He showed almost no emotion whatsoever when you told him about Hayley's allegations. Nothing at all until his family was mentioned. He clearly doesn't want them around. If this kid is telling the truth, why the panic over his family?' Jane wondered aloud. 'Melanie, I'll leave it to you to call St John's library tomorrow. Get some details from his friends who were at the bar with him, especially the girl Megan. Also, find out who his parents are. I'd be interested to meet Mr and Mrs West. Maybe his parents walking into the picture will loosen his tongue.'

CHAPTER FOUR

MELANIE GIBSON looked up as she heard Jane walk into the CID room early on Monday morning.

'Some interesting news about West's father. Turns out Daddy's a diplomat,' said Melanie.

'In this country?'

'Yes, at the American Embassy in London. He's in charge of economic relations between Britain and the United States.'

Jane's shoulders dropped. She let out a slow sigh. Investigating rape was hard enough, but throwing a diplomat into the equation was only going to complicate things. Not a good start to the week.

'Where is he now?'

'I just got off the phone with the embassy. He flies in from France at one o'clock this afternoon. I'm going with DC Mason this morning to check out West's alibi.'

'And Hayley Bannerman?'

'She's already on her way in. Her father phoned to say she was quite keen to get this over with. Kathy Spencer is already here. I think she's waiting at the front desk for them to arrive.'

*

Dr Charles Bannerman parked his Volvo estate in the police car park. Walking around the large, dark blue car, he opened the door for his daughter. Hayley faltered as she rose unsteadily to her feet. He took hold of her arm and gave her what he hoped was a reassuring smile. In twenty years as a GP he had helped many patients get through various traumas, including rape, but he was finding it difficult to keep his emotions detached to help his daughter. He and Hayley had become very close since the death of his wife and he'd proudly watched her grow into a beautiful and confident young woman. It tore him apart to see the hollow look in the eyes of the fragile girl standing in front of him.

'I know this is going to be hard but you're your mother's daughter and have always been as strong as she was,' he said.

Gently squeezing her hand, he locked the car and they walked towards the station steps.

DS Kathryn Spencer watched them from a window overlooking the car park. Five years in the sexual offences unit had taught her that rape victims were often easier to deal with than their families; husbands who could not cope, parents that did not understand. On more than one occasion she had watched the families actually blame the victim. She was relieved at how supportive the father had been so far.

She walked over and unlocked the front door, holding it open as they came in.

Kathryn smiled, asked how Hayley was feeling and led them to a room at the end of the corridor. The Rape Suite. Despite efforts to try and give the room a relaxed, comfortable atmosphere of a living room, it still had a sterile feel. Soft yellow paisley curtains, pale yellow walls and dark blue carpet made a half-hearted attempt at relaxing victims. A well-worn sofa and two armchairs had been arranged around a large coffee table scattered with out-of-date magazines. A television with children's videos stacked neatly underneath stood against one wall. A pale blue door in the far corner led to a small surgical room where the police surgeon could examine victims and take samples. A two-way mirror covered a four-feet square of the wall next to the door to the surgical room so officers could watch interviews without intruding.

Kathryn offered them a chair. Hayley sat close to her father on the large sofa.

'Coffee?'

Dr Bannerman looked at his daughter, who shook her head.

'Thank you, but I think we'd both rather just get this over with,' he said.

'I appreciate that Dr Bannerman. We'll get started.'

Kathryn turned to Hayley, whose eyes were red, her face pale. The girl clutched a very damp, screwed-up tissue. Kathy reached over to a small bookshelf, picked up a packet of tissues and placed them on the coffee table.

'I need to get another officer to sit in on the interview with me and make notes. I'll be back in a couple of minutes.'

'Will it be a woman?' Hayley asked nervously, tears welling up in her eyes.

Kathryn looked sympathetically at the girl. 'It will,' she said as she rose to leave the room, desperately hoping a female officer would be available.

Kathryn saw Jane in her office.

'Just to let you know, I'm about to interview Hayley Bannerman. She's requested that the other officer present be a woman.'

'I think Melanie is busy with something at the moment. Go and collar DC Sam Parker. I think she's grabbing a coffee in the canteen. While you're questioning Hayley, find out if she knows anything about Jennifer Clarke, the young girl who died back in January. I'll be watching from behind the glass.'

*

Hayley Bannerman shifted distractedly on the sofa, staring at her hands as she twisted the tissue around her fingers.

'We were all out punting on the river, then we decided to go to Henry's for a drink. It was about lunchtime, I think. I didn't really know him. He'd only just started hanging around with our group a few weeks ago.'

Hayley hesitated and looked to her father for reassurance.

Spencer encouraged her to continue.

'You're doing well, Hayley. This is really helping us. What happened after you had drinks at the pub?'

'I started to feel a bit dizzy after I finished the drink, like I was going to be sick. I don't know why. I'd only had one drink. I got up to leave and he and my friend Megan both helped me back to my room. It starts to get a little bit hazy after that. I lay down on the bed and they left. I remember he came back into the room later. Megan had gone. I was so thirsty. He walked around the room, looking at my things. He gave me a drink of water but I was still thirsty. Things started to go blank after that. I'm sorry...I'm sorry.'

'It's all right, Hayley. Just tell us everything you can remember.'

'I woke up a bit later. My friend Megan was by my bedside. I'm not really sure what time it was. I felt dizzy and sort of, well, disorientated. I went to the bathroom to throw up. I didn't have any underwear on but I don't remember having taken them off. When I went to the bathroom, I knew I'd had sex.'

She looked uncomfortable and embarrassed. Kathryn's heart went out to her, having to relive these details in front of two strangers and her father. Hayley pressed on, staring down at her hands and avoiding eye contact.

'I was sore, you know, and when I looked in the mirror I could see bruises starting to show on my neck. I was confused and upset. I couldn't remember what happened. I didn't know what to do and so Megan called Dad in Norwich. That's when he came and got me.'

As a GP, Hayley's father had immediately realised something was seriously wrong. His daughter seemed disorientated and unsteady on her feet, as if she was drunk, but she didn't smell of alcohol. Besides, he knew she didn't drink much. Her dilated pupils and her unquenchable thirst made him suspect she may have been drugged. The bruising on her neck worried him, too. His daughter was extremely distraught, crying continually. He had not been able to get much sense out of her so he took Hayley straight to Addenbrooke's Hospital to have her checked over.

Hidden behind the two-way mirror, Jane groaned inwardly as she watched Hayley giving her statement. The bruises on her throat meant only one thing, the bastard had tried to strangle her. She was determined that this case wouldn't end, as so many invariably did, with the suspect walking free, leaving his victim racked with guilt, anger and shame.

As Jane made her way back to her office, she noticed an unfamiliar face with Steve. She motioned Steve into her office.

'Who's the new guy?'

'DC Dan Miller, the new detective Divisional Headquarters told us about last week. I'm giving him the grand tour.'

'It never rains but pours in this place,' said Jane looking at Dan through the glass. He was desperately trying to look completely absorbed in a file on Steve's desk to overcome the uncomfortable situation of being in a room of busy people he didn't know, with nothing to do.

'Okay,' she added. 'You've got ten minutes to give him the full tour before I call the team together. We've got to get on West's tail.'

Jane walked out of the goldfish bowl to introduce herself to Dan. He was barely five feet six inches tall, in his early thirties with already-thinning dark hair.

'DI Blackburn,' she said, thrusting out her hand. 'We're a bit informal here, you can call me Jane in the office. Good to have a new face around. Steve's going to give you a quick tour, then we've got a team meeting in about ten minutes. There's quite a lot going on at the moment. You'll have to hit the ground running. What made you put in for the transfer?'

'Family commitments. My parents have moved to this area. My wife Julie's folks are only fifty miles away. We thought it was more convenient to be in this part of the country,' he explained.

'How long did you spend in Manchester and Newcastle?'

The new recruit looked surprised as she continued, 'Did you spend any time in West Cumbria?'

Dan hadn't noticed but the whole office was watching him.

'I did,' he said. 'My father was a research scientist before he retired and we spent six years living near the nuclear plant at Sellafield, where he worked. I was born in the North East and spent my first few years there. I started my police career in Manchester, ma'am, sorry... Jane'

The office broke into a cheer. Melanie reluctantly tossed a ten pound note to Gary, who said with a grin, 'That'll teach you to be a disbeliever.'

'Thank you, thank you.' Jane acknowledged the clapping, 'Get on with whatever you were doing. Show's over.'

Turning to Dan she said, 'I'll leave you in Steve's capable hands. Ten minutes and then I want the whole office together.'

Steve grinned at the disbelieving look on Dan's face.

'She must have read my file,' said Dan.

'You know how police bureaucracy works. Your paperwork won't catch up with you for another month. Jane's father was in the Navy so as a child she moved around a lot. She has a natural gift for spotting and copying accents. When she first joined the force she realised the importance of being able to pinpoint accents and dialects. She's given up a lot of her free time to develop her skill. She's had help from a couple of linguistics professors. Believe me, it's saved us hours of work in the past.

Handy little hobby. Okay, on with the tour.'

'This is Jill, our secretary. Do yourself a favour, don't call her the office clerk, she doesn't like it,' said Steve approaching the tidiest desk in the office. 'There's nothing this lady doesn't know about what goes on in this place...'

'And what is supposed to be going on?' Jill interrupted with a grin.

'If you're unsure about anything, don't waste your time with us. We've no bloody idea. Ask Jill. I suggest you make friends with this lady if you want to keep ahead of the game around here.'

Jill rose from her seat to shake Dan's hand. For the second time in ten minutes, a look of astonishment flashed across Dan's face. At 5'11", Jill towered over him. She was in her late twenties and wore a constant expression that said, "Been there, done that". A young PC appeared from behind Dan, fresh-faced and enthusiastic. He handed Jill a buff folder and said nervously, 'Um, Jill, how about the cinema tonight? The new Clooney film's on.'

She snatched the file from his hand and, with a dismissive wave of her hand, abruptly ended the conversation by announcing she was on a fat-head free diet. Steve and Dan looked at her in awe, then roared with laughter as the wounded PC shamefully scurried back downstairs.

'So what's it like working for a woman?' Dan asked as they moved on.

'Jane's great to work for. Efficient, no-nonsense, demanding. She's one of those people you don't have to call "Ma'am" or "Boss" for you to realise she is definitely in charge. Some of the top brass think she's too informal with her staff, but she gets results. Like you, I moved back here to be close to my family. After I started, I copped the odd racist remark around the station. She pulled me in and told me I was smart, university-educated, happily married and had half the women in the office after me, of course I was going to attract some racist remarks, it was all that was left to attack. Then she asked me how I thought she felt being a woman in the force and taking that kind of thing every day. It was just the boost I needed.'

Steve looked at his watch.

'We'd better head back for the meeting. Time to see her in action.'

CHAPTER FIVE

JANE WAVED a piece of paper in the air.

'Before we get started ladies and gentlemen, we've been sent another memo from The Dream Team.'

A groan erupted across the crowded CID room.

Dan shot Steve a confused look. 'The Dream Team?' he whispered.

'Head office. Normally from Assistant Chief Constable Edwards.'

Jane read from the memorandum.

'Performance indicators show that this month your Division has fallen below the mean average for your expected yearly targets.'

A cry of 'Rubbish' came from the back of the room. Jane held up her hand and went on.

'I note that whilst your burglary, robbery and theft arrests, along with your detection figures, are the highest in the force, sadly you have been let down by your failure to meet the targets for your telephone answering response times.'

Jane could now barely be heard above the laughter and shouts. She fought on reading the memo, desperately trying to keep a straight face.

'Another target which resulted from consultation with your Community Forum was that your detectives should be patrolling in uniform at least four hours a week, which formed part of my "High visibility - see and be seen" objective.'

'Those of you who can still get into your uniforms!' Jane said, smiling.

'I also note that you failed to achieve your "Detective hours patrolling target" for the second month in a row. You previously gave the excuse that your officers were engaged in robbery objective: detecting crime. I trust that you will not use that old chestnut again. Remember my key words to success - the three E's: efficiency, economy and effectiveness. Particular emphasis should be placed on the first two.'

Fighting to be heard above a chorus of booing and jeering, Jane said, 'Okay, okay, for the benefit of the ignorant among us, could somebody please translate.'

'Be better coppers and spend less money,' came another shout to a room of laughter.

Jane waved the memo in the air and brought the room back to silence. She raised her hand. 'Not one word until I have finished the last paragraph.'

'Finally, it has come to my attention that you failed to release officers from operational duty last month to play in the force band, namely two violinists and a piccolo player. The omission of these musicians was noted during the band's performance at the police authority dinner. The Chief Constable specifically allows these men to play in duty time and the officers should accordingly be released.
Please remember the force phrase for 2002 - Failing to plan is planning to fail.'

The rest of Jane's words were totally lost as mayhem erupted in the room. The three offending officers all looked distinctly uncomfortable as the others played invisible violins and piccolos. Jane screwed the memo into a neat, round ball and threw it at Gary Johnson. He caught it and tossed it back behind his head. Melanie snatched it out of the air and threw it cleanly into the wastepaper bin. She took a bow to a round of applause.

Jane held up her hands and the noise died down.

'Right, now that we've got the important stuff out of the way, let's get down to our "customer service"', Jane said.

She ran through the facts of the date rape case, gave them details from Hayley Bannerman's statement and the possible link with the death of Jennifer Clarke.

'There's an added twist with this one, folks. Daddy's a US diplomat based in London. Expect trouble. No doubt he'll descend with a circus of lawyers so I want our facts accurate and our evidence cast iron. Chris, can you and Dan check over West's room at college? See what you can find. This guy may like to keep trophies of his conquests, like videos of the attack. Check his computer, e-mails, internet sites. You know the drill. Matt, start questioning tutors, college mates. See what you can find out. Get the names of any past girlfriends. We'll have a word with them and see if they can give us any insights. Steve, I want you and Melanie to interview West again, see if he's ready to talk.'

West would be even more arrogant after a night in the cells. Jane was sure his arrogance would be his downfall.

'You all know how hard it is to get these bastards convicted so let's not let this be another one that gets away,' she said, signalling the end of the meeting. They all stood up and began filing back to their desks when Jane called to them.

'One more thing before we go, may I just remind you that Bill is on Crimewatch tonight and we're running the usual sweepstake. Jill's got it set up. So we'll meet in the Cricketer's Arms at 9.30. Somebody pick a charity for this week.'

Melanie called out the name of a local children's charity.

'Agreed. Now, let's get started.'

*

Sterling West sat with his lawyer, Caroline Everett, in the back of a chauffeur-driven car on the way to Parkside police station.

The diplomat clutched his cell phone tightly to his ear as the authoritative voice echoed down the line.

'Where are you now?'

'We're heading to the police station. They're keeping him there for questioning while they do some further investigation.'

'Has he said anything to incriminate himself?'

'I don't think so. He certainly hasn't been charged yet. What should we do? Do you know anybody who can help?'

'Don't be a fool. Wait and see what happens before you charge around like a bull to a flag and show your hand. He hasn't even been charged yet. The sooner we get him out of that damn country the better. Have you got his passport ready?'

'We were told he may have to hand in his passport if he's charged.'

'Then get another one sorted. Keep me informed.'

West hung up the phone and turned to the pretty blonde lawyer.

'So, what did your father-in-law have to say?' she asked.

CHAPTER SIX

STEVE CHENEY poked his head around Jane's office door, his brow furrowed in a frown.

'We've just finished interviewing Charles West.'

'By the look on your face, I take it we didn't get a full confession. Are we any closer?'

'He's getting nervous and edgy. He even started to imply she willingly had sex.'

'So he must have admitted that he was actually in the room with her?'

'Yeah. He didn't have a lot of choice when he learned his fingerprints had been found all over the room, including on the mug he used to give Hayley a drink.'

'He could just have admitted being in the room and claimed he only gave her a glass of water. Why the sudden change of heart and admit having sex with her?'

'During the interview, a PC came in to tell us West's father and lawyer were on their way. Suddenly, he seemed to panic and he coughed to having sex with the girl, though he claims it was with her consent. He refuses to say anything more now, though, without his lawyer. He refused to let us take any samples for DNA testing. It's like...' Steve hesitated.

'What else were you going to say. Go with your instincts.' Jane insisted.

'My gut feeing is that he not only raped Hayley but he was trying to strangle her, too. West meant to kill this girl. Hayley is only alive because he was disturbed when Megan came to the door. The evidence we're getting from forensics supports it. I'm also 100 per cent sure that Jennifer Clarke would still be alive today if she hadn't been drugged by Charles West. When we were in the interview room together, I just wanted to put my fist straight into that arrogant, self-confident face. But every time we mentioned his parents, or more specifically his father, a look of terror suddenly flashed across his face. The kid is running scared, but not of us. What sort of parent can instil that much fear in their own child?'

At that moment Jill knocked and entered the goldfish bowl.

'Jane, Superintendent Benson wants to see you.'

Whenever Jill used 'Superintendent' before Benson's name, it was their code that trouble was looming.

'Did he say what it was about?'

'No, but he has the American's father and lawyer with him.'

Jane turned to Steve, 'Looks like I'm about to find out exactly what sort of parent can do that.'

Her relationship with Benson, the head of the station, had slowly deteriorated over the four years since John's death. She had been lucky that their friends had not pushed Jane out of their social circle now she was single. They were genuine friends. Friends who'd helped her through the darkest days of her life. Almost by accident, she had acquired the three things Benson most craved in life: social standing, respect and admiration among her team and independent wealth.

At one of Sally Goodman's dinner parties she'd found herself sitting opposite Chief Constable Robert Taylor and as the evening wore on, Jane and his wife Caroline became like old pals. Their friendship had grown strong over the last three years. Jane had never bothered to put herself up for promotion because she enjoyed being a DI. It didn't help that Robert Taylor often deliberately teased her about promotion in front of Benson. There was also the fact that that she didn't need her job.

On John's death she had discovered he had secretly and successfully been playing the stock market. That and the fact he was insured to the hilt, had left her wealthy. She could never work out which part of her life irritated a social snob like Benson the most.

As she walked into his office, Benson was handing a cup of coffee to a man in his early fifties, wearing a Savile Row suit and hand-made Italian shoes. A blonde in a black Chanel suit sat next to him. A small, expensive ladies' attaché case leaned against her chair.

'This is Mr West, the young boy Charles West's father, and his lawyer Ms Caroline Everett,' said Benson, the china cup and saucer still in his hand.

West held out his hand to Jane. She ignored him and turned to Benson.

'The boy is over eighteen years old, sir. In this country that makes him a man.'

Sterling West continued his conversation with Benson.

'Of course, we'll endeavour to help you as much as we can. However, you must realise this experience has been devastating for my son. Have you finished your questioning? Why is he still being held?'

Jane locked her eyes on him. 'Your son', she emphasised, 'is still helping us with our enquiries. This hasn't exactly been a barrel of laughs for the victim, Hayley Bannerman, either.'

West snapped back, 'I'm only interested in my son, not that attention-grabbing liar.' Jane seethed with anger. She ignored West and turned to Benson. 'Charles West has refused to give us a DNA sample. I need your permission to take a non-intimate sample.'

The diplomat shot to his feet, spilling coffee as he thumped his cup down on Benson's desk, 'You can't do that without my son's consent.'

'Yes I can,' replied Jane. 'All I need is a few hairs from his head. Whether your son gives his permission or not, I can forcibly take them.'

'That's barbaric,' West spluttered.

'So is rape, Mr West. I'm sure you're as keen as I am to have this cleared up.'

Ms Everett intervened and tried to quell the rising tension in the room.

'Mr West, please calm down. The Detective Sergeant is right. They are able to take certain samples from your son without his consent. Of course, it all depends on whether Superintendent Benson gives his permission.'

Jane watched the lawyer flash Benson a 24-carat smile. Sterling West's manner changed instantly. He pleaded deferentially to Benson.

'Surely, Superintendent, two intelligent and reasonable men of our standing can come up with a less, shall we say disruptive, way of dealing with this situation.'

Jane wanted to scream at Benson to wake up. Superintendents were all the same. Most of them had reached as far up the ladder as they were ever going to go. Big fish in small ponds and were almost always impressed by rank and standing. She could see Benson was being taken in by them. He turned to Jane.

'Do you think this is necessary, Inspector?'

Jane simmered just below boiling point. She turned on him, 'Yes, sir, I believe this is absolutely necessary, with or without the young man's permission. May I remind you that just possessing GHB is now illegal and carries a possible two-year jail sentence.'

She couldn't help herself as the words rolled off her tongue, 'Under normal circumstances sir, there would be no question about the necessity and we would not even be discussing this in front of a suspect's lawyer and parent.'

An uncomfortable silence fell over the room. Benson gave West Senior a weak-chinned, almost apologetic smile.

'I'm sorry, Mr West, but, to help this investigation along, I am granting permission for my officers to take non-intimate samples from your son.'

You bastard, thought Jane, furious that in front of West and a defence lawyer, Benson had made her fight for his permission to take the samples.

'If that's all, sir, I really must get back to work.'

Without bothering to wait for an answer, Jane turned and left the office. Ms Everett called after her.

'Sergeant, sergeant!'

Jane continued down the corridor. An old trick, she thought bitterly, addressing someone by an inferior rank. She was not going to play into the lawyer's hand by turning around.

Finally, the lawyer corrected herself.

'Sorry...inspector.'

Jane stopped and turned.

'I need to talk to my client.'

'When you have finished your morning coffee with the superintendent, I'll be more than happy to show you to Interview Room Four.'

CHAPTER SEVEN

JANE FURIOUSLY paced the floor of her tiny office as she gave Steve a blow-by-blow account of her meeting with Sterling West and his lawyer. Jane rarely swore, but the names of Benson, West and Everett were all followed by a string of colourful expletives.

Steve sat quietly, knowing better than to interrupt, letting her get all her anger and frustration off her chest.

'How many people have we got working on this?' Jane asked.

'At the moment I'd say at least half the team,' Steve said, doing a very rough calculation.

'Spend twenty minutes phoning each team member and get them told. I want meticulous notes on this one. I want every dot and comma recorded. I don't want this case thrown out because of a technicality.'

'But we haven't even charged him yet.'

'I don't care, Steve. I want this kept scrupulously clean right from the word go. The Wests' lawyer is going to give us trouble.'

She finally paused long enough to look up at Steve's face, her anger spent.

'Sorry, Steve. The rant's over now. There is one piece of good news. I managed to drag an okay out of Benson to take samples for DNA testing. It was bloody hard work though.'

'Charles West is in the cells now. I'll head down,' said Steve.

'I'll join you. I'm in need of a bit of sport.'

Roger Lewis, the station Custody Officer, was a tough, no-

nonsense man who did things by the letter of the law, whether they were convenient or not. He was in his middle fifties and coming up to retirement.

'Afternoon, Roger.'

Lewis finished writing in the logbook he was filling out before looking up at Jane. He shook his head in exasperation. 'I've had a crap day and the cells are full from last night's dope operation. What do you want, Inspector? I'm pretty busy.'

The noise in the cellblock was deafening. A number of PCs in civilian clothes, with the help of two sniffer dogs, had trawled the streets and pubs for people with drugs in their possession. Because some police forces elsewhere in the UK were now turning a blind eye to anyone carrying cannabis and Ecstasy for personal use, the town centre search had netted a far larger haul of bodies than anyone had expected. Roger had been called in at three o'clock in the morning to help sort out the chaos. Jane could now see the stress he was under. There were bodies everywhere, on the chairs, on the floor, spilling out of two filled cells. A couple of young PCs were desperately trying to restore some form of order.

'You're going to miss us all when you retire you know.' Jane's humour was lost on Lewis just at that moment. She continued. 'I need to take a DNA sample from Charles West. He's decided not to co-operate. He's about to see his lawyer and I need to get this done before the interview.'

Roger looked concerned. 'If you go charging into a cell with four PCs, we're going to have a riot on our hands. I'll get a couple of officers sent to Interview Room One. I suggest you take him there.'

Jane smiled. 'Thanks Roger. Whose bright idea was the drugs initiative anyway?'

'Take a guess.'

'ACC Edwards?'

'Got it in one. This is the result of the new safer streets initiative. Why is it whenever they come up with these new bloody initiatives we get landed with the work? Anyway, it's nice to hear you and Benson are getting on as well as ever.'

Jane had always been amazed at how quickly news travelled in a nick.

'Sometimes I just think I'm here to amuse you lot,' she said.

'Be careful, Jane. Benson doesn't make a move for the good of anybody's career but his own.'

Jane and Steve watched a PC handcuff Charles West and lead him from the cells to the interview room.

'I've just had a thought,' said Steve. 'Why not let our pretty young DC, Melanie Gibson, take the sample. After all, they're already old friends.'

'Excellent idea. Where is she?'

A phone call sent Gibson running down the stairs from CID towards Interview Room One.

As the PC led West into the room, two more constables stood in the corridor outside. Jane and Steve followed the American in. A brief flash of fear crossed West's face, quickly replaced with a look of defiance.

'So, this is where you get rough is it?' he scoffed.

Jane looked across at the young PC who had led him into the room. He was just months out of training college, as young and as green as they came.

'Tell me PC...' Jane hesitated.

'Clive, ma'am. PC Clive.'

'When was the last time you beat someone up?'

He paused for a moment. 'That would be about eleven years ago ma'am, when I got into a fight with my brother in the garden.'

Jane turned to West. 'I think you've been watching too much TV.'

At that moment, Benson walked into the room. 'Mr West, Detective Inspector Blackburn has requested a DNA sample. Do you give permission for this sample to be taken?'

'No!' he barked.

'Do you understand the consequences of your answer, Mr West? We can take the sample anyway, without your consent, by force if necessary.'

Jane watched the colour drain from West's face as it began to dawn on him what was going on.

Benson continued, 'I am now giving my officers permission to take the sample forcibly.'

Jane followed him out into the corridor. 'When you're finished here, send him to Interview Room Four. His father and lawyer are waiting. For God's sake Blackburn, try a little diplomacy here.'

When Jane went back into Interview Room One, Melanie Gibson was already wearing pale cream surgical gloves and holding a small, clear self-seal plastic bag.

'Take a seat, Mr West,' Jane said.

The two PCs who had been waiting in the corridor entered the room and stood either side of West and sat the American forcibly down in the chair. Melanie leaned over him. 'We can do this the easy way or the hard way,' she said.

Holding the sample bag in her left hand, she reached out with her right to get hold of half a dozen hairs on his scalp. West flinched, pulling his head back out of Melanie's reach, the suddenness and forcefulness of the movement made her jump.

'All right, the hard way it is.'

The two officers pulled him to his feet, pinning him to the wall while Clive held his head still. Melanie reached up, took hold of six or seven hairs and yanked.

West winced at the sharp, stinging pain.

'Hold him there,' said Melanie as she slowly and carefully

inspected the hairs in her hand to make sure they all still had roots attached. She deliberately took her time while West remained pinned to the wall.

'Okay. I have what I need,' she said finally, turning to leave the room.

Jane walked over to West. 'I am now going to instruct the officers to let go of you. I advise you not to do anything stupid.'

As they let go of West, he almost buckled as his knees suddenly took the full weight of his body.

'Gentlemen, take him to Interview Room Four. You'll find his lawyer waiting there.'

Jane allowed herself a satisfied smile as she watched West being led down the corridor. The case was in the bag.

CHAPTER EIGHT

DESPITE BENSON'S attempt to transform the station canteen into a 'cafeteria', the food was still unappetising. Jane toyed with a bowl of leaden pasta as Steve placed a green salad and a glass of orange juice on the table.

'Do you have any vices?' asked Jane, as he sat down.

He smiled. 'Only Anne. '

She watched his eyes light up. They were so in love, so involved. Jane admired them for that.

'So, what do we have planned for this afternoon?' Steve continued.

'I thought we'd re-interview Robert Hughes, the lad who gave West his alibi in the Jennifer Clarke case.'

Steve pulled out his notebook and flicked over the pages. 'At the time of the original interview back in November, he was staying at a flat on Mill Road,' he said.

'Which end of Mill Road?'

'The wrong side. Across the railway, near Brookside Hospital. Typical run-down student digs.'

'And?' said Jane, suspecting there was more.

'Well, I phoned the University to find out if he still lived there but it turns out he's moved up in the world. He's now living just around the corner, in Melbourne Place. Definitely the right side of the tracks.'

'Well, isn't that interesting. Did they say when he moved?'

'Apparently, he changed his address after he returned to college from the Christmas break.'

'That's only six or seven weeks after the party where Jennifer Clarke collapsed.'

Steve went on. 'I've skimmed over his original interview. Turns out Robert Hughes went to a small comprehensive in County Durham. Consett, you know, where the steel works closed putting most of the town out of work. He's bright, four A levels, hard-working. His parents couldn't support him financially, so he has to work while he's at uni. He has two part-time jobs.'

'Expensive new digs for an impoverished university student. I wonder who gave him a helping hand across the tracks? Do we know where he is at the moment?'

'The University say he's at home recovering from the flu.'

The house in Melbourne Place was a double-fronted, three-story terrace on a beautiful, tree-lined street opposite a small primary school. As Jane opened the gate to the large well-kept garden, she looked at Steve with a raised eyebrow.

'Very nice. How much do you think this costs?'

'Eight hundred, nine hundred a month, maybe. His explanation on how he can afford this is going to be interesting.'

A set of stone stairs led down to a large two-bedroom basement apartment. Jane rang the small brass buzzer marked Flat 1A.

'Hello?' said a snuffly voice on the intercom.

'Mr Hughes?'

'Look, I don't know what you're selling but go away or I'll call the police.'

'We are the police, Mr Hughes. We have a few questions we'd like to ask.'

There was a moment's silence. Then the sniffling came back. 'I'm ill. I've got the flu. Can't we make this another time?'

'We could always do this down at the station, Mr Hughes.' said Steve.

The front door opened. A gangly 20-year-old stood in the doorway. Dried-out night sweats had left his ginger hair a matted mess. Robert Hughes looked dishevelled. He was dressed in several layers of clothing. His eyes and nose were streaming.

They followed him into the living room. It was well-furnished with tailored drapes on the windows. A small gas fire was on full blast despite the warm May weather. Steve and Jane found the heat stifling. Hughes picked up an old blanket from the large sofa and wrapped it tight around him. He motioned to them to take a seat.

'We're here to discuss the statement you made after the party last November where Jennifer Clarke was raped before she collapsed into a coma,' Jane said, watching his face for a reaction.

Hughes closed his eyes and groaned. 'Not that again. I've already told you everything I know.'

In his distinctive north west Durham accent, that was neither the Geordie spoken in Newcastle nor the Macam of Sunderland, Hughes began to go through his statement almost word for word, reciting it like a well-known story.

Jane interrupted him. 'We already have that version, Mr Hughes. Is there anything you might like to add to your statement, under the circumstances?'

'Under what circumstances?' asked Hughes, his watery eyes suddenly wide open, darting between Jane and Steve.

'We've arrested Charles West and are interviewing him in connection with a different rape,' said Jane.

'What do you mean? He hasn't done anything. Why don't you just give the guy a break?'

'Tell me Robert, when did you move into this flat? You must have to work very hard to keep up with the bills.'

'I have two part-time jobs and I'm still managing to do my

university studies.'

'This flat must cost about nine hundred pounds a month to rent, plus council tax and heating and lighting.'

'Students don't pay council tax,' he sniffed.

'Even so, they must be two very good part-time jobs to pay for all this. Detective Sergeant, could you take out your notebook?' Jane tossed Steve a glance. 'Now, Robert, if you'd just tell us where you work and how much you're paid.'

'I don't have to say anything,' he said petulantly.

'Of course, there's another way of dealing with this.'

'Yeah?' said Hughes.

'We can get a court order to look at your bank accounts.'

Scanning the room, Steve suddenly noticed a photograph on the mantle piece above the fire. He picked it up and handed it to Jane.

'How often do you go skiing, Mr Hughes?' Jane paused. 'With Charles West?'

Hughes fidgeted in his seat. He looked down at his feet to avoid eye contact.

'Withholding evidence or falsifying a statement carries a penalty of imprisonment. Did you know that Mr Hughes? In your statement back in November you said Charles West never left your sight all night. Care to add anything to that Mr Hughes?'

'He was...' Hughes faltered. 'More or less.'

'More or less?' Jane repeated, slowly sounding out every syllable.

'He said he went to the toilet.'

'How long was he gone?'

'Ten minutes, tops. I was talking to one of the other students, a girl.'

'Did you look at your watch at any point while he was gone?'

'No.'

'So it could have been longer if you were distracted by a pretty girl? Even twenty or thirty minutes?'

Hughes stayed quiet.

'Whose idea was it for you to say West never left your side?'

'It was when you lot started pulling in everyone at the party. We just thought we'd make it easy for ourselves. But I had no idea he would do anything like that.'

Jane rose to her feet, cutting him short.

'You're a bloody idiot. Do you realise the harm you may have caused? You're coming down to the station with us now to revise your statement. I don't care how ill you are. Do you understand?'

The boy didn't protest.

CHAPTER NINE

RAISING HER voice above the din of fifteen detectives at work in the CID room, Jane said, 'Ladies and gentlemen, we'll have a meeting in fifteen minutes to bring everyone up to date on the West case.'

Detective Sergeant Gary Johnson caught Jane's eye. Even though it was nearly twenty five degrees outside and not much less indoors, he was still wearing a permanently crumpled sports jacket. Johnson had been passed over for promotion on more than one occasion. Instead of inspector's pips, he wore a chip on both shoulders. That still did not stop him from being a damn good detective and he bore no resentment towards Jane.

'You might want to delay the meeting for a short time, JB,' he said.

Jane shot him a quizzical look, 'Why?'

'A girl walked in off the street half an hour ago, said she wanted to talk about West and asked if she could see a female officer,' Gary explained. 'She's in the Rape Suite with Kathy Spencer.'

'I'll go down and see what's going on. In the meantime, Robert Hughes is in Interview Room Two. Remember him? West's alibi in the Jennifer Clarke case. We brought him in to "revise" the statement we took from him in November. Turns out West's alibi wasn't so watertight after all. I want you to take the new statement and don't be too bloody polite about it, either.'

'Is that an official okay to ruffle his feathers?' Johnson asked looking gleeful.

'You can pluck him bald for all I care.'

Through the two-way mirror, Jane watched a slightly overweight, dark-haired girl of about nineteen or twenty sitting on the edge of the Rape Suite sofa, obviously uncomfortable at being there. Flicking a switch on the wall allowed Jane to hear the conversation between Spencer and the girl.

'Chuck West made a drink for me. I don't remember finishing it. The next thing I can recall was waking up. My clothes felt odd.'

'What do you mean "odd"?' Spencer asked.

'Well, you know when you go swimming and you get dressed without having dried yourself properly, nothing quite fits. Nothing is quite in the right place. That sort of feeling.'

'What makes you sure you hadn't just passed out from a few too many drinks?'

'If I'd been anyone else, I'd have doubted myself, but I was brought up on my Dad's home brew wine. Some of it was so alcoholic it would have pushed Russian vodka off the scale. I can hold my drink and I only had one.'

Tears rolled down the girl's cheek. Jane saw an opportunity to knock on the door and call Spencer out of the room.

'Gary told me you were down here. I've been listening on the intercom. What do you think?'

'She seems genuine,' said Spencer.

'Has she told you why she didn't come forward sooner?'

'Too intelligent for her own good,' said Kathryn flicking through her notes. 'Four grade 'A' A levels, had the pick of any university in the country, any college at Cambridge. She's angry, she feels stupid for letting herself get into that situation and she's too ready to question herself. Also, it was a good week later before her memory started to return, and by then she had little to no evidence to back up her story.'

'So what made her turn up today?'

'Guilt. West's arrest is the talk of St John's college. She was pretty shaken up when she heard. She was on a bridge over the Cam yesterday morning as West and Hayley went past on the punt. She felt that if she'd only told someone about West then maybe Hayley would have been spared the ordeal she's gone through.'

'Take a statement from her and make sure she's offered some counselling.'

'I've already sorted out a meeting for her at the Rape Crisis Centre.'

'We're having a team meeting in the office in five minutes. Pull in a WPC to look after the girl. I'd like you there.'

Jane perched on the edge of Steve's desk, cradling a cup of black tea in her hands.

'Okay, ladies and gentlemen, to bring you up to date. At the moment Gary Johnson is interviewing Robert Hughes, the guy who gave West his alibi back in November. He's now downstairs adding parts of his statement, which he may have "overlooked". What else do we know?'

Steve kicked off. 'Forensics have sent back the results on Hayley's blood and urine samples. She definitely had traces of the date rape drug gamma-hydroxybutyrate, GHB. We won't know until tomorrow if his DNA results match the semen specimens taken from Hayley.'

Jane looked around the room and frowned. 'Okay, who did I send to check West's room?'

A hand shot up among the sea of faces in the crowded CID room. Considering the amount of stick he'd received throughout his career, DC Chris 'Sherlock' Holmes was a remarkably pleasant, even-tempered man. 'West's computer revealed he likes to surf internet porn sites, hetrosexual sex, no paedo. A couple of dirty magazines were lying around plus the odd X-rated video.'

'Sounds like Gary's bedroom,' a voice piped up from among the group.

Chris continued amid the laughter. 'Nothing too out of the ordinary for your average college kid, until forensics started digging in the toilet cistern. They found a small, clear glass jar with GHB in it, cleverly hidden in the water. GHB has lots of street names, like GBH - because it does your head in. It's also known as Blue Heaven or Blue Verve. Forensics think he made up a home-brew of this drug himself to beat the new restrictions on buying GHB.'

'Good God,' said Jane. 'Do we know how much more of the stuff he has?'

'Not yet. Forensics are still looking.'

'Okay, I want you to go back to the dean of St John's. West can't have made the GHB on his own, he must have had help. I want a full list of any friends or acquaintances who are doing some kind of science degree. If he's making and storing this stuff, I want to know where. Get the list today and start interviewing everyone on it. Kathryn, can you tell us about Claire Reece?'

As Kathy Spencer gave the team brief details of the girl who'd walked in off the street, Jane's mind wandered over the new details. If Claire had been raped and kept it quiet, how many others women had he done this to? How many more victims were out there?

Kathy continued. 'The girl was quite genuine and level-headed, not the sort to make up such a story to be the centre of attention. Quite the opposite in fact.'

'If Claire has kept quiet, there may be more out there,' Jane cut in. Melanie, you and Kathryn have a discreet word with some of the other women on West's course and in the college, see if anyone else has been raped and not reported it.'

Moments later Jane wrapped up the meeting. 'Keep going but I'm convinced we already have enough evidence to charge West without waiting for the DNA sample.'

At seven o'clock that evening Jane and Steve sat opposite West in the interview room.

'We had an interesting chat to some of your ex-girlfriends today,' Jane said. 'You're in deep trouble this time. Traces of the date rape drug, GHB, in Hayley's blood and urine samples match the GHB we found hidden in your room at the college. I expect DNA from your hair will match the semen samples taken from her. Anything you want to tell us?'

West looked at Jane with venom. 'You can't touch me,' he snapped.

'I believe we already have. Charles West I'm charging you with the rape and assault of Hayley Bannerman.'

Jane watched the blood drain from the American's face. As she rose to leave she told him, 'I suggest you have another little chat with your lawyer.'

CHAPTER TEN

AS AN ELDER statesman of the US House of Representatives, the Congressman for Georgia liked to keep people waiting. Because he was chairman, he always made a point of making the nine members of the Committee on Standards of Official Conduct wait a full five minutes. He sat in his office as the minutes ticked by while they seethed in the committee room next door. A young intern knocked at the open door and walked towards him. He didn't know her name. If he was honest, he didn't know any of their names but he could tell this one was nervous.

'Congressman,' she said, approaching his mahogany desk. 'Mr West is on the phone, calling from England.'

'I'll get back to him later.'

She hesitated. His face was expressionless and that intimidated her more.

'I'm sorry Congressman, but he did insist it was urgent.'

'Then I'll have to make the committee wait a little longer, won't I?'

After she'd closed the door, he picked up the phone. 'Sterling, my boy. And how is the English weather treating you?'

Sterling West was fifty-two years old and being called "my boy" always annoyed him. West could never work out if the old man did it to intimidate his son-in-law, or whether it just made the Congressman feel younger.

'Charles has been charged with rape and assault,' he said.

The line was silent. West wasn't sure if it was just the satellite delay on the phone or perhaps, for once, the Congressman was too stunned to speak.

The line exploded to life. 'How the hell could you let this happen? I thought you'd sorted this situation out! For Christ's sake, don't let him say anything. Find out what's going on and phone me back later. I'm about to go into a meeting.'

The Congressman slammed down the phone, left his office and took his seat at the head of the long, mahogany table in Room HT-2 where the committee convened. Twelve maroon leather chairs surrounded the table in the cream-coloured room inside the Capitol building. The Congressman sat with his back to a large window with a magnificent view from Capitol Hill down the Mall towards the Washington Monument.

The committee of ten members, five from each party, had been joined by two more congressman, part of a sub-committee formed to investigate a complaint made against a Congressman for Texas. They were here to report their findings and give their recommendations on the political fate of their colleague. This was never an easy task and the tension around the table was palpable.

The chairman called the meeting to order. 'Ladies and gentlemen, we've all read the report of the sub-committee. I believe we should take action and go ahead with a full investigation.'

Norma Long, Congresswoman from the corn-belt state of Iowa, looked up from the report in front of her.

'With all due respect Mr Chairman, the evidence is at best slim and at worst practically non-existent. To go ahead with an expensive investigation would be a waste of possibly hundreds of thousands of tax dollars...'

She stopped her speech mid-sentence. It was obvious the Chairman was not listening.

He held up his hand and said, 'I'm sorry you feel that ensuring the House's reputation and integrity is not sufficient justification for a proper, valid investigation. I have sat on this Committee since the 105th Congress and not once in those six years have I allowed the tax dollar to override the principles which it is our duty to uphold.'

Congresswoman Long seethed at his condescending tone but she decided not to press the issue. Everyone around that table knew the Chairman's principles and concern for integrity were not the real motivation behind his decision to instigate a full investigation. There'd been long-standing tension between the two men since the Congressman for Texas had successfully managed to block the Chairman's proposed amendments for a new Bill on energy.

Besides it was an open secret among members of the House that the Chairman was using this committee to enhance his image as an elder statesman. In spite of his wealth, he had never managed to reach a political position high enough to match his family's aspirations for him. He'd been elected as Governor of Connecticut, taking over from his father. In the late seventies, after failing to win the nomination for Republican presidential candidate, he was elected into Congress by the slimmest of margins, as Representative for Georgia. In any other family, this would have been seen as the height of political success. To his dynasty, it was a poor second. Embittered, but still filled with the family's arrogance and pride, he was now committed to using this small pocket of power to his own ends.

He brought the meeting to a swift close.

'Ladies and gentlemen, we will now vote on whether the affairs of the Congressman for Texas should undergo a full investigation. It is my belief that the committee should undertake this course of action.'

No one voted against him.

*

Although it was only three in the afternoon, the Congressman poured himself a large brandy. He sat in the big leather chair behind his desk and rubbed his temples. He had to think quickly. He flicked through his mental list of contacts. He'd have to call on a large favour to sort out this problem. He'd played the game long enough to know that if you dig deep enough into a person's past, you'll always find some dark little secret they'd rather keep under the carpet. That's when you had them. He picked up the phone. It was time to re-acquaint someone with their darkest secret.

*

Sir Phillip Roberts was alone in his office in Victoria Street, London, five minutes walk from the Houses of Parliament. He had recently been appointed Director of the Judicial Group, a department of the Lord Chancellor's Office, after years spent carefully forging his career as a civil servant. He was proud of his new role and took his position seriously.

'Phillip? It's Charles.'

Roberts instantly recognised the American accent. Nausea rose up inside him. Bitter-tasting bile burned the back of his throat. He had been expecting this call for a long time. As the years passed he'd lived in denial, clinging to the hope that he would never hear the voice again. Fear of this moment had always lurked just below the surface. His life had moved on. He had been promoted twice. His little indiscretion had been forgotten but the pride he felt in his achievements was always tarnished by dread.

"Phillip, I have a little favour to ask."

CHAPTER ELEVEN

WORDS IN the witness statement Jane was trying to read seemed to swim across the page. It was getting late. She checked her watch. Nine fifteen, almost time to head across to the pub. She quickly checked the overnight court list to see which magistrate would preside over West's hearing. It was Arthur Bowen. She felt comforted, he was renowned for being tough on offenders and Jane usually agreed with his decisions. With Bowen in charge, any application for bail was likely to be thrown out. Jane picked up her jacket and bag.

Steve and his wife Anne walked into the Cricketer's just before 9.30pm. This cosy little pub not far from the station was favoured by the officers. The cops hardly noticed the dark red chairs and Sixties-pattern carpet. They were more interested in the pool tables and large screen TV.

'Do I look all right?' Anne asked as she pulled at the new pair of trousers she had just bought.

'You look fine, honey. You always look fine. Don't worry.'

They entered the smoky atmosphere. Most of the team were already sat around the television at the far end of the bar. As usual, Jane was in the thick of the crowd, organising them, making sure glasses were full. Gary Johnson was telling yet another long-winded story of his adventures as a young cop in the Met. Steve almost thought he saw a look of relief cross Jane's face when she looked up and saw them.

Jane stepped forward, greeting Anne warmly. Steve's boss and his wife had become close, using each other to blow off steam about work and life in general. They would often sit and chat for hours. Somehow, Jane had always managed to never allow the relationship to cross over into work.

'Hi, Anne,' she said. 'How's little James?'

'He's been a terror lately. This morning he flushed one of his new shoes down the toilet and the day went downhill from there. We've left him with poor Mum tonight. I almost ran out the door.'

Jane laughed sympathetically. 'Even my Richard wasn't that bad.'

She looked up and caught sight of a young man walking hesitantly through the door of the pub, looking lost.

'Here's Dan, the new man on the team. Steve's probably told you about him. I'll introduce you.'

Jane made her way to the bar and came back with a pint, a gin and tonic and Dan in tow.

'This is the reason we're here,' Jane told him, looking towards the TV screen. 'One of our lads, DS Bill Parker, is on Crimewatch tonight. Bill's a brilliant copper, a first-rate man but he has a slight speech impediment. We've got a bet running on how long it will take him to say a particular word.'

Steve called Jill over and she wrote Dan's name in an empty space on a sheet, marked up in five-second intervals.

'Now what happens?' Dan asked.

'We sit, wait and count,' Jane explained. 'If your name is beside the closest time you win.'

The programme had already started. Smartly-dressed presenter, Nick Ross, was going through the week's Most Wanted list. When a picture of a burglar with a particularly crooked nose appeared on the screen, Sherlock Holmes piped up, 'Look, my ex-wife!'

Nick Ross went on to describe an armed robbery on a security van that had happened in Cambridge a couple of weeks ago.

The police desperately wanted a breakthrough.

'With us tonight we have Detective Sergeant Bill Parker of Parkside station in Cambridge,' he said.

A cheer went up in the pub. Someone called out, 'Start the stopwatch, Jill!'

The bar fell silent as Parker went on to explain how two robbers had held up a filling station with a shotgun, leaving staff and customers terrified. E-fits of two men appeared on the screen.

Then Nick Ross looked straight at the camera. 'What were you doing that morning? If the slightest thing jogs your memory, an oddly parked car in the area or something that just didn't seem right, please phone Parkside Police Station, the number's below, or call us here at Crimewatch.'

All eyes were fixed on Parker as Ross gave him the last word, 'May I remind the viewers that these two suspects are particularly dangerous crinimals…'

Laughter erupted and drowned out the rest of Parker's sentence. The watch stopped at two minutes forty-six.

Dan turned to Steve 'Did I hear that right? *Crinimal.*'

'Yes, we have a DS who can't say the word criminal.'

CHAPTER TWELVE

STEVE STRODE into Jane's office late on Tuesday morning, relief written all over his face. 'We've done it. The magistrate has granted police custody pending trial. West is safely locked up in a cell. At first he hesitated, but once the prosecuting solicitor told him how West had already interfered with a witness in the Jennifer Clarke case, it was in the bag.'

He allowed himself a wry smile, 'You should have seen his father's face when the decision was announced. No wonder the kid's terrified of him. He even scared me. The magistrate has also placed reporting restrictions on the names of everyone involved, which should make our life a little easier for a while.'

Jane spent the rest of the day making inroads into the rapidly-expanding mountain of paperwork that was threatening to cover her entire desk top.

She drove home that evening still smarting at a how a mix-up at the lab meant the results of the DNA tests on the hair they'd taken from Charles West still hadn't arrived. As Jane pulled into the driveway of the large 1930s redbrick, detached house she noticed a light glowing in the garage. As she strained her tired brain trying to remember whether she'd left the light on, the beginnings of a headache pulsed in her temple.

Slowly and quietly, she opened the side door to the garage, her heart thumping in time with the throbbing in her head. In the far corner, a man leaned over the old MG, his back to her and his upper body half inside the open-topped car as if he was searching for something. Jane moved her right hand noiselessly, edging it along a shelf close by, and picked up a spanner. She crept up behind him. She was so close now she could hear him breathing but he didn't stir. In a quick, well-practiced movement, she wrapped her left hand around his neck and held the spanner to his head with the other.

'Police! You're nicked!'

The man struggled to free himself from her grasp, shock etched on his face. He was in his early seventies, with a head of thick silver hair. He was slim, with a slight tan and large brown eyes. He held his hand to his heart, shook his head with a laugh and gave her a warm hug.

'For Heaven's sake Jane, you're going to give your old Dad a heart attack one of these days, creeping up on me like that.'

He'd never been able to stay angry at her for long, even when she'd been an infuriating, headstrong teenager.

'It's your own fault,' she told him. 'What have I told you about snooping in my garage at all hours? You could be anyone. Anyway, how's Mum?'

'Fine. She's having a couple of ladies over tonight so I thought I'd make my escape and drop in to say hello. How are you? You really ought to take it easy. You look like you haven't slept in days.'

'I haven't, but don't ask. Work's been a bit crazy lately and I've had an awful couple of days. I could do with a strong coffee. Want to join me?'

'I thought you'd never ask. I'd love one.'

As they walked into the house, Jane hit the play button on the answer phone. Just one message. Her son Richard wanted her to call him back.

'What does he want?' asked her father.

'He's an eighteen year old who hasn't phoned his mother in weeks. That can only mean one thing, money. I'd better give him a call in case it's important.'

To Jane's surprise, a girl answered the phone and mumbled 'hello' in a sleepy voice.

'Um, hello. It's Richard's mum. Is he there?'

'Oh, hi Mrs Blackburn. He's right here. I'll put him on.'

'Well, well. Anything you'd like to tell your mother?' she teased when he answered. 'She sounds nice. Is she intelligent?'

'God, Mum, that's enough. Glad you called, though. There is something I've been meaning to talk to you about.'

'How much will it cost me?'

'I'm insulted,' he said with mock indignation. 'You've never been one for small talk have you? All right, if that's how we're playing then I'll get right down to business. I've been offered the chance to crew on this brilliant boat in the Fastnet Race but I really need to get a new life jacket. I need one that's fitted with a satellite-tracking device and, to cut a long story short, I was hoping you could help finance it. Think of it as an early birthday present.'

'All right, I'll think about it. Tell me which one you need and how much I'm up for and I'll see what I can do. Grandpa's dropped in for coffee so I'd better go and see what he's up to. Give me a call with the details. Have you found a part-time job yet?'

There was silence at the other end of the line. Jane continued, 'Richard, please promise me you'll do something with your life. I know you're having a year off to sail but you worry me. I think you should give some thought to which university you want to go to. And stop cringing, I know what you're up to.'

Richard immediately stopped wincing and glanced involuntarily around the room. His mother had always had a sixth sense about what he was up to and she had a way of making him feel like a child again.

'I thought I'd join the time-honoured tradition of following in the footsteps of my mother and grandfather and join the Navy.

What do you think? I rather fancy myself in whites,' he said, hoping a flippant remark would distract his mother from a conversation he'd been dreading. Jane frowned at the mention of her naval career. The brutal way it had come to an abrupt end was a dark, brooding cloud that still hung over her.

It wasn't her son's fault. She shook the memory out of her head and said, 'I should have known better than to get a sensible conversation out of you. We'll talk about it later, young man.'

Richard groaned and they said their goodbyes.

Her father was in the kitchen fixing two cups of coffee. The smell began to make her feel a little more human again.

'How's he doing?' he asked.

'He's fine. And, yes, he was after money. Dad, have you and Mum thought about what to buy him for his birthday? I may be able to suggest something.'

CHAPTER THIRTEEN

Bay of Biscay, Tuesday May 7. 11pm

THE SPANIARD looked down at the body, slumped against the tyre of a bashed-up Ford Taunus on cargo deck Four. The needle was still in the boy's right hand, clasped tightly into a now-rigid fist. He knew instantly this was no accidental overdose. He thumped the deck. He had grown to like Will Davies.

Whispering beside the dead teenager, he pleaded, 'Why didn't you come and see me if you'd seen anything?'

Covering the boy with his jacket, the Spaniard left the deck and took a lift up five floors to the crew deck. He found Marco Alessandri in the games room, playing pool with the rest of his cronies. Struggling to control his anger, the Spaniard whispered angrily in Alessandri's face.

'What the hell were you thinking? You've put this whole operation in even more jeopardy by killing the boy.'

Alessandri's face contorted in fury, his coal-black eyes blazed. He grabbed the Spaniard by the arm and led him into the narrow corridor outside.

'You idiot,' he spat contemptuously. 'Do you want the whole ship to hear? This is still my operation. I say what happens. The kid had seen things. He knew too much and had to be shut up. He could have ruined the whole thing. Besides, no one will question it. The boy was obviously a junkie. Just keep your mouth shut and your head down if you don't want to end up like him.'

The Spaniard went back to his cabin. His companion was already there.

'The kid's been killed,' he said.

His companion felt a sense of foreboding. He knew the Italians were volatile and the situation was getting worse. 'How?' he asked.

'They've set it up to look like he overdosed on heroin. Marco said the kid knew too much. He must have found out about the drugs. I wasn't given any more details. Let's just say Marco wasn't in the mood for idle chat.' He nursed his aching arm, still throbbing from the Italian's vice-like grip. 'I'll have a word with the boy's bunk mate later, before we dock in England, see what I can find out.'

'What are they going to do with the body?'

'They could just throw the body overboard but at some stage questions will be asked about a missing crew member. I think they will have to inform the captain but we know he won't ask too many questions. My guess is they'll wait until we dock when they'll notify the Port Authority that the boy died of a self-inflicted overdose. They'll get away with it, as long as the Brits don't dig too hard.'

His companion could see the weight of Will's death sitting heavily on his shoulders. He tried to ease his friend's guilt, 'There was nothing we could have done about without jeopardising the whole operation. You know that.'

Iain Robertson, Master of the *Star Supreme* was an ex-Royal Navy skipper and liked his men to call him 'Captain'. He only had a couple of years to go until retirement after an unblemished forty-year career at sea. Everything he'd worked for since he'd started as a cabin boy on a Clyde paddle steamer was now at risk. Slumped at the desk in his office on the crew deck below the bridge, he reflected on his own stupidity.

Explaining a dead body to the British Port Authorities was

going to be a lot more difficult than bribing a few Turkish officials.

He picked up the satellite phone on his desk and called the Harbour Master at Tilbury Docks on the Thames estuary at the gateway to London. He gave a brief explanation of how the body of an 18-year-old British crew member had been found on a car deck, probable cause of death: heroin overdose.

The Harbour Master asked where the body was being held.

'We cleared one of the cold storage units and put him in there,' explained Robertson.

'When do you dock?'

'Eighteen hundred hours today.'

'I'll inform the Coroner and the Health Board now. Nothing must move on or off the Star Supreme, and that includes your crew, until the authorities have given you the all clear. It would help me if you'd contact your shipping agents so they can send somebody with the police to break the news to the crewman's family.'

'I'll do that now,' said the Captain.

Robertson replaced the hand-set. He knew what was coming. The Port Authority would double-check the boy had not died of any infectious diseases. They would then insist the ship's entire food stocks were replaced. A private ambulance would be waiting, as well as the Port Police, to move the body to the morgue. All he had to do was keep a cool head, get the ship to America, and then he would be free of them, once and for all.

CHAPTER FOURTEEN

HENRY FIELD had already telephoned three times for Jane before she arrived in the office at twenty past ten. Her morning had already gone badly. A trip to the dentist had left her nursing a sore mouth. The dental surgeon had moaned the whole time about getting two parking tickets.

'Parking fines, Eileen, are nothing to do with me,' Jane told her tetchily. 'You want to murder that husband of yours, then I'll get involved.'

'I'll keep that in mind,' said the dentist by way of an apology.

Jane threw her bag over the back of her chair and called Field's office at the Crown Prosecution Service. Jane liked Henry. He was extremely diligent and would go that extra mile in pursuit of the truth. Inside the courtroom he was like a terrier, locking his jaw into the case and refusing to let go. But once he walked down the court steps he reverted into his other persona, the quiet bachelor who was a fantastic cook and genial dinner party host.

'Henry, what's up? Please don't give me any bad news. I've just spent half an hour in the dentist's chair and my mouth's killing me.'

'Sorry, Jane, but your day is about to get worse. West's solicitor has made an appeal to a judge in chambers to overturn the magistrate's decision. It's being heard in the next couple of hours. I've got the file in front of me. I'm short staffed this morning and there's only two people I can pass this on to.'

'How experienced are they?'

'Not very, but if we have proof this American has been interfering with witnesses, it should be a pretty straightforward affair. He's not going to get bail.'

'This case has become important, Henry. Is there any chance of you fighting it yourself?'

'It's fairly routine, Jane, and I'm terribly busy.'

Jane stayed silent, waiting for Henry to give in.

'Okay, if it means that much to you. Meet me at the Crown Court. We have a circuit judge on today. His clerk has said he will hear the case in chambers once the court has broken for lunch. I could do with being brought up to speed.'

'Brought up to speed, Henry? You've been listening to too many politically-correct probation officers.'

Henry let her slight dig pass. 'Meet me down here as soon as you can.'

Jane put down the receiver. She was furious. She should have realised West and his lawyer would put up a bitter fight.

*

Cambridge courts building is a mixture of Victorian Gothic and late 1970s additions slapped on without much thought or care. Jane spied Henry Field talking to a couple of barristers dressed in their wigs and gowns. He broke off his conversation and gently manoeuvered her towards a small side room.

'Let's go in here and you can tell me what's going on,' he said.

Jane knew Henry would have already read the file and by now probably knew almost as much about the case she did, so she didn't bother wasting time by repeating the bare facts.

'West's father is a US diplomat in London. I think that has more to do with the appeal than anything else.'

'So, how do you want me to play this?'

'We received the DNA results this morning. His DNA matches the semen samples taken from both Hayley

Bannerman and Jennifer Clarke. We know they were both drugged using the same chemical that we found in his bathroom. The case against him is watertight. More importantly for this hearing, West has already bought off a witness once before, in the Clarke case. We should be okay if we emphasise this strongly. You know the view judges take on that. We need to win this one. I have a feeling that West will flee if he's released.'

A court officer popped his head around the door.

'His Honour has broken early for lunch. You're on,' he told the lawyer.

Henry turned to Jane. 'Wait and I'll try and get you called in.'

Jane took a seat outside the courtroom door as Henry walked in with West's lawyer, Ms Everett. Confident, Jane thought, almost smug. Henry was a good solicitor, though, and had rarely let her down in the past. She checked her watch repeatedly. Twenty minutes passed. It seemed like an eternity.

Eventually, the door opened. Caroline Everett still had that smug smile plastered across her face. Deep furrows rutted Henry's brow. He didn't need to tell her the outcome.

'Nice doing business with you, Mr Field,' Caroline Everett said as she swept past him. She stopped in her tracks and turned to Jane. 'A word of advice Mrs Blackburn. You're wasting your time here. We both know you couldn't make your case against my client stand up if it was nailed to the ground.'

Jane sprang to her feet but Henry intervened. 'Please, not one word. Quiet,' he said as West's lawyer swaggered down the corridor without looking back.

Henry gently, but firmly, took Jane's arm and led her out of the court and across the car park to his navy blue Renault. She did not protest. They walked in silence. Once inside the car, Jane turned and looked at him. 'What the hell happened in there, Henry?'

He looked perplexed. 'I've known Judge Hammond for twelve years and I'm telling you, Jane, that decision had been made before we even got into those chambers.'

'Are you sure?'

'I realise I'll never have your instincts. You're a bloody good detective, but after twenty-three years in the CPS, even I can see this was a foregone conclusion. There was nothing I could have said that would have changed the outcome. Somehow, somewhere, a deal has been done.'

Jane almost stammered with fury, 'I can't believe it. How do we find out what's gone on? Do we know anybody in the Lord Chancellor's Office?'

'How much effort is this really worth, Jane?'

'You want me to ask Jennifer Clarke's parents or Hayley Bannerman or Claire Reece whether it's worth it?' she said angrily, immediately regretting her tone. He was on her side.

'Okay, tell you what I'll do,' said Henry. 'I'm in London at the Crown Prosecution office tomorrow afternoon. It shouldn't be too difficult to find out if somebody out of the ordinary has been making contact with the Judge. Meanwhile we can start here. We both know who's the biggest gossip in town.'

'Toby Harding,' Jane said instantly.

'If anyone knows anything, it's him. No intrigue is too small for that man. He's defending in Court Two this afternoon. Why not leave a message with his clerk? Oh, by the way, there is a little bit of good news. The only concession I managed to get out of the Judge was that Charles West had to hand in his passport and he has to report at the station here in Cambridge every day by ten o'clock. He didn't lift the reporting restrictions either.'

CHAPTER FIFTEEN

JANE SLAMMED her office door, almost taking it off the hinges. She jumped at the noise and wondered how the door was still intact after all the abuse it had withstood over the years. Steve gave her a few minutes before following her into the office, closing the door quietly behind him.

'The judge released him,' she said, her eyes blazing.

'What?' Steve couldn't believe his ears. 'Surely you and Henry told the judge about his interference with the witness?'

Jane turned on Cheney, 'Don't ever tell me how to do my job. I didn't even get a look in.'

She slumped in her chair, holding her head in her hands. The pair of them sat in total silence for several minutes. Slowly, Jane raised her head and looked at Steve.

'I'm sorry. I wasn't even allowed in the Judge's chamber. West's lawyer saw to that. Henry tried his best but he told me the decision had been a foregone conclusion. He thinks someone got to the judge.'

'Is he sure? I just can't believe it.'

'I know, that's what I thought, but how else can you explain it? Henry's never seen anything like it before.'

'What do we do now?' Steve asked.

'I need to do a bit of digging, starting with Toby Harding. Meanwhile, Henry's going to ask a couple of questions at the Crown offices in London tomorrow. The father seems to have more influential friends than I realised. But first we'd better make some phone calls. You phone Jennifer's parents and I'll call Claire Reece and Hayley Bannerman. I don't want any of them finding this out on the college grapevine.'

As Steve got up to leave the office, Jane said, 'We haven't lost totally. West has to present himself at the station by ten o'clock every morning. Tell the desk. I want him collared first thing when he arrives tomorrow so we can do some more questioning.'

Jane pulled up a seat in the cafeteria and sat down alongside four of her officers, all looking tired and defeated.

'From the looks on your faces you must have heard then,' she said.

'Heard what?' asked Matt.

'The judge has let West go. He's out on bail.'

From the silence that greeted her, they obviously hadn't heard.

At last one of them spoke up, 'Well, we're not going to see him again.'

'Thanks, Matt. I needed to hear that. So why the long faces?'

'Al Smith's son, the boy who's in hospital with a lung problem, wants a toy Spiderman for his birthday but nobody can get their hands on one,' explained Matt. 'This has been tougher than the Bedford Level Strangler investigation.'

'Important stuff, then lads.' She instantly regretted her cynicism. They were hard-bitten coppers who spent their lives dealing with the scum of this world. Helping children, from whatever walk of life, was one of the best ways policemen found to stop themselves sinking into the cesspool.

'All right,' Jane sighed. 'I'm up for a bit of a distraction at the moment. I'll see what I can do.'

She returned to her office and made a quick call to the press officer of Brown's department store who she'd met at one of Sally's dinner parties.

'Edward? Hi, it's Jane Blackburn. I have a little favour to ask. I need a Spiderman for one of the officers' kids.'

'Sorry, Jane. I couldn't help you out even if I wanted to. We're only expecting thirty more in and there's a waiting list ten times that long already.'

'The young boy is ill in hospital. Please.'

'Well, maybe if the store could use it for a bit of publicity, we might be able to arrange something.'

'No. I'd rather there wasn't any publicity. Please, Ed.'

Edward Harrison hesitated for a moment then relented. 'All right, have someone come around to collect it tomorrow afternoon. But if this gets out then I'll be on your doorstep looking for a job.'

Jane returned triumphantly to the cafeteria. Around the table sat fifty-four years of policing experience and she'd managed to solve the problem with one phone call. She leaned over to Matt, 'Operation Spiderman is underway. Have someone send a squad car to Brown's department store to collect the package tomorrow afternoon.'

'Well done, boss,' said Matt.

'That's fine,' Jane said grinning. 'Because you now all owe me an hour's overtime!'

CHAPTER SIXTEEN

SIMON ANDERS had been an undertaker all his working life. Over the course of thirty years in the business he had helped to bury people he had known, even those he had loved, but this was one of the hardest things he'd ever had to do. His practised hands moved deftly over the boy's torso, washing away the stains left by the pathology lab. It had been a long time since he had last washed a body.

Simon had turned the small family firm he'd inherited into a large operation with four partners and a staff of twenty. He normally left the job of washing down bodies to his assistants, but when he'd received the phone call from Brian Davies, he promised to take care of the boy personally. Brian was Simon's oldest friend. They'd been pals almost all their lives and Simon was godfather to Brian's son, Will. Simon had two daughters and as he gently washed the boy's body his mind filled with memories of the child he had known and cherished like the son he never had.

Will Davies had been fit all his short life, a natural athlete. Simon remembered how Will had endured teasing from his friends for refusing to eat junk food. He smiled, recalling the upset Will had caused his father when, at fourteen, he declared that he had become a vegetarian.

Brian Davies ran a small building company, along with his two older sons. His youngest son, Will, had wanted to see something of the world before marriage and a mortgage tied him to a life in his father's company. The cheapest and easiest way was to earn his passage as a deck hand on whatever ship was willing to take on young and eager seamen. His mother, Helen, had always proudly showed off Will's letters, telling them about new friends and faces, new places he had seen. He never complained about his work, the long hours of drudgery in between ports.

Simon gently dressed the boy in the coffin shroud he'd wear until his parents brought down the clothes he would be buried in. Then he called in an assistant to place the body in the cool room. The undertaker needed to make a phone call. Something was not right.

Anders flicked through his address book to find Bill Donaldson's home telephone number. The phone rang twice before the coroner for Cambridgeshire answered.

'Hello, Bill. This is Simon Anders. Sorry about bothering you at home at this hour but I need to speak to you about Will Davies. I received his body this afternoon.'

'Yes, the drug overdose. I brought his file home to read. Isn't he the son of Brian Davies, the builder?'

'Yes.'

'So what can I do for you?'

Bill could hear the hesitation in the undertaker's voice. Simon wasn't one to phone up and ask questions unless there was a good reason.

'Listen, you know you encouraged all the undertakers in the area to go on a seminar after that case of the doctor up north who killed dozens of his patients.'

'Shipman,' the coroner prompted.

'Yes, that's the one. The course was basically to make us more conscious of situations where things didn't quite add up.'

'And you think this is the case with this boy?'

'Yes, but before we go any further Bill, I have to declare an interest. I've known Will all his life.'

'And I've known you a long time, Simon, and I'm willing to trust your instincts. So what's wrong?'

'He was a health nut, Bill. Over the years I've seen the bodies of many drug users who have died of an overdose and Will just doesn't fit the usual profile. There were no track marks on his body at all.'

'Maybe he snorted it.'

'His nose shows no signs of drug taking. It just doesn't seem right.'

'I'll tell you what I'll do. I'll give Harold, the Coroner's Officer, a ring tomorrow morning. He's based down at the police station on a Thursday. I'll ask him to see if Jane Blackburn can give us a hand. In the meantime, I'll read the file this evening and see if anything unusual leaps out of the paperwork.'

'Sorry about that. Hope you didn't have anything planned.'

'No. I can't think of a better way to spend an evening. How's your golf going?'

'I've dropped two on my handicap because I haven't been out for so long. Too busy playing detective!'

Simon put down the phone. He debated whether to tell Brian of his call to the coroner. He decided not to. The boy's mother and father had already been through enough.

CHAPTER SEVENTEEN

HAROLD SMITH had been retired from the force for more than ten years but his part-time job as Coroner's Officer meant he could still stay in touch with policemen. He was pushing sixty but still working kept him young. His thirty years of experience on the force was never wasted, he was on good terms with almost everyone in the station and many officers often picked his brains.

He'd already made a phone call to the CID room upstairs and knew Jane hadn't arrived in the office. So he waited at the front desk, hoping to ambush her on the way in. He didn't have to wait long.

'Detective Inspector Blackburn,' he announced as Jane scurried through the front door.

'Inspector Smith,' Jane replied, stopping in her tracks and turning to face Harold. 'How can I help you on this pleasant, sunny day? How's Jean?'

'She's fine. We've the first of the season's flower shows coming up and she's hoping her sweet peas will take top honours this year. Look, Jane, I'm here at the request of the Coroner. He wondered if you could pop in at lunchtime for a few minutes.'

Jane thought for a moment. 'I'm busy at lunchtime and most of my day seems to be mapped out but I've half an hour to spare, so I could go over to his office now.'

'I know he's in clearing up paperwork this morning, so if you give him a quick call, I'm sure that'll be fine. He's keen to see you.'

In the CID room, Jane gave Jill a pile of paperwork to sort through and told her, 'If anyone needs me I'm off to see Bill Donaldson. Won't be too long.'

Taking an unmarked station car, Jane headed north along Sydney Street and into St Andrew's Street. The Coroner's office was above a small clothing shop opposite the Shire Hall. In England, coroners are usually local solicitors who do the job part-time. Donaldson's office had not changed in over forty-five years. Bill could see no reason for spending money on decoration. 'The dead don't care, criminals have bigger things to worry about and no client likes to see a rich solicitor,' was his favourite saying. This had always amused Jane because she knew Bill had at least four semi-rare classic cars in his garage at home.

Donaldson's long-suffering secretary, who years ago had lost her sense of humour, waved Jane through into Bill's den of an office. She stepped over the gaping cracks in the lino and sat on the edge of a threadbare armchair. Bill Donaldson sat at a large partners' desk, books piled at each corner, papers strewn across the middle.

He looked up from the muddle and stood and walked over to the armchair. Bill was in his early sixties, slightly built with short, thinning grey hair. His three-piece suit was far too heavy for the warm weather. She looked down and saw he was wearing brown brogues and no socks.

'Jane. Nice to see you. I haven't heard from you in a while.'

'Sorry I haven't passed any business your way, but if Dad doesn't leave the MG alone then you could have another customer on your books!'

Bill had always enjoyed Jane's morbid sense of humour.

'Would you like some coffee?' he asked.

'That depends. What sort of mood is Margaret in today?'

Bill shook his head in despair. 'Not one of her better days, I'm afraid.'

'Then I'll pass, if you don't mind.'

Bill slumped in the other armchair, a pained look on his face, 'I'd let her go if it wasn't for the fact she knows more about my business than I do. Besides, I'm not that brave.' He looked absent-mindedly out of the window. 'So how is the MG?'

'Looking good,' Jane said. 'My re-chromed headlights are back from the restorers. I'll think we'll give you a run for your money in the August car rally.'

'I accept the challenge. Now, I hate to do this to you, Jane, because I know how busy you are but an interesting little case landed on my desk yesterday and I think it raises a few questions.'

He handed Jane a manila folder with the name WILLIAM JOHN DAVIES written on the cover in black felt pen.

'I haven't a lot of time,' Jane said. 'Could you give me a quick summary?'

'A local boy, eighteen years old, died while he was working on a car transporter ship bound for Tilbury. You know the ones, they export new cars for various car companies around the world. Apparently, he died in the Bay of Biscay and his body was kept in the ship's cold store until they reached the dock.'

'Along with their food? Nice.'

'The ship docked on Wednesday and the Coroner in Essex phoned to ask if I wanted the boy's body kept in transit so it could be sent straight to Cambridge to help his family.'

'How did he die? What does the post mortem say?'

'Heroin overdose.'

'You still haven't explained why you think this was suspicious,' Jane said, flicking through the report.

'Look at the pathologist's report from the post mortem. The heroin found in his system was almost one hundred per cent pure. It hadn't been cut with anything.'

Jane fell silent for a moment as she quickly scanned the PM report. After a couple of minutes she said, 'I agree no one takes one hundred per cent heroin but...' Bill stopped her.

'I received a phone call last night from the undertaker, Simon Anders. He knows the family quite well. He's convinced the cause of death just doesn't add up. Apparently the kid was an absolute health nut who wouldn't take so much as an aspirin.'

'Track marks?' Jane asked.

'None, other than the shot that apparently killed him. Otherwise, Simon said that the kid looked as if he was fit as a fiddle. That's what made him call me. I was wondering if you'd have a look into it.'

'It does sound a little odd, Bill, but your timing's not great. We've had a bit of a nightmare case on at the moment.'

'You mean the young American? It's the talk of the courts at the moment.'

'Yes,' shrugged Jane. 'It's going to keep me well and truly occupied for a while. Have you got the details of the boy's ship?'

'You'll find them in the file. I can get Margaret to run you off a copy.'

'Okay.' Jane said at last. 'You know I can't promise anything at the moment but I'll make a few phone calls and see what I can find out. When's the funeral?'

'Tomorrow, three o'clock. Burial.'

'I'll do my best.'

Steve was heading out of the CID room as Jane arrived.

'I'm just going down to see if West has signed in yet,' he said.

'Good idea,' she said. 'Is there anybody around with a bit of spare time on their hands?'

Steve let out a laugh. 'Tell me, again, what's spare time?'

'You remember, those few minutes between leaving work and

falling into bed exhausted.'

'Well, Dan isn't snowed under at the moment, being new in the office. He could get Matt to help him out. Why?'

'The Coroner has asked me to check out a suspicious death on a ship.'

'A ship? We're forty miles from the nearest sea.'

'Bill Donaldson has done me a few pretty big favours in the past and I want to try and help him out on this one. Now go and check on West and let me know if our young VIP has deigned to call on us.'

DCs Dan Miller and Matt Mason crammed around Jane's desk as she briefed them about the death of Will Davies.

'He was a crewman on the *Star Supreme*,' she explained. 'I need you to contact the Port Authority at Tilbury and find out where the ship is now. It's registered in Korea. Track down the parent company and speak to their shipping agents. The agents will probably be based at Tilbury. Also, I want the pair of you to have a word with the boy's mother and father. I don't need to tell you to go gently with the parents.'

Jane passed them a copy of the coroner's file. 'I don't expect you to spend hours on this. I'll see you early afternoon and you can give me a summary,' she said.

Their conversation was cut short as Steve pushed his way past Dan and leaned over Jane's desk.

'West didn't appear this morning. I've had the address where he is supposed to be staying checked out. His flatmates haven't seen him since yesterday evening.'

Jane leapt to her feet and checked her watch. Quarter past eleven.

She was gripped by a combination of anger and dread. 'Fuck, I knew it,' she exploded. 'Let's rattle Ms Everett's cage. I hope to God we're not too late.'

CHAPTER EIGHTEEN

THE TWO DETECTIVES were in no mood to take a seat in reception at the expensively decorated offices of Brown, Strange and Wilson solicitors. They followed the receptionist along an airy corridor. Halfway down she stopped and politely knocked on a door. A small brass plaque read: Caroline Everett, Junior Partner.

'Come in,' said a voice they both recognised.

Jane signalled Steve to bend down. She put her face close to his ear and whispered, 'West is a diplomat's son. Remember, Benson wants us to approach this with diplomacy and discretion and as your senior officer I expect you to follow the Superintendent's direction.'

Before he could reply, Jane barged past the receptionist. Caroline Everett was sitting behind a large oak desk, with neatly stacked case notes, a lap-top, the morning's mail and a cup of coffee on it.

'Where is he?' Jane demanded, her face flushed with frustration.

Caroline Everett, lifted her head from the case notes she was studying, her lips formed in a condescending smile.

'Inspector Blackburn. Delighted.'

'I'm sorry, Caroline,' the receptionist stammered apologetically. 'They just barged past me.'

'That's all right Jackie. I'll deal with this.'

Steve closed the door as the receptionist left, still shaken by the intrusion.

'So, where is he?' Jane asked again.

'And who might you be referring to Inspector? We're a busy firm and I've many clients.'

'You know exactly who I'm talking about. Where's Charles West?'

'I take it he didn't observe his bail conditions by checking in this morning,' the lawyer said matter-of-factly.

'You know full well he didn't.'

'If you'd take a seat Inspector, I'll make some enquiries.'

Jane and Steve watched the hint of a nervous smile betray her cool and composed exterior as she picked up the phone.

'Mr West please. This is Caroline Everett, his son's solicitor.'

Jane's eyes, now dark with anger, never left the solicitor.

'Mr West. This is Caroline Everett. I've been advised that your son did not check in at the police station this morning. I wonder if you could…'

As she fell silent, the colour slowly drained from her softly tanned skin.

'But…but Mr West, surely you understand you were required to hand in his passport. You have broken the bail conditions by…'

Jane leapt round the desk, grabbed the phone out of her hand and yelled Sterling West's name down the phone. The line was already dead.

Caroline Everett's cool veneer slipped as she protested, 'I had no idea, really.'

Jane thumped the desk, 'Spare me, sweetheart. You knew this was going to happen!'

Steve stepped forward and stopped Jane to calm her down, but she was having none of it. Sometimes he did not understand the demons that drove her on. As a policeman you have to learn that you cannot win every fight, there's always another day. But not Jane, she would and could beat herself up over the smallest of injustices. This one was eating her alive. Why?

Caroline Everett continued pleading her innocence. 'You must understand. I had absolutely no idea...'

Jane looked the girl straight in the eye. 'You're as much a puppet here as I am. Somebody else has been pulling strings for that kid and I'm going to find out who it is.'

The DI reached out and swiped both hands across the desk, sending papers and coffee flying. Caroline Everett watched her lap top bounce off the wall and on to the floor.

The noise brought people from nearby offices rushing in. An elderly gentleman in his mid-sixties scanned the chaos and confronted Jane.

'Good God! What happened here?'

Jane recognised Ian Wilkins, the firm's Senior Partner. She pointed at Caroline Everett, who still sat wide-eyed surveying the carnage of her designer office.

'Your Junior Associate here has assisted a suspected rapist to flee the country.'

'That does not give you the right to come barging into these offices in such a manner, Inspector,' Wilkins protested.

'It gives me every right. You're not the one who had to interview his victims, Mr Wilkins. You're not the one who had to watch her daughter die in a coma because of your client. Be warned, I will have Charles West extradited to stand trial, even if it means going to Washington and dragging him back myself.'

As Jane had barged her way out she heard Ian Wilkins calling to the receptionist, 'Get Superintendent Benson on the phone. I'll be in my office.'

CHAPTER NINETEEN

JANE WAS halfway down the street before Steve eventually caught up with her. He grabbed her arm to slow her down.

'That was an interesting lesson in diplomacy and discretion,' he said, desperately trying to diffuse the situation. 'Come on, let's go back to the office. Via the Cricketers,' he added as an afterthought.

Jane's cell phone rang as they entered the pub.

It was Dan Miller. 'We're on our way back to the station. We've just met Will Davies's parents.'

She told them to forget the office and instead brief them in the pub.

Ten minutes later Dan and Matt arrived to find Jane sitting next to Steve in the far corner of the lounge bar, a small cloud of depression hanging over their table.

'Who died?' Dan asked.

'We've been on the front line with some solicitors. Another time,' replied Jane. 'What have you got on Davies?'

'Well, we've got some really good news.'

'Good,' sighed Jane. 'We bloody well need it.'

Miller looked at Jane and then back at Steve. 'Has something happened we should know about?'

'Our DI here, the model of diplomacy I was telling you about on the office tour, has just trashed the office of Charles West's solicitor'

Miller looked at Jane in admiration. 'Impressive. Why?'

'West has already broken his bail conditions. Didn't show up at the station this morning. Turns out he's now sitting safely in America.'

Miller almost choked on the glass of orange juice he was drinking.

'We're not one hundred percent sure the lawyer was involved,' Steve added.

'Are you seriously telling me she didn't even suspect that this was going to happen?' Jane protested.

Steve looked at her. 'Yeah, you're right. She must have known.'

'So,' Jane said. 'Give us the good news.'

'The ship the boy was serving on, the *Star Supreme*, is still at the docks. We spoke to a Mr ..' Dan hesitated as he flicked through his notes. 'A...Mr Thompson, from the Harbour Master's Office in Tilbury. Apparently the ship has developed trouble with the hydraulics on the loading ramp. He seemed pretty pissed off about it because it was causing him no end of trouble.'

'Do we know how long it's going to be stuck there?' Jane asked.

'According to him, engineers will be working on it for at least the next two or three days.'

'What do we know about the shipping agent and the parent company?' Jane enquired.

'The shipping agents are A & E Grant, based at Tilbury docks. We have a phone number for the parent company in Pusan, South Korea. They've probably already closed for business today, but we'll call them from the office this afternoon and see if we can contact anyone.'

'And Will's parents?'

'Really nice couple, hardworking, decent. They run a small building firm where Will's two older brothers work. The mother was too devastated to talk but we managed to get Mr

Davies to take a walk in the garden and he said right from the start that he didn't believe Will was a drug addict. We told him the Coroner had asked us to make a few more enquiries. He kept telling us his son was a health freak.'

Dan nodded in Matt's direction. 'Mason here asked if we could have a quick look around the boy's room.'

'So, what did you see?' Jane asked, turning her attention on the other young officer.

'God', she thought, 'I'm getting old. They're getting younger by the day'.

Matt Mason had been in Jane's office for six months. He hadn't made a dramatic impression in that time, but he'd kept his nose clean and hadn't fouled up on anything. He painted a picture of the room. 'Small. Single bed. Manchester United fan, swimming, cricket trophies and athletics trophies on the shelves. Big map of the world on one wall with postcards stuck around it. His mother had been tracking the ship's progress around the globe. At that point the father was overcome with emotion, so we took our cue and left.'

'The funeral is tomorrow afternoon. I want you two to bring your best suits into the office. If Steve and I can't make it to the funeral, you two can go in our place. If you haven't got a black tie, buy one. Funerals are like magnets, they attract all sorts of people. Let's see who turns up.'

Jane flipped open her phone and called Jill.

'Anything going on I should know about?'

'There are a few messages. The most important is from Superintendent Benson.'

'On a scale of one to ten, how bad?'

'Try one hundred and eleven,' said Jill. 'Sounds like you've been making friends at Brown, Strange & Wilson.'

'I guess you could say that,' Jane said sheepishly. She was going to be crucified for her little outburst and was already beginning to regret it. 'Anything else?'

'No. Everything else can wait.'

'Steve and I are going to Tilbury this afternoon to inspect a ship and make some enquiries on behalf of the Coroner. We probably won't be back until late this evening.'

'How convenient.' Jill said with a laugh. 'I'll try and hold off Benson. See you tomorrow.'

Steve looked at Jane. 'So, I take it we're off to Tilbury, then?'

'Come on. If you're a good boy I'll buy you an ice cream. You drive. That glass of wine has gone straight to my head.'

CHAPTER TWENTY

HUGE WAREHOUSES, some a hundred feet high and nearly half a mile long, dwarfed the station car. Steve slowly followed signs directing them towards Dock 39, where the *Star Supreme* was berthed.

'Look at all those cars.' Steve exclaimed, pointing over to the left. 'There must be a couple of thousand.'

Jane stared out at row upon row of smart new Japanese cars, still covered with a bright white plastic to protect their roofs and bonnets. They were neatly lined up across an area the size of several football pitches.

Another sign for Dock 39 sent them weaving along a quayside between huge stacks of shipping containers. Steve braked to allow a giant straddle carrier to pass. The massive girder structure, sat on eight huge tractor wheels, looked like a vehicle from the War Of The Worlds. A driver sitting in a small glass cabin 30ft off the ground, deftly manoeuvred the weird-looking crane to pick up a metal container as big as a living room. A warning alarm screeched constantly to remind anyone nearby to get out of the way.

Jane grinned at Steve, 'I think we'll sit here for a while and let it pass. I'm not describing that machine on an insurance form.'

'Are you prepared to admit we're lost yet?' Steve asked, uncertain where to go next.

'There's a guy over there working on a boat. We can ask him where we are.'

Jane climbed out of the passenger seat and strolled over to the edge of the dock. She looked down on a man in his early seventies. He wore a dark blue overcoat with a high roll-neck sweater underneath. His head and face were covered in thick white hair. His weathered cheeks and hands told her he'd spent his life on the water.

'Excuse me,' Jane said loudly. 'We're a bit lost. We're looking for Dock 39.'

'Well, you're standing on Dock 39,' he said in a West Country accent. He didn't look up and carried on coiling a rope he held in his gnarled hands. 'If you're looking for a particular ship,' he continued, straightening his back to look up at Jane. His dark grey eyes seemed to twinkle. 'The best thing you can do, Miss, is go to the Harbour Master's office, just around from those containers.' He pointed to three red containers stacked on top of each other to her left.

The small red brick Victorian Harbour Master's office was hidden among canyons of containers. Jane and Cheney walked into a large ground-floor office. In one corner stood a bookcase, filled to overflowing with magazines and books on maritime law. A large, hand-painted map of the port filled the entire back wall. Fifty or sixty wooden boats, each with its name neatly written on the top, were attached to the map with magnets. Every model boat indicated the position of a ship in the dock. The words Port of Tilbury were displayed across the top of the map in large gold lettering. Underneath, someone had stuck a yellow post-it note proclaiming "For sale".

Jane held out her hand to a portly man sat behind a desk. She guessed he was in his early forties but a slightly greying beard made him look older than he really was. She and Cheney pulled out their warrant cards, which he read slowly and carefully.

'You here about the body, then?' he asked, finally.

'Yes,' replied Jane. 'I'm sorry, I don't have your name.'

'Thomas Hobson. I've been Harbour Master here for nine

years and it's only the second time I've had to deal with a body. First one was a suicide. Drove his car clean off Dock 36. Seven years ago now.'

He pointed to his left, as if Jane and Steve could actually see Dock 36, through the bookcase.

'Terrible business.' Hobson went on. 'He was a young lad, too.'

'I see. We're actually looking for the *Star Supreme*. I understand you were contacted when she docked.'

'The master radioed ahead to warn Port Authorities and the port police they had a body on board. When they docked, the Health Authority were first on board, but because the lad didn't die of a disease...' Hobson stopped mid-sentence to check through a report in a grey file to make sure he had his facts straight. 'Yes, here it is. "Drug overdose, possible suicide. No health risk." Like I was saying, because it wasn't a disease, they instantly contacted the Coroner, and then it was no longer my problem.'

Hobson seemed visibly relieved the body was no longer his problem.

'You've no idea how much paperwork a body can generate,' he said.

Jane thought guiltily of the paperwork weighing down her desk and shot Steve a let's-be-polite-and-get-out-of-here look.

'If you could just point out the *Star Supreme* on your map, we'll be going,' Jane said.

'She's there.' Hobson jabbed a chubby finger on a model boat stuck to the map. She was in a berth a quarter of a mile from the harbour master's office.

'Been tied up there for nearly three days already. We like to get them in on one tide and out on the next. Caused no end of problems she has.'

'Do you know how much longer she'll be here?' Jane asked.

Hobson explained that after the Zeebrugge ferry disaster in Belgium, which claimed the lives of nearly two hundred passengers, ships were not allowed to put to sea from the UK that were not totally sealed.

'On the back of the *Star Supreme* is the biggest hydraulic ramp you've ever seen. Helps them load and unload the cars. It got stuck,' said the harbour master. 'The authority that issues certificates of sea-worthiness has been seriously touchy about having these things checked when they go wrong. I expect it will be repaired tomorrow, but then the master has to wait to have the certificate re-issued, which could delay the ship another three or four days.'

Jane took advantage of the slight pause in the conversation to thank Hobson and make their exit. She wasn't sure when they'd get another chance.

There was no mistaking the *Star Supreme*. Her sheer size silenced them momentarily. Jane and Steve stepped out of the car and stood looking at a wall of steel that rose into the air like a pale blue cliff.

'Just look at that thing,' said Steve in awe. 'It's got to be at least one hundred and fifty feet high. It looks bigger than the police station.'

The name *Star Supreme* was written on her stern in English and again in what Jane presumed to be Korean. The rear roll-on, roll-off ramp jutted awkwardly from the stern, suspended one third of the way from the closed position. The other ramp, on the starboard side, facing the dock was shut.

Jane could see the boat wasn't fully laden. The red paint of its Plimsoll line rode high out of the water. The only way on board looked to be up a set of metal stairs placed between the harbour and a small doorway, halfway up the side of the ship, normally used by pilots to get on and off at sea.

About twenty feet above the pilot's port was a forty-feet-long open-railed gangway. Apart from a similar gangway near the ship's nose there wasn't a window or porthole in sight.

There was no alternative, Jane would have to tackle the steps. Despite having spent nearly seven years in the Royal Navy, she'd never been comfortable about climbing open steps above water. Gulping deeply, she stepped onto the gangway. Her stomach churned as she looked down through the metal grill of the step at the black water twenty feet below. Palms sweating, she gripped the rail tighter and looked up at tiny black hole of the pilot door fifty feet above. Just then she caught sight of a dark-haired figure in crewman's orange overalls staring directly at her from the gangway above the pilot's door. As Jane fixed him with her gaze he took a step back and disappeared into the ship.

*

It wasn't Jane the Spaniard was watching intently but Cheney just a pace behind her on the gangplank. The Spaniard could spot a plain-clothes cop a mile off. His muscles tensed as a feeling of unease enveloped him. Everything they'd worked for was under threat. He turned to find his cabin mate.

CHAPTER TWENTY-ONE

TWO CREWMEN, wearing hard hats and overalls, met the detectives at the top of the gangplank. One looked Malaysian, the other had dark, Mediterranean features.

Jane reached for her badge, turned to the Malaysian and said, 'We'd like to speak to the ship's master please.'

The swarthy one answered, 'Why you want the Captain?'

Definitely Italian, thought Jane. He was 5'9" tall with the strong, stocky build of a rugby player. His dark brown eyes were hard and cold. There was nothing forgiving or soft about his features. His severe short black hair, could barely be seen under the hard hat. Jane took half a step forward, deliberately invading his space.

'The Master's office is on which deck?' she demanded. The Italian didn't reply. He made her feel edgy. Why were they being so deliberately obstructive?

She tried again. 'I'm here to speak to the Master. Take me there, now.'

The Italian did not blink. Finally the Malaysian spoke, quietly and reluctantly, 'This way. I take you.'

*

The Spaniard shook his cabin mate awake. He had been on the duty watch all night and struggled to collect his senses, but there was no mistaking the urgency in the Spaniard's voice.

'You'd better come,' he hissed. 'Two officials have just come on board. A man and a woman.'

'They could just be from the Port Authority,' said his pal, resting on one elbow in the cramped bottom bunk.

'No. Too well dressed,' said the Spaniard. 'They were police. No doubt about it. It's got to be about Will. Why don't they keep their noses out of this? We can't afford any trouble, particularly now we're so close.'

Swinging his legs out of bed, the Spaniard's companion pulled on his trousers in one quick movement. They locked the cabin and headed towards the crew mess room, deliberately taking a long way round. Over the long months on the boat they had become familiar with every corridor and room on the ship. It didn't take the pair long to find the two detectives, still being escorted to the Captain's office. The tall man led the way, talking to the Malaysian about the ship and its cargo. The woman had fallen behind, stopping occasionally to have a close look in rooms off the maze of corridors.

The Spaniard turned to his cabin mate, 'You'd better keep an eye on the Italians. You know how jumpy they're getting. Especially Francesco. I think he's using.'

His companion looked startled. 'Then we really have a dangerous situation on our hands. A drug user with a gun will do anything.'

Jane sat facing a brown-haired man in his late fifties. He had the world-weary expression of one who had seen everything and for whom life held few surprises. Her eyes flicked to his huge hands clasped on top of the desk and then to the broad shoulders. His physique seemed almost at odds with his quiet Scottish accent, the hard edges softened from years abroad. He was probably originally from Greenock, Jane noted.

'There really isn't much more I can tell you about the lad,' said Captain Iain Robertson. 'He was generally well liked and got on with his duties.'

'What were his duties?' Jane asked.

'Supervision of the loading and unloading of cars, checking of the holds and, while we're at sea, general watch and maintenance work. Will often spoke about his parents in Cambridge. That's why I arranged with the authorities at Tilbury to have his body sent there.'

'Did you realise he had a drug problem?' Steve asked.

The Captain kept looking straight at Jane. 'I see all of life on board this ship and I've learned not to make assumptions or ask too many questions. Though I have to confess, I was very surprised when the lad was found dead.'

'Where was he found?'

'Car Deck Four. It costs £20,000 a day to keep this ship going. We couldn't afford to put into a French port when we were so close to Tilbury. So, we wrapped the needle in foil and kept him the best way we could, in the deep freeze. As it happens, we're losing money because we're still here. We should have been turned around in twelve hours.'

The Captain appeared to be genuinely concerned for the lad. Jane could not understand why the boy's death was so obviously playing on the mind of someone who saw crew members come and go at almost every port the ship docked.

Jane got to her feet. 'Thank you for helping us. Would it be possible to see Deck Four, the boy's quarters and to speak to anyone on board he may have been friendly with.'

'You'll want to speak to the young Greek lad, his cabin mate. He seemed to strike up quite a friendship with our two Spanish crewmen as well. I'll have one of my men show you around.'

The dead boy's cabin was barely ten feet by eight. Two bunk beds hung from one wall with a tiny desk underneath a small window. The only other furniture was one chair and two tall, grey lockers. One of them had Will's name on the door. Steve opened it. Most of Will's possessions had left the ship with his body but his clothes, shoes and overalls still hung there. Jane poked her nose into the tiny bathroom, which was far too small for a bath. Instead it had a small shower on one side, a toilet, sink and mirror on the other.

Jane thanked God that when she'd been in the Navy, women did not go to sea.

'I've seen prison cells with better facilities than this,' she exclaimed.

Steve had been going through the pockets on one of Will's shirts. He held up a small red notebook filled with comic drawings.

'Our lad was obviously a bit of a cartoonist', Steve said, handing the book to Jane. Underneath some of the sketches were hastily scrawled passages, the letters slanted towards the top right hand corner of each page.

Holding a page open for Steve to see, she said 'This kid had an interesting imagination.'

They heard the buzz of a heated conversation going on out in the corridor. Jane turned. A boy of about eighteen or nineteen stood in the doorway. He was tall with jet-black hair. Puberty had left its punishing scars, his dark olive skin was badly pock-marked. This was obviously Will's cabin mate, she recognised him from the photos on the cabin wall.

'Can you speak English?' she asked the young Greek.

'Yes. We all have to speak English on board. I'm Demos Katsaris.'

'How long have you worked on board?' Jane asked.

'I've only been on this ship eight months now. When it heads back to the Mediterranean I'm getting off and going home to Athens.'

'Why?'

The boy went to say something but stopped himself. Fear flashed in his eyes.

'Were you and Will good friends?' Jane added, deliberately

switching the conversation.

'We had some good times when we got a few hours shore leave.'

The boy was obviously wary of saying too much. She tried another tack.

'Do you work long hours?'

'When you're trapped on board a ship, there isn't much more to do. We work twelve, fourteen, sixteen hours a day sometimes.'

'Those are long days for a young man.'

His eyes flashed again, this time with indignation. 'I'm nineteen next month. I'm as strong as anybody else here. I can take care of myself.'

'I'm sure you can, Demos. It must be hard losing your cabin-mate. Did you realise he was a heroin addict?'

'Will never took anything in his life. He wasn't a drug user.'

His eyes darted across to the crewman stood in the doorway.

'I'd better get back to my duties,' the youth said, struggling to hide his emotions.

Steve took out his wallet, removed a business card and placed it on the table.

'If you can think of anything else, give us a call.'

They watched Demos turn and walk quickly out of the room.

On the way to Deck Four, Steve paused, letting the crewman pull six or seven feet in front.

'Why did we stop questioning him? He obviously knew something,' Steve whispered.

Jane hit back. 'That kid was scared. He wasn't going to say anything else in front of our guide. Maybe we'll get the opportunity of speaking to him some time later on his own.'

Almost as if he sensed he was being talked about, the crewman turned to Jane and Steve. He was obviously annoyed that they were lagging behind again. He also resented the fact he'd had to cut into his shore leave to show them around.

'This way.'

It wasn't a request.

CHAPTER TWENTY-TWO

DECK FOUR was immense, at least the size of two-and-a-half football pitches. Almost every square inch was jam-packed with cars. The majority were brand new and neatly parked. Against the far wall, fifteen old rusting wrecks littered the deck in an untidy row.

'That,' the crewman said pointing, 'is where the boy was found dead. He was resting against the wheel of one of those cars.'

Jane noticed a CCTV camera on the ceiling almost above her head. The lens wasn't pointing towards where Will had been found. How convenient, she thought. She looked more closely and saw the small red light on the back wasn't lit. The damn thing wasn't even working.

'I'd like to speak to the Spanish crewmen the Captain mentioned had been friendly with Will. I think one of them found his body,' Jane said.

'I will take you back to the galley and bring them to you,' said the crewman, half hoping the tour was over. 'This way please.'

A few minutes later their guide pointed towards a dark-haired man sitting alone at a table near the far wall of the canteen where the twenty-three crewmen ate their meals. The nine officers had their own restaurant.

'There's one of them. I'll go and find the other,' said the guide.

Jane and Cheney walked over to the table and sat down without asking. The Spaniard kept on shovelling food into his mouth with gusto, like he was eating the meal of the condemned.

The detectives showed him their ID.

'We're asking a few questions about Will Davies. We understand you and he were friends,' said Steve.

The Spaniard shrugged his shoulders but didn't look up. He kept on eating. If he'd bothered to raise his eyes he'd have seen the look of absolute disgust on Jane's face. He looked as though he hadn't washed or shaved properly for weeks. He was sun-tanned and a hint of grey in his jet-black hair suggested he was in his early forties. Steve was getting angry at the man's sheer bad manners.

Jane turned to Steve. 'I could do with a cup of coffee. We're clearly going to be here some time. He obviously can't speak English well. Maybe we should have him off the ship to be interviewed through an interpreter.'

The Spaniard's hazel eyes suddenly lifted and fixed on Jane. 'So', he thought, 'it's the woman who's in charge'.

Steve smiled as he turned away. 'Now we have your full attention, mate,' he said under his breath.

The Spaniard put down his knife and fork, pulled a matchstick from his pocket, blew off a lump of orange fluff, and began cleaning his teeth with the sliver of wood. Then he picked up his cup and started slurping coffee.

Jane sat perfectly still. She said, 'I have no intention of going away. I know you can speak English, so let's do this the easy way. You knew the dead boy?'

'Yeah.'

'How well?'

The Spaniard shrugged. 'You know. He was a shipmate. We spoke occasionally.'

'What about?'

'Stuff. Nothing in particular.'

This guy was beginning to seriously annoy her. In a calm voice that hid her irritation, she asked, 'Did you realise he was a user?'

For a split second he flinched. Then it was gone.

Jane carried on, 'I understand you found the body. That can't have been easy.'

'Hey, I been at sea for twenty-two years. I seen dead bodies before.' For the second time his eyes gave him away. Steve returned with two cups of coffee just as the tour guide appeared with the other Spaniard.

Jane told him, 'Your friend here has been a little unco-operative. Perhaps you can give us a little more information.'

'Will, he was nice kid. He play darts well and he beat me all the time at pool. He was funny.' A look of genuine sorrow appeared on his face.

At least this one had got the message, Jane thought. He appeared to be more helpful. He stood just under six feet, with slicked-back thinning hair and dark brown eyes. He was about ten years younger than his companion. Again, he looked as though he hadn't seen a bathroom in weeks, and God only knows what the pair of them had been eating. Whatever it was, Jane could smell it.

The first one interrupted. 'It's a rule of the sea. You don't get too close to your shipmates. They come and go too quickly.'

'What position was the body in when you found it?' asked Jane.

He hesitated for a moment then said, "Will, he was leaning against one of the car tyres. Lying over to one side, with the syringe still in his right hand.'

Alarm bells rang in her head. These two just didn't add up. For a start their accents were all wrong. During her seven years in the Navy, Jane had been stationed in Gibraltar and had spent nearly all her holiday time exploring Spain. She rose to her feet.

'I'll be back in a minute, I'm just going to use the bathroom,' Jane explained. She walked out of the galley, along the corridor, down two flights of stairs and found the boy's cabin. She opened the door and looked around. Pinned on the wall was a photograph of two smiling faces, two young men enjoying themselves. Will and his Greek friend, glasses in hand. As she took the photograph from the wall, she realised what it was that had been nagging in her brain.

A voice behind her made her jump. She turned to find the menacing Italian who she'd met at the top of the gang plank. He certainly had a lot more to say for himself this time. The only problem, he was ranting in his native tongue.

'I don't understand. Do you speak English?'

He was in her face, 'Why don't you just leave. The boy was a junkie. The whole ship knows it.'

His raised voice brought another Italian to the room. They started shouting at each other. The second Italian bustled the first one out of the cabin.

'I apologise for my friend. I think he's just upset because he liked the boy very much.'

'It's time we were leaving anyway,' Jane said, tucking the photograph safely inside her jacket pocket.

The Spanish crewmen watched the two detectives make their way down the steep gang-plank steps.

'Do you think our little act fooled her?'

'Not for one second.'

*

'I'll drive,' Jane said as Steve unlocked the unmarked car. 'I need to think.'

'Okay, you can drive, but I'm not putting up with the music.'

'What?'

'Driving, you're quite good at that, but you don't ever listen to decent music.'

Steve was a jazz fan but Jane didn't care what she was

listening to as long as it was loud. She flung her jacket on the parcel shelf and settled herself into the driver's seat.

'Did you think any of that was odd?' she asked. Steve slowly turned and looked at her.

'Right, so let's recap,' he said. 'We met a Scottish captain who was clearly unco-operative because he was stuck in port, a young Greek lad who was obviously frightened and two Spanish men who had the manners of pigs. No, that all seemed normal to me.'

'Sarcasm, Sergeant Cheney, is not one of your virtues. When I went back to Will's cabin...'

'Pretending to go to the loo,' Steve interrupted.

'There was an Italian there who was extremely angry that I was in the kid's room.'

'Why did you go back?'

'It was the photograph on the wall, the one of the two lads drinking. The Greek held a glass in his right hand, but Will held his with his left.'

Jane showed him the picture, then she took Will's sketchbook from her handbag and flicked through until she found the pages with writing on them.

'I'm no handwriting expert,' she said, 'but that looks to me like the writing of a left-handed person.'

She handed the book to Steve. 'Why did the Spaniard say that he found the needle in Will's right hand?' Steve asked. 'You think the two Spanish murdered the lad?'

Jane started the engine. 'I don't know, but the Coroner was right. It doesn't bloody add up. We'll make a few more phone calls in the morning and find out as much as we can about the ship. They're stuck here until the weekend.'

CHAPTER TWENTY-THREE

FRIDAY MORNING brought crushing news. The Crown Prosecution Service was 'examining the economic viability of instigating extradition procedures in the West case'. In other words, the pen-pushers were working out whether it was cost-effective to bring to justice a man who had raped three girls and been responsible to for the death of one of them.

'Bastards,' Jane said, slamming down the phone. She held her head in her hands. Economic viability. Somebody come down here and ask his victims whether it's economically viable to have this bastard prosecuted.

'Something wrong, Inspector?'

Jane found herself staring straight at the sharply-pressed lines on Benson's black uniform trousers. In the middle of a heat wave he was still wearing his jacket with the silver buttons done up.

'The CPS is...' Benson held up his hands, stopping her mid-sentence.

'I know. I was informed yesterday.'

'And why wasn't I informed yesterday?' Jane asked. 'This is my case, you know.'

'You deliberately chose to ignore my phone call yesterday,' he said coldly.

Jane felt the controlled anger in his voice.

'We're both busy people, so I'm going to come straight to the point. I want this obsession with the West case to end now. Do you understand Detective Inspector? I want you to spend less time telling the CPS how to do their jobs and more time doing your own.'

Jane stared at him in disbelief. 'Three girls have been raped and one of the cases is probably manslaughter. I'm going to do my job and make sure the man responsible stands up in a dock.'

Benson leaned over the desk, 'What you will do, Detective Inspector, is exactly what I tell you. I think you're forgetting who runs the show. Do you think the rest of us are only here to pick up the backlog of cases while you swan around on a whim? If you've got too much time on your hands then I've got plenty of other cases to keep you busy. Also, I do not want senior solicitors like Ian Wilkins phoning me up and complaining about your disgraceful behaviour. I will not have this station's reputation sullied in that way.'

Jane got to her feet, walked around her desk and slightly opened her office door. Staring straight into Benson's eyes, she said, without raising her voice, 'The only reason this station has such an excellent reputation is because of the hard work and dedication the CID team puts into its cases, along with excellent ground work by your uniforms. Your pro-active policing initiatives haven't contributed one jot to this station's efficiency. Don't be under the illusion they have.'

She picked up her jacket and left. Benson called after her, 'Where do you think you're going?'

She glanced at her watch, 'I've a funeral to attend.'

*

Will Davies's funeral was already underway when Jane arrived at St Margaret's-in-the-Field church in Cherry Hinton, a suburb on the south-east outskirts of the city. The modern Protestant church, with its huge expanses of glass and wood, was full. Jane and Steve stood with friends and acquaintances who could not get in. The service was piped through a speaker by the entrance.

The two officers kept a respectful distance as eventually the coffin, carried by Will's father, two brothers, an uncle and two cousins came out of the church into the graveyard. His mother followed directly behind the plain oak coffin. She sobbed gently, her face ashen white against her cinder black dress. Two younger women, her daughters-in-law Jane guessed, helped her along. The Reverend Peter Reid spoke clearly and loudly as the bearers lowered the coffin into the earth.

Steve whispered into Jane's ear, 'See anybody unusual?'

'Not from where I'm standing,' she said.

'Then I'd better buy you a pair of platform shoes, because I can see Will's bunk mate.'

'Where?'

'Over on the far side of the grave.'

'I didn't see him come out of the church,' said Jane who had closely examined the faces of everyone in the slow procession that had followed Will's coffin to the graveside. She'd thought it odd that no one from the ship was there, not even the Captain or a representative. Although she knew that often foreign crewmen were not allowed shore leave in the UK in case they jumped ship.

'I don't think he did,' said Steve. 'He seemed to just appear from the far end of the graveyard.'

'Make your way around to him, but don't make a fuss and scare the kid witless,' Jane said, her voice barely above a whisper.

By now, mourners were leaving the churchyard. One of the brothers and the two daughters-in-law were asking them all to join them for tea or a stiff drink. The elder brother stood next to the vicar, shaking hands and thanking each mourner as they left the churchyard. Will's parents were left, clinging to each other, staring into the grave.

Jane tried desperately to keep her own emotions in check. Four years ago it had been her standing at the graveside with her son, saying goodbye to John. It wasn't only funerals that triggered off the memories. It was little things, sudden smells, little words, moments of thoughtfulness. She watched Cheney walking towards her with Demos. The boy seemed more relaxed today. She wondered why. He was dressed in the same smart khaki pants, pale blue shirt and dark jacket he'd worn in the photograph on their cabin wall.

Jane shook hands with Demos, then came straight to the point. 'We're beginning to get the picture that Will's death was not the simple overdose it has been made out to be. Just so we can tidy up some loose ends, do you mind if we ask a couple of questions?'

Demos shook his head.

'Did Will seem depressed at the time of the accident, moody, anything wrong?'

'No, not that I noticed. Will started talking to me one night about parking cars in the wrong area and...'

The young Greek fought to find the right English words. 'How do you call it? Grey, that's it. There was a grey powder coming out of the car. I think he said it was a Mercedes. The Italians made him put it on Deck Four.'

Steve and Jane exchanged puzzled glances. 'Did he tell you any more?' Steve asked.

'No, I think one of the Italians was starting to, oh, what is the word I am looking for? Not good, unhappy, how do Will say, creepy. He also said maybe he not get back on the ship after we dock in England.'

'Did anybody else know that?' Jane asked.

'The Spaniards. I think he also talked to the Spaniards.'

'Have you been told when the ship is leaving?'

'Yes. High tide tonight. At eight o'clock. That is why I have to go now and get my train.'

The repairs had obviously taken less time than the captain had expected.

'We're going back to the ship ourselves,' Jane said. 'We could give you a lift.'

'We are?' Steve asked with a quizzical look.

Demos protested. 'No. I must not be seen with you.'

'The Seamen's Mission is just outside the port. We could drop you off there and no one would see you.'

'No,' Demos said firmly. Jane could see the fear in his eyes.

By the time Jane and Steve arrived at the ship it was already six thirty in the evening. They were beginning to think they should have gone back on the train with Demos. The Friday afternoon parking lot, laughingly called the M25, had turned a normal fifty-minute drive into two hours. Captain Iain Robertson was already under pressure, without having two police officers invading his bridge.

'You'll have to keep this brief, Inspector. This ship is about to catch the tide.'

Jane stayed calm. 'I'm just here to satisfy my curiosity, tidy up one or two loose ends.'

'Then hurry up,' Robertson said, 'Satisfy your curiosity and get off my ship.'

'We'd like another look around Deck Four,' Jane said briskly.

With less than an hour to cast-off, Robertson had no crew to spare. 'You know where it is,' he said finally.

*

As Steve pushed the huge metal door, Jane's eyes scanned across the sea of brand-new cars packed on to Deck Four. In the far corner, next to a pale green bulkhead she spotted the row of beaten-up motors. Each car was secured to the deck with yellow webbing bindings attached to the wheels. It was like walking through knitting. Steve tripped and steadied himself on the bonnet of a small red hatchback.

'What are we going to do?' he asked as he picked himself up.

'Find out if Demos was telling us the truth. If we do find any drugs in the Mercedes then we'll just leave and give Customs a call,' said Jane stepping over the yellow web.

'We should have given them a ring first anyway,' he said.

'We don't know whether we've been told the truth yet. One quick look and we're out of here,' Jane replied. At that moment she spotted the old black Mercedes.

'It isn't damaged on this side. It must be the other.' Before Steve could stop her, she climbed on to the bonnet, slid across it and jumped off the driver's side.

'Here it is,' she said, crouching down by a gash in the sill. 'Have you got an evidence bag in your pocket?'

'Now there's something I carry around every day,' Steve said sarcastically.

Jane took a small envelope from her shoulder bag and, using a pen, pushed remnants of a grey powder into it. She folded it neatly and put it back into her bag. Steve looked around nervously. He could feel the giant engines throbbing somewhere deep below the deck.

'Are you done?'

'Yes. Why?'

'Can we leave now? We've just collected evidence that's not even going to get to court because we've done it without a warrant and...' he turned and didn't finish his sentence.

'What?'

'We're being watched, over there,' said Steve, pointing towards the far end of the car deck.

The two Italian cousins were closing in fast.

Jane stared at Steve. 'This doesn't look good. Let's go!'

The hairs on the back of her neck began to stand on end. Her instincts screamed at her to get off the ship.

The younger Italian raised his arm.

'Jesus, he's got a gun!' Steve shouted.

CHAPTER TWENTY-FOUR

THE DETECTIVES hit the deck. Jane cursed as she scraped her left leg on the steel flooring. Slowly they eased themselves up into a crouching position behind the cover of a brand-new saloon. They watched the orange-clad figure clambering over the webbing straps towards the Mercedes. The Glock 9mm pistol in his right hand bobbed up and down in time with his ungainly stride. His cousin, two steps behind, did not seem to be armed.

As the gunman closed in, Jane sized up the situation. Their only hope was to sneak between the rows of cars towards the door they'd come in. When they came to the last row of cars, they would still have to cross a thirty-feet gap to the door with no cover. They would be out in the open. Totally exposed.

Jane slipped off her black shoes. The loafers' leather soles would have made a deafening racket on the steel floor. She looked at Steve and jabbed her finger towards the door. He nodded. Hardly daring to breathe, they clambered over the webbing straps edging along the narrow alleyways between the cars. Fear numbed the pain caused by the crab-like movement. Her thighs hadn't ached so much since PT sessions at police training school. Tripping over a binding, Jane fell. Steve reached out, his huge hand grabbed a clump of her jacket to stop her hitting the deck.

They'd reached the protection of the last line of cars. Survival was just ten yards away. Just six or seven strides for Steve, perhaps twelve steps for Jane, and they'd be through the heavy metal door and into the safety of the stairwell.

Hidden from the Italian's view behind the cover of a silver hatchback, Jane looked at Steve.

'Are you ready?' she asked.

Jane didn't wait to see him nod. She sprinted across the open space and wrestled with the iron handle, desperately trying to force the door open. Steve was two paces behind. He didn't see the Italian raise the Glock. He didn't see the barrel flame. The lead-nosed bullet, travelling at 1,400 feet per second, had shattered Cheney's spinal cord by the time Jane heard the gunshot. As Steve was propelled forward he felt no pain. He saw the faces of his wife and their toddler son smiling in the sunshine. As the bullet, now squashed to a flat disc, tore through his heart, he saw another face. A face he hadn't seen in years. His grandfather was waiting.

Cheney was already dead by the time the second and third shots rang out. All twelve stones, dead weight, slammed Jane against the door. The force knocked her legs from under her and she crashed to the deck. Her eyes stung from the blood running down her face. For a split-second panic consumed her. She wanted to vomit. The whole world was running in slow motion. She forced her leaden legs to work as she struggled to her feet. Her heart thundered as she lunged for the door handle. Pushing her weight down on the bar, it moved seemingly without effort. As she pulled the door towards her, two more shots rang out.

Her worst nightmare appeared out of a haze of claret and cordite. The Spaniards were on the other side of the door. There was to be no escape. The tall Spaniard brought his fist down on her neck, sending her spinning. Jane fell onto Steve's body. She felt the warmth of his blood on her chest and neck. Jane tried desperately to force herself back onto her feet. She could make out distant voices screaming and arguing, like echoes in a mist, then she heard no more.

The hot-head Italian was now by the Spaniard's side, grinning, proud of what he'd done. As he started to relive the shooting, the Spaniard's fist hit his jaw, sending him reeling onto the deck. The second Spaniard's boot held his arm. The taller of the pair bent down and tore the gun from his hand. The Italian squealed in pain.

'You fucking idiot. Do you realise what you've just done?'

He didn't give him a chance to answer as his boot connected with the Italian's body. The cousin sprang forward, but Spaniard held the gun towards his face.

Just then, Marco Alessandri appeared through the door. He surveyed the carnage and snarled, 'Close the door. Put the bodies in the boot of the car. We leave port in less than an hour.'

'How the hell are we going to get these bodies off the ship?' demanded the Spaniard. 'The port's swarming with people trying to get us away on the tide.'

Marco exploded, 'I'm in charge here and don't you forget it.'

'Just what are you in charge of? A fanatic with a gun and his lunatic cousin? You're going to be lucky to walk away with your life once the syndicate find out about this. You haven't shot two drug-pushing nobodies here. These are fucking English police.'

The Spaniard turned to the cousins. ' Clean yourselves up and go back to your work stations before you're missed.'

Marco was not used to having his authority questioned. Hatred of the Spaniards burned like a furnace. This was not the time, he would deal with them later.

'Shoot her,' he told them. 'Hide the bodies in one of the old cars. We'll dump them overboard once we're in the English Channel.'

As Marco turned to walk off the deck, a shot rang out. He saw Jane's body twitch. She felt nothing.

CHAPTER TWENTY-FIVE

SLOWLY AND painfully, Jane's senses came back to her. She could feel the movement of the ship. Her head pounded. Searing pain numbed her arms and legs. She opened her eyes but found it difficult to focus, like she was in a pond. Gradually her blurred vision cleared. She was on the bottom bunk of a small cabin, similar to Will's. She was unable to move her body, but she could lift her head. As her focus sharpened, she realised her legs and arms had been tightly bound with webbing tape. She gasped, but no air entered her mouth. In her panic she snorted through her nose. Her mouth must be taped up. Desperately she kicked her brain into gear. Then she remembered. God, Steve was dead. How am I going to tell Anne? What have they done with him? Her thoughts raced. Why am I still alive? I have to get off this ship. Tears of anger trickled down her cheeks. Anger at her own stupidity. She could have found something else to do that Friday afternoon. They didn't need to be on this ship. She could have phoned the port police and let them deal with it. Her eagerness to conquer her own demons and constantly prove to herself she was good at her job had cost a good friend his life.

The cabin door opened slowly and one of the two scruffy Spaniards stepped in. He busied himself emptying his pockets, placing various items on a small table to her right. He crouched down to look down at Jane, his face close to hers. She struggled to back away, as far into the corner as her bindings would allow. He pinned her to the bed, his eyes boring into her.

'You must lie still. Keep quiet. It's the only way to save your life. I'm going to take the gag off your mouth. You must keep quiet,' he hissed.

He ripped the gag off with all the finesse of a sadistic nurse in an over-worked casualty department.

'You bastard. You fucking bastard. You've killed Steve...' Jane didn't get a chance to finish her tirade. The Spaniard placed his hand across her mouth and said in a harsh whisper, 'If you don't keep quiet I will kill you. Do you understand?'

Jane winced as a sharp pain stabbed inside her head. Her wide eyes followed the Spaniard as he took out a pocket-knife. Fighting down a panic attack, her senses were on red alert.

He began cutting the bindings. 'Look, I'm sorry. I'm sorry we couldn't get to you both in time, before he was killed,' he said. All trace of a Spanish accent had vanished.

'You're American?' Jane spluttered.

He sat on the floor on the other side of the cramped cabin, looking at her. 'Yeh, the gang of Italians on this boat are part of a big drug-running syndicate. It was unfortunate that you and your partner...'

'Unfortunate?', Jane exploded. 'You killed probably the best officer in my team and you're calling it unfortunate.' As she swung her legs round to sit up, the pain in her head and shoulder made her feel dizzy. She fell back onto the bed, overcome by nausea.

He leapt onto the bunk, his hand covering her mouth again. 'You don't understand the risk we've taken to keep you alive,' he hissed. 'You have to be quiet, we're all in danger here.'

His hand, still clamped over her lips, smelled of oil. He carried on talking, his voice just above a whisper, 'We knew they were dangerous. We knew they'd killed the boy. It wasn't suicide. In less than a week this boat will dock in New York and the heroin will be unloaded. We've tagged the drugs and we'll be able to find out where they're stored.'

Jane's eyes burned with anger, 'And that justifies two deaths?'

Gradually it began to dawn on her that this American wasn't part of the gang, but some kind of law enforcement officer, part of the US Drugs Enforcement Administration, perhaps. He felt her body relax underneath his.

'I'm Special Agent Logan of the Federal Bureau of Investigation,' he said getting to his feet. 'What you do now is up to you.'

Jane, still struggling to get her brain firing on all cylinders, pulled herself up onto her elbows.

'What's happened to Steve's body?' she asked.

'It was disposed of.'

'You just threw him overboard?' she asked in disbelief.

'We made it look like you both went overboard.'

She flared up again. 'Why didn't you just hide him in a car somewhere, so he can have a decent burial?'

This woman is becoming a pain, thought Logan. 'Don't forget darlin', you came crashing in on this,' he said coldly. 'I have to go back to work. Try to sleep off your sore head. We have a shower and a john over there. You're in danger so stay in the cabin.'

He reached into a canvas bag stowed under the bottom bunk.

'You'd better change into those,' he said, flinging an old pair of jeans and a shirt at her. 'You're covered in blood.'

After Logan left, Jane locked the cabin door and climbed into the tiny shower. The water ran pink as she washed away Steve's blood. Towelling herself down, she took in her surroundings. This was a mirror image of Will's cabin. She must be on the port side of the ship, she thought. Putting on the blue button-down shirt, her eyes slowly scanned the bookshelf. All the books were in Spanish, all of them looked unread. One at a time, she took each book off the shelf and flicked through the pages. As she removed the last two paperbacks she noticed a blue and white packet of Ducados cigarettes had fallen behind them. She left well alone.

Jane climbed up on to the top bunk. She was exhausted but the adrenalin rush was keeping her awake, she couldn't clear her brain of the image of Steve lying lifeless on that deck. Voices outside broke her train of thought. She was sure at least one of them was Italian. The door handle rattled. She pressed herself hard against the bulkhead as the door opened. She looked down on a stocky man with thinning hair. Jane leapt. Momentum and bodyweight forced him onto his haunches. She grabbed his right arm and pushed it up his back. With one knee pressing hard into the small of his back, she pushed him to the ground, hissing in his ear 'And you are?'

'Manuel Diego.'

The voice came from behind her. It was Logan. He quickly closed the cabin door, and as he pulled Jane to her feet, he added, 'Otherwise known as Special Agent Scott Newman, my partner.'

Jane climbed back onto the top bunk. Scott rose to his feet. Blood trickled from a small cut on the top of his left cheek. He was three inches shorter than Logan. A burly man with thinning hair jet black and olive skin, Jane guessed he was the younger, by a good ten years. He looked angrily at Logan as he dabbed the wound, 'How the hell are we going to keep this wild cat quiet?'

'You could have prevented all of this.' said Jane. The two men looked up at her.

'And just how did you figure that one out?' Logan protested.

'You could have warned us.'

'Without blowing our cover?'

The two men sat down on the bottom bunk and ignored her.

'How are we going to hide her for the next week?'

'She'll just have to hide in the cabin.'

'We have to go to the galley and eat, otherwise we'll be missed,' said Newman.

Logan turned to Jane. 'You stay in here. Don't move.'

CHAPTER TWENTY-SIX

ONLY ONE thing was certain. Jane had no choice but to trust the Americans. Her survival now depended on them. That inescapable conclusion didn't stop her checking every inch of the cabin. Their clothes and documents revealed nothing. God, they were good. Their papers looked genuine. Among them were fake half-written letters to fictitious families back in Spain. Even their toothbrushes had 'Hecho en Espana', Made in Spain, stamped on them. There was absolutely nothing to give them away as FBI men.

She leapt back onto the top bunk as the Americans returned. The two men sat side by side discussing her as if she wasn't there.

'This operation's going downhill, and fast,' Newman said. 'Our lives are all in danger now. We've no choice, we're going to have to tell her everything.'

Logan nodded. He stood up and turned to face Jane.

'So you've remembered I'm here, then?' she said, sarcasm masking her fear.

'Look,' Logan explained, 'Let me tell you what we know about the gang who killed your partner.' Jane sat up. Logan leaned against the cabin wall while Newman perched on the bottom bunk.

He took her back almost six months to the cold January day he and Scott were summoned to FBI headquarters in Washington. They were late. As they walked into the conference room at the far end of the lobby, their boss, Head of Operations, Senior

Special Agent Chris Tenant looked up. 'Take your seats gentleman. Now we can begin.'

Logan caught Tenant's eye. His boss was wearing a 'we're about to be pissed on' look.

John Carl, Assistant Director in Charge of the FBI's Washington Field Office, sat at the far end of the table.

'Gentleman, this is Mr Arthur Robson and Ms Ellen McLean from the DEA,' Carl explained. 'They're running an operation investigating an international drug-running ring. They have infiltrated a cartel smuggling heroin onto car transporting ships. The consignments are being concealed in vehicles and exported to various ports around the world.'

Newman interrupted, 'So what's this got to do with us?'

Carl was obviously annoyed at the interruption. He continued, 'I believe it would be easier at this point if the DEA explained the operation to you themselves.'

Arthur Robson's severe haircut, dark brown eyes and gold-rimmed glasses made his already-hard features look like they'd been chiselled from granite. He spoke with the authority of a man always deferred to and never interrupted.

'Thank you, John. Four months ago we managed to infiltrate a cartel importing drugs into Europe and North America. This cartel of a group of businessmen, some of them well known, carry out a lucrative sideline under the cover of a legitimate import/ export business. They're based in New York, the point of entry for three-quarters of the heroin from that area. We believe the cartel has cornered the US market in the importation of heroin from south-west Asia, particularly from Afghanistan. We're talking a billion dollar business. If you could just open the briefing notes we have provided for you, gentlemen, you will find the estimated figures on page three.'

Logan and Newman picked up the briefing documents from the table in front of them and flicked to page three.

Robson continued, 'It's estimated that close to fifteen metric tonnes of heroin was imported into the United States last year. The largest source is South America, but figures from the DEA's Heroin Signature Program show heroin imported from south-west Asia now comprises about six to eight per cent of the market. As you can see, this is big business. Over the last decade, up to twenty two billion dollars was spent on heroin in the US. The opium crop in Afghanistan is now the largest producer in the world, accounting for nearly three quarters of the illicit opium on the world market during 2000. Efforts to persuade Afghan farmers to stop producing opium since the War on Terrorism began after 9/11 are likely to fail. Production in 2002 may be double the previous years. This far outstrips the increase in production in the "Golden Triangle" of south-east Asia. Europe is the primary target for south-west Asian heroin, but we're seeing an increase in the consumption of the drug in the US. Compared to South American heroin it's cheap, wholesale prices range from forty thousand to a hundred and ninety thousand dollars a kilogram. It sells on the street for between a thousand and two thousand dollars per pure gram. It has a high-retail purity. It's about eighty per cent pure when it's imported into the country.'

Ellen McLean spoke up, seamlessly picking up where Robson had left off. She was in her early thirties with short, sandy hair, a round face and blue eyes. From where Logan was sitting it was clear that the weight of this investigation was taking its toll. She looked like she had not seen a decent night's sleep in weeks.

'This drug-running operation presently involves over thirty men in three countries.'

Carl interrupted her, 'If this operation is so big, why has this cartel never come to our attention before?'

'They make a point of recruiting men and women with only minor misdemeanours, bent enough to get involved but no real criminal records. Now, if I could press on...As you can see from the map on page four, ships collect new cars from Japan. They're transported on to South Korea, then to the Mediterranean, stopping in Cyprus, Turkey, Italy and Spain. Next they go to France, then England before crossing the Atlantic to New York. From the East Coast, the ships cross to Africa, dropping off used cars and heavy machinery.'

McLean pressed on at a remorseless pace, barely allowing them time to digest the material in front of them.

'The raw heroin comes from Afghanistan. It is refined in Turkey, then stashed in used cars at ports in Turkey and Cyprus, which are then loaded into the ships. The Master of the ship we're currently interested in, the *Star Supreme* is Iain Robertson. We know he has heavy gambling debts and, although he's not a member of the cartel, we suspect he's being paid to turn a blind eye. Now if you turn to page five, gentleman, you will see photographs of four Italians. They're all related and we believe they are working on the ship for the cartel.'

Logan looked down at the faces. You could have passed these men in the street without batting an eyelid. That had always been the difficulty with their job. This wasn't the movies. They didn't wander the shadows in dark coats and dramatic music didn't strike up when they entered the room.

'The leader is the eldest brother, Marco Alessandri,' McLean continued, pointing to the first photograph. 'The next two, Angelo Alessandri, Marco's brother, and their cousin Salvatore Baretti are very loyal foot soldiers. The hot-head of the group is the younger cousin, Francesco Macchietto.'

Tenant became more and more edgy as he listened to McLean. He was the head of one of the FBI's largest and busiest branches and resented interference by the drugs agency. Working with the DEA had spelled nothing but trouble for him in the past and he knew he was about to be cornered again.

'Forgive me for interrupting here gentlemen, sorry, lady and gentlemen,' Tenant corrected himself. 'But as Agent Newman said earlier, where do we fit into this?'

'If you turn to the next page, you'll see a photograph of our agent who has managed to infiltrate the cartel,' McLean said.

As Tenant thumbed the page, his question was immediately answered. The face staring out could have been Logan's twin brother. Apart from a few more grey hairs and a much deeper tan, they were practically identical.

'His name is Martin Allen,' Robson said. 'Three days ago he was taken into hospital suffering from a stomach complaint. He has been diagnosed with cancer. He was due to join the ship on Monday. He'd worked his way into the cartel's confidence much more quickly than we'd anticipated and he was being sent aboard to keep an eye on the Italians.'

'Why?' Tenant asked.

'The businessmen are getting increasingly worried about the Italians. It seems the youngest cousin is out of control. We believe he has already killed a crewmember when the ship was in the Far East. Their recklessness is putting the whole operation in jeopardy,' said Robson.

'Why hasn't the cartel just pulled the Italians off the boat?'

'They know the operation inside out and it's too late and too risky for them to pull in fresh men at this stage. The last piece of information Allen gave us before he was hospitalised was that the cartel had managed to stockpile enough heroin at various points across North America to shut down the operation for eighteen months. This is to be their last run. We need to track the heroin once it is off-loaded in New York so we can find the mother load.'

Logan came straight to the point, 'And you want me to take Allen's place?'

'Yes,' said McLean, again taking the helm in the DEA tag team. 'We've spent hours trawling through Government computer files looking for an agent who closely resembles him. Your file stats tell us you speak Italian and Spanish. Allen was disguised as a Spaniard and you will need to be able to speak Spanish fluently..'

Tenant interrupted. Twenty-two years in the FBI had taught him that this operation would tie up one of his best men for months, stretching the already overworked department to breaking point. Besides, a previous joint FBI/DEA had cost the life of one of his men. He wanted to be damn sure another one wasn't going to be killed.

'What safeguards are there if anything goes wrong?' he asked.

'The ship is under constant surveillance by satellite. They will also be given a tracking device,' Robson said.

Tenant interrupted again, his anger barely hidden, 'You said they. Where does Newman come into this?'

'Allen's contact at the cartel phoned him and said he was sending along a 'bodyguard' to accompany him on the ship.'

'And how are you going to replace him with me?' asked Newman.

'The Italians don't know who's coming. They've only been told to expect two Spaniards but they don't know what either of these men look like. They'll accept Newman as the other Spaniard.'

'When do we go?'

'You're booked on an American Airlines flight to Japan, where you'll have twenty-four hours to acclimatise yourselves. Your itinerary is on the last page. As you can see, one of our men will meet you in Japan, your American passports will be taken off you and you will be issued with appropriate clothing before you join the ship. I've also given you a brief profile of the four men you are about to meet. It is important not to underestimate Marco Alessandri. He believes he is being groomed for the inner circle of the cartel and will not be happy about being babysat. He will see you as a threat to his authority. This guy will be out to prove himself. '

Jane looked at Logan. Those hazel eyes had softened. Fighting to take in all that she'd just been told, Jane said, 'I don't even know your first name.'

'Just Logan. I like to be called Logan.'

'So "Just Logan" what happens now?'

'Simple,' Newman said. 'All we have to do is get the drugs back to the US and you can fly home.'

'It may not be as easy as that,' Jane replied. 'Once my station realises we are both missing all hell will break loose and it's likely this ship will be stopped by a gunboat, even in international waters.'

Logan and Newman looked at each other.

*

The four Italians were alone around the pool table in the recreation room. The cousins were quiet, but Marco's brain was racing. He turned to his brother. 'I don't trust them.'

'What?' Angelo asked, struggling to follow the line of thinking.

'The Spaniards. I don't trust them.'

'So what are you going to do?'

'Later tonight I'll bribe the radio officer to use the satellite phone and speak to Joey. He'll get some questions answered for us. In the meantime keep your eye on them. I checked on the duty roster, they're on watch tonight, so we'll have to keep it in turns. You can have the first stretch.'

His brother protested, nodding his head towards the cousins, 'Do you trust them any more than the Spaniards?'

CHAPTER TWENTY-SEVEN

WHEN LOGAN and Newman left the cabin for their night shift, Jane tried to focus on everything the FBI men had revealed about their operation. She wondered if she would ever be able to bring the Italians to justice for murdering Steve and Will but her temples pounded as if a herd of wild elephants was running amok inside her head. Jane closed her eyes to ease the pain. She was fast asleep when Logan returned later and placed a couple of apples and a chunk of bread on the cabin table. He called her name but she didn't reply. She was curled up in a tight ball. He placed another blanket over her. Her face looked relaxed for the first time. The fear had gone.

How much of a liability was she going to be? Logan wondered. Surely as an English law enforcement officer she had to be fairly strong, but he had his doubts.

Jane drifted into consciousness again. She had only been asleep for a few hours but was feeling more alive. She had no idea of the time but the cabin was no longer pitch black. Dawn must be breaking, she thought. Again she could hear voices in the corridor. They were talking Italian, fast. She gently wedged open the door a fraction and, peering through the narrow gap she could just see them. She heard them mention Newman and Logan's Spanish names. Whatever was going on, it did not bode well for the Americans. She waited for the corridor to clear.

Logan and Newman were on the bow of the boat as the first rays of the sun glowed red behind them. The ship had left the

English Channel and was now in the Atlantic. Their watch would be ending in an hour. Scott didn't see or hear the Italian behind him. He felt the thud of the heavy wrench cracking his skull, warm blood running down the back of his neck, then nothing. Logan didn't have time to react to the noise of Newman hitting the deck before he felt the cold barrel of a gun on the back of his neck.

'So, my friend. Let's go down to Deck Four and find out who you really are.' The Italian's English had suddenly become very fluent, not the halting pidgin he'd been speaking until then. The FBI men weren't the only phonies around here, Logan thought, as he began protesting in Spanish.

'Don't insult my intelligence. Your friend is four inches too tall and forty pounds too heavy to be Diego,' said Marco Alessandri.

He waved his gun and herded Logan towards the steps. The Italian's brother and his cousin, Salvatore, dragged Newman behind them. The American was still out cold as they dropped him onto the floor of Deck Four where only hours before he'd washed away Steve's blood.

Logan hadn't had a chance to say anything when the wrench hit him in the face, he felt the heavy metal head of the tool split open his cheek. He had no time to recover as the blows rained down thick and fast. Steel cracked against bone as he desperately tried to shield his body with his arms. He cried out in pain as the wrench made contact with his kidneys.

'Por favor,' he gasped, trying to keep his Spanish going.

Marco placed his hand on Angelo's arm, as his brother raised the wrench to bring down it down again on Logan, curled up on the floor.

'Don't knock this one out. We need him awake to answer our questions,' Marco said.

Salvatore grabbed a chunk of Logan's hair, lifting his head off the floor.

'Who are you? Who do you work for?' Salvatore snarled.

Congealed blood caked Logan's eyes. His brain screamed at him to stay focused. His mouth was bone dry. He struggled to speak but the words still came out in Spanish.

'You're not Spanish, and if you're not going to tell us who you really are then let my cousin help you.'

Blows rained down again.

'Stop!' a voice rang out from across the car deck.

Logan watched Angelo hold the wrench high in the air.

The youngest cousin Franceso was striding across the webbing.

'Why?' Marco shouted.

'Ask him why the woman is alive and still on this ship,' said Francesco, suddenly feeling important.

In the stunned silence Logan could feel his own pulse in his swelling face. His eyes closing up, he could taste blood running down the back of his throat.

'Where did you see her?' Marco asked impatiently.

'Deck Three.'

Marco looked down at Logan, 'So, you didn't shoot her after all. You will live to regret that.'

He turned to Francesco, 'Get her. Kill her if necessary, just find her.'

'It'll be my pleasure.'

Jane had realised instantly she was on the wrong deck. Remembering the second set of steps at the stern, she climbed onto Deck Four. Slowly and carefully, she made her way between the cars, just as the Italians had sneaked up on her and Steve.

'Help him out with his memory,' Marco told Angelo.

Logan winced as the brother's foot connected with his already-tender kidney. Through slits he looked at Newman.

Beyond his partner's body he made out Jane's hands and feet as she crouched behind two cars. A second later he caught sight of her face as she lay on the deck, stunned at being totally powerless again to save someone at the hands of the Italians.

Marco picked Logan up by the scruff of the neck.

'Killing the English policeman is going to be nothing compared to the pleasure of killing you, my friend, whoever you are. You'll have the chance to think about what you have done as you will die slowly.'

He released his grip on the collar, letting Logan's head thump back on the deck.

'What are we going to do with them?' Salvatore asked.

Take them to the open gangway on the portside bow. Throw them overboard. Tie them together, they'll sink faster.'

Marco stared down at Logan's mashed face. 'Like I said, my friend, you will die slowly together.'

'Surely you'll give a condemned man one last request.' Logan rasped in English. 'I'd like a cigarette.'

Jane couldn't believe Logan was going out of his way to anger his captors even more. Why the hell does he want cigarettes? she thought. Her nose had told her neither of the Americans smoked. Then she remembered the packet of Spanish cigarettes hidden behind the books in their cabin.

Logan groaned as Salvatore's boot pummelled his kidneys again. He turned his head towards Newman. Jane was gone.

CHAPTER TWENTY-EIGHT

JAMES CHENEY woke his mother at ten past five on Saturday morning. Anne rolled over in bed. 'Steve, it's got to be your turn.' Her husband wasn't there to hear her. She climbed out of bed and slipped on her dressing gown. As she picked up the four-year-old boy in her arms, she gave him a hug.

'Come on, Daddy must have been working all night. Let's go and find out how many bad guys he's caught,' she whispered.

They wandered downstairs. Anne called Steve's name but no reply came. She glanced at the kitchen clock, nineteen minutes past five. She waited until six o'clock then picked up the phone and dialled Steve's mobile. She placed the phone back on the receiver when she reached his cell phone answering service.

'Odd. No reply,' she muttered to herself.

She made herself a cup of coffee and wondered where Steve could be. It wasn't unusual for him to stay out all night working but it was unlike him not to be contactable by mobile. James ate his breakfast and tugged at her dressing gown.

'Put the cartoon on the telly, Mum.'

Anne found the remote control and turned the TV channel to the Power Rangers. She left the boy watching the screen while she went to the hall phone, found the number in her address book and dialled. The phone at Parkside station was answered quickly.

'Hi. This is Anne Cheney, Detective Sergeant Cheney's wife. Is he there?'

'I don't think there is anybody in the CID room at the

moment Mrs Cheney.'

'Are they out on a special job?'

'I think they must have been.'

'I can't get any reply from his mobile phone and he was out all night,' Anne said, trying to sound unconcerned. 'It's just he normally calls me to say he won't be coming home. It's unusual not to be able to get hold of him.'

'Just as well you're an understanding woman, Mrs Cheney. I'll have a ring round and get back to you in about a half an hour.'

'Thanks,' she said and hung up.

Sergeant Tim Roberts wandered upstairs. He had only been on duty for just over an hour but didn't know of any major operation going on. He called Jane Blackburn's mobile phone. No reply. He rang her home and reached the answer phone. The next person on his list was Steve himself, so he skipped to Gary Johnson's mobile number. The voice on the end of the phone was half asleep.

'I'm asleep and it's six thirty on Saturday morning, so whoever is on the end of this bloody phone must have something important to say.'

'Gary, it's Tim here. Is there anything going on?'

'There's lots of things going on. Which bloody 'going on' are you talking about?'

'I've had Anne Cheney on the phone trying to find out where her husband is. Was there a night-time operation or anything?'

'Not that they were involved in. Have you phoned the DI?'

'Neither of her phones are answering either.'

He now had Gary's full attention.

'Phone Jill at home and find out if the DI said anything to her. Also check the diary upstairs. I'm coming in.'

CHAPTER TWENTY-NINE

JANE KNEW the lift was too risky. She bounded up yet another flight of metal stairs, ignoring the throbbing ache in her body. Adrenaline and fear were keeping her going. She had to get back to Logan's cabin. The cigarettes had to be important or he wouldn't have mentioned them, but it didn't make sense. Nothing that had happened on this ship made sense. She knew she had at least a few more minutes. It would take them that long to drag Logan and carry the dead weight of Newman's unconscious body practically the whole length of the ship.

She heard voices above her. Korean. They were waiting for the lift. She was in the stair well directly below them. She held her breath. Hurry. At last the lift appeared. She let out a long sigh, then gasped her way up another four flights of steps.

The dimly-lit crew deck corridor was clear. She sprinted the last few yards and almost fell into the FBI men's cabin. Jane pushed all the books off the shelf and grabbed the cigarettes in their blue and white paper packet. She lifted up her shirt and placed the cigarette packet underneath her bra, wedging them tight. She frantically searched through the top draw of the desk and found the small Swiss army knife Logan had used to cut her bindings.

Jane's mind ran through the ship's layout. Her best chance of survival was the pilot's door on the port side on Car Deck Five. She opened the knife blade and dashed back down the corridor. From the stairs, she spied the Italian lurking in the well below. Thinking fast, she cut across the landing and scrambled down the other set of stairs. She prayed he hadn't seen her.

Logan kicked out backwards as Angelo forced him onto the open gangway twenty five feet above the sea, foaming as the huge bows chewed through the water. Angelo gasped as Logan's right boot struck him in the solar plexus. The Italian buckled. Salvatore swung the wrench like a club, knocking Logan to the metal deck. He fell down on top of Newman who groaned but still didn't open his eyes. Marco held the gun to Logan's head as Salvatore tied the two FBI men together. With one tug, the three Italians pulled Logan and Newman to their feet. A split-second later they were catapulted through an open gate in the guard rail and into the Atlantic Ocean.

At the other end of the ship, Jane frantically tried to open the pilots' port. It worked on a hydraulic system. To her left a list of instructions and cautions were written in four languages. She followed the instructions. As she pressed the red button to finally open the door, an orange warning light began to flash above her head. A siren was now sounding as the door slowly opened.

Jane ignored it and looked into the murky green sea below. If she jumped too she'd never find them. Was she too late already? A shot rang out, shattering the warning light, covering her in shards of orange plastic. She could not take her eyes off the water for a moment. A second shot, this time closer. She crouched in the doorway.

Logan struggled with all his might to push Newman's dead weight back up to the surface. He'd managed to fill his lungs with air, but he knew his friend hadn't.

Francesco steadied his nerves and pointed the handgun square at the back of Jane's head. She could now see them. Their crew suits like orange jetsam in the water. She took a couple of deep breaths to fill her lungs. Christ, she thought, I wish I had a better idea than this. She jumped just as Francesco pulled the trigger.

CHAPTER THIRTY

SUPERINTENDENT Douglas Benson was, for once, doing some real police work. Instead of issuing initiatives, he was sat behind Jane's desk in the CID room at Parkside Station giving out orders. Less than an hour after Anne Cheney's phone call, the CID room was filling up as word spread that Jane and Steve were missing. Their cars were still in the car park and the red CID pool Ford Mondeo they'd driven away in was missing. Benson had already exploded at Jill in front of the whole room when she explained that she seemed to be the last person Jane had spoken to before departing to Tilbury. The Superintendent demanded to know what Jane had been doing in Tilbury checking on a boat. His sarcastic remark about Tilbury not being on their patch was ignored. In fact, the whole room ignored him, turning instead to Gary Johnson for their instructions. Dan had already phoned the harbour to check the pool car was at the docks. The Harbour Master sent two men out to look.

Dan told Gary about the shipping agents he had spoken to the day before.

'The best thing you can do here is go down there and see for yourselves,' said Johnson.

Benson stepped in. 'With all due respect DS Johnson, I'm the senior officer here, I'll give the orders and carry out this investigation the way I see fit. ACC Edwards and the Chief Constable have informed me they have full confidence...' Gary stopped him.

'With all due respect,' Johnson almost spat. 'You're nothing but a desk jockey. Two of our colleagues are missing. If you think it's more important to inform your superiors before you find out what's even going on, you couldn't be more wrong. Jane and Steve keep the strike rate of this CID one of the highest in the country. We're not going to let you and the Dream Team keep us from doing our job properly.'

Benson erupted but Gary wasn't listening. He turned to Dan, 'Who went with you the other day?'

'Matt.'

'Then call him in. You're going to Tilbury to find out what's going on. I want the full background to the case Jane and Steve were working on. Someone phone the coroner, at home. Phone the boy's parents. They must know something about the company he was working for. Phone fucking Santa Claus. I don't care, just get phoning.'

Gary turned to leave the office but Benson blocked his path.

'I'll see you dismissed for this,' said the Superintendent, his cheeks flushed with rage.

'You'll have to find a witness first.'

Benson looked around the room. All eyes were on him for a moment and, as one, the detectives turned away and started hitting the phones.

Johnson walked down to the front desk to speak to Tim Roberts.

'Phone Steve's wife,' he told the sergeant.

'What do I tell her?'

'Tell her what you know. Steve had been asked to do an investigation for the coroner and his mobile batteries have obviously gone dead. Somebody's trying to get hold of him now.'

CHAPTER THIRTY-ONE

SHE ONLY had time to scream 'Logaaaan!!!' before the Atlantic engulfed her like a freezing shroud. Jane fought to keep the air in her lungs as the bitterly cold water sent her whole body into spasm. She broke the surface gasping for breath. Her eyes stung as she frantically looked around. The water boiled as the *Star Supreme* churned a channel through the choppy sea. She saw Logan and Scott briefly as they bobbed on the crest of a wave no more than twenty yards away. Then she saw them disappear under the water.

Breathing hard, Jane swam towards them as they appeared again almost in grabbing distance. With Newman's body strapped to him, Logan was dying in front of her. She dived, squinting in the murky water, her eyes stung with the salt. She reached for them but missed. She kicked again and again, struggling against the force of the water and grabbed Logan by the back of his overalls. The two of them were just too heavy for her to pull. She struggled with the knife to try and break them free.

Summoning almost his last ounce of energy Logan kicked to help Jane bring them to the surface. Her lungs were bursting and her brain ached with the cold. They were never going to make it. Logan was beginning to feel dizzy and blackout. He kicked harder. A split-second later they surfaced.

Logan coughed and spluttered. Jane started to cut the rope that bound them together like Siamese twins, all the time struggling against the propeller drag drawing them ever closer

140

to the ship. She gulped another breath and plunged her head back under the water, squinting and feeling the cord as she sawed at it with the knife. It seemed to be taking forever. Suddenly the two of them were free. Logan took hold of Scott's arm and at the same time Jane grabbed his shirt.

As they pulled Newman, Jane yelled, 'When I shout "now," swim away from the ship.'

He could just hear Jane's voice above the churning noise of the water and the boat's engines. The rush of the water and the noise were almost deafening.

'We're almost there. Now!' She shouted. Logan felt the pull of the water slacken and they began to be propelled away from the boat, dragging Scott as best they could.

Jane could feel Scott struggle back to life. He opened his eyes and began to cough. Now is not a good time for you to wake up, she thought. The water slowly calmed. Logan and Jane held Scott as he began to flail his legs. They watched the ship slowly ease away from them, the noise dying down.

Scott was still drowsy and almost incoherent. Jane looked at Logan, and between gasps, told him to take off his trousers.

'Does this mean we're on a date?' he asked, a lopsided grin appearing on his ash-coloured face.

Jane looked at him, her eyes fierce with anger, 'It's a bloody male thing, isn't it. Stupid, flippant remarks at the worst moments.' She coughed as she got a mouth full of salty water.

Logan, kicked off his boots, struggled out of the trousers of his orange two-piece suit and handed them to her. Jane had already taken hers off and was tying knots into the ends of the trouser legs. Lifting the blue denims above her head, she brought them back down, forcing air into the legs. She tried as best she could to hold the waist end together in her hand. She lifted Scott's right arm and placed the inflated trousers under his armpit and pushed Logan's trousers under the other arm.

'You've got to stay with us, Scott.'

She turned to Logan. 'If you've a plan for getting us out of this one, I'd be keen to hear it. Why did you want the cigarettes?'

'Did you get them?' he asked incredulously.

Jane let go of Scott, reached inside her sodden shirt and pulled out the soaking wet packet of cigarettes.

Logan grinned. 'Anything else interesting down there?' he said as he grabbed the pack off her.

His cold hands trembled as he struggled to open the packet.

'So what is it?'

'Our ticket out of here. Inside this packet is a satellite navigational tracking device.'

CHAPTER THIRTY-TWO

CHRIS TENANT, Head of Operations at the FBI's Washington Field Office, picked up the phone on the second ring, cursing and hoping the call had not disturbed his wife. It was just after 1.30 in the morning.

'Sir, we've had a courtesy call from the DEA to say that they've picked up a signal from Logan and Newman's tracking device.'

Tenant huffed and said sarcastically, 'Courtesy, eh?' His mind focused instantly.

'Where?'

'In the Atlantic, off the west coast of Ireland. Satellite shows the signal is almost stationary but the ship is still moving so at least one of them must be in the sea. We've already alerted the Irish Marine Rescue Service. They've got a base at Shannon. We've given the co-ordinates so that they can home in on the tracking device.'

Tenant silently cursed the DEA. He asked, 'How long before air-sea rescue can be there?'

'About fifty minutes.'

'Get Shannon's phone number so I can find out what's going on myself. I'm coming in.'

He gently leaned over, kissed his wife and whispered, 'I'm going into the office, honey.'

She turned and looked at him, 'One of these days you and I are going to get out of this bed together.'

He kissed the top of her shoulder and murmured, 'As long as

we always get in together. I'll call you from the office.'

*

Scott's life was ebbing away. The colour had drained from his face, his lips were blue. Jane kept talking to him, asking him questions about how he and Logan had met. Scott didn't respond, so Logan explained how the pair had known each other for five years. Their partnership hadn't got off to an auspicious start. Newman had given Logan a right-hander, which had left him smarting for days. It had been quick thinking on Newman's part and had rescued them from a drug bust that had gone badly wrong. The pair had been part of a three-man team working undercover but one of the drug runners had recognised Logan as an FBI agent. In the chaos that followed, Newman managed to drag Logan out of the room just as the code call was given that sent fifty FBI and DEA agents running in to make the bust. From then Logan had taken the new recruit under his wing and their friendship had grown.

All the time she listened she never took her eyes off Scott, desperate to get some kind of response. 'Is there anybody special in your life?' she asked.

'I can tell you every woman I've had,' Newman mumbled, his eyes flickering for the first time.

'How long do you think we've been in the water?' Logan asked.

'About forty five to fifty minutes,' Jane said, looking at her military watch, the one memento she'd kept of her time in the Royal Navy.

Resting her left arm on Logan's shoulder to steady herself, Jane started to rub Scott's arms in a futile attempt to keep up his body temperature.

'Next there was a pretty little blonde with blue eyes,' Scott said.

'How many are we up to, Scott?' she asked, silently praying help would come soon.

'Nine.'

Jane focused all the energy she had left on the two men who had saved her life. Her mind drifted to John, then to Richard. Would she ever see her son again? How would he cope with her death after losing John? She thought of all the times she had teased him about his sailing, his girlfriends, him just growing up too fast. She began to regret not telling him often enough how much she loved him. She watched Logan, he was strong. His face was beginning to swell up, the saltwater must be stinging his wounds. She thought of the strangest things. Would Richard remember where the strong box was with her life insurance policies in it? Would her mother remember where the will was? She reached over and gently pushed Newman's wet hair out of his eyes.

'Are you still with us?' she asked.

'Yes,' he said, half smiling through the pain. He could not work out which hurt him more his back, his head or his shoulders. She refilled the two pairs of trousers with air and put them back under Newman.

God, she thought, treading water for this long is hard work. She turned her attention to Logan. His right eye was almost closed now.

'You look bloody awful,' she said.

'This date isn't going well, is it?' he smiled.

Jane smiled back. Despite all this, he still had a sense of humour.

'Hey,' she said, 'I got a man to take his trousers off. It's going okay for me!'

He'd been wrong on the boat. This woman was tough and resilient. He liked that. He liked it a lot.

Five minutes later Logan shouted, 'Listen!'

He had their full attention. They were all silent. They could hear the low hum of beating rotor blades.

'There,' said Jane, pointing at a red dot low on the horizon.

The Sea King helicopter swept back and forth, edging ever closer, until eventually it hovered two hundred feet above them.

The numbness that had drained their energy evaporated as complete relief overwhelmed Jane and Logan. Newman was too far gone to realise that they were about to saved. The helicopter was now hovering thirty feet above them as a figure on the winch line descended slowly. The line stopped just above their heads. They could just make out the winch man's words above the noise and down draft.

'I need you to separate so I can pick you up one at a time.'

Jane looked at the winch man and pointed frantically at Scott. The Irishman, clad in a drysuit, helmet and wearing huge fins, dropped into the sea beside the injured FBI man. As Logan held him up, Jane helped him place the strap over Scott's head and pulled his arms through. Seconds later, Scott rose out of the sea.

The noise inside the helicopter was deafening. Wrapped in a foil thermal blanket, ear defenders clamped around her head, it was impossible for them to talk.

Jane watched Logan. He seemed to be ignoring her totally, all his attention focused on Scott strapped to a stretcher in the fuselage. A saline drip hung above the makeshift bed. A paramedic was monitoring his pulse.

The winch operator moved over to check Jane. He leaned closer, 'What's your name?'.

'Jane Blackburn, Detective Inspector Jane Blackburn."

'Two FBI agents and a detective inspector. Are you listening to this, sir?' he announced over the intercom to the rest of the crew.

'This story's gonna be worth a read,' said the pilot.

'How long before we arrive?' Jane asked.

'We'll be there in twenty minutes. Just sit tight. Are you warm enough?'

Jane could feel the circulation slowly returning.

*

It was just after 2am when Tenant arrived in his office at the FBI building.

'Sir, we've just been informed that both Logan and Newman have been pulled from the sea along with a third person. They're at the Marine base in Shannon, being checked over by medics,' said the duty officer.

'Three? Who's the third?' Tenant asked.

'An English policewoman.'

'Only those two could pick up a goddamn woman in the middle of the Atlantic.'

CHAPTER THIRTY-THREE

JANE PULLED the comforting towelling robe close to her body.

'Apart from the nasty bruise on the back of your head, you're going to be fine,' said the doctor. 'How did you get that?'

Jane pointed to Logan. 'He did it.' Logan shrugged.

'If you have a shower, you'll warm up quicker,' the doctor advised.

'I need to make a phone call first.'

'Phone calls are best left until after the shower, food and rest,' the physician said with typical Irish philosophy.

'This is a call I don't want to make but I have to.'

She picked up the receiver in the small office off the medical room at Shannon Marine base and dialled the direct line to the CID room in Cambridge. Jane was surprised to hear Jill's voice early on a Saturday morning.

Jill almost screamed at hearing her boss's voice, 'Jane, where've you been? You've no idea the chaos that's going on here! We've had half the county looking for you and Steve. The ACC's in the Super's office. We're expecting the Chief Constable any minute.'

'Who's there?' she asked.

'Tim, Gary, they're all here.'

'Let me speak to Gary.' She could hear the phone being placed on the desk, then Johnson came on.

'God, Jane, it's good to hear your voice. We were beginning to think you and Steve had eloped. Where are you?'

148

'I'm going to tell you something and then I want you to put me through to Benson's office. I'll leave you to inform the rest of the office.'

There was never an easy way of breaking the news that someone had died. She had done it dozens of times. But it was never any easier.

'Steve's been killed,' she said, there was no way to soften the blow. 'I'll inform Benson now. Make sure everybody knows. Are you listening to me Gary?'

Gary Johnson, who always had a quip for every occasion, could only say, 'Yes.'

'I'm in Southern Ireland. Make sure it's you who goes with Benson to inform Anne. Promise me you won't let him go on his own. Make sure you help Anne. Send over Sarah Larkin, the Welfare Officer, too. Now put me through.'

A moment later Benson came on the line. 'Jane, Johnson tells me you're in Southern Ireland. What's happened?'

For a moment, only a slight moment, Jane thought she could sense concern in Benson's voice, but then realised it was probably worry about his own position rather than her well-being.

'I'll fill you in with the details when I get back, but I have to inform you that Detective Sergeant Steve Cheney has been killed on duty. He was shot.'

There was a moment's silence at the other end. 'Christ, Jane. What the hell's gone on?'

Jane hesitated, then willed herself on. She was determined not to let Benson hear her falter. 'We stumbled on a drug running operation. Two American FBI agents were on board...'

'We were just about to call the Navy to have them intercept the ship. The coast guard told us it was already in international waters. Where's DS Cheney's body?'

'According to the Americans, he was thrown overboard near

the Goodwin Sands.'

'How could you let that happen and what were you doing in Tilbury? We don't have the resources for all this. Why did you let this happen?'

Jane exploded with fury. 'There wasn't a lot I could do about it! I was unconscious at the time.'

She slammed down the phone and, finally, the tears flowed.

As the line went dead Benson turned to ACC Edwards. 'She's gone too bloody far this time. Her maverick actions have caused the death of an officer.'

'When's she coming in?' asked the Assistant Chief. 'Mr Taylor will have to be informed.'

Benson thought to himself, Not even her friend Taylor can get her out of this one,

'I'm not sure when she'll be back. Maybe later today.'

Erin, a young woman with a soft Irish accent, found Jane slumped on the desk, tears rolling down her face. She put her arms round Jane's shoulders and gently led her to a large bathroom upstairs. 'You'll find towels in the top drawer and plenty of clothes. I'll go and get you some coffee and sandwiches,' Erin said.

Jane let her dressing gown drop to the floor and stepped into the shower. She stood directly underneath the showerhead, letting the water pound the top of her scalp and rush down the back of her neck. It stung the bruising but didn't wash away the memory of the blows. Jane had always enjoyed showers, quite often doing her best thinking there. No one to see or disturb her, but the weight on her shoulders was getting heavier. It didn't matter how hard she scrubbed her body, she could not wash away the feeling of total despair. Slowly the tears came as the realisation of what had happened began to truly sink in. For the first time since the shooting she grieved for Steve. She let her body fall against the white tiled wall as she slowly slid down on to the floor of the shower, the weight pushing her down. Kneeling, she began to rock, the only way to ease her pain. Seeing Steve's body as she closed her eyes only made her cries louder. John, the one person she could always talk to, was no longer there. She wished she were dead.

CHAPTER THIRTY-FOUR

LOGAN REPLACED the receiver. Scott looked across at him from the bed in the medical centre. 'What did Tenant say?' Newman asked.

'He wanted to know how we could pick up a woman in the ocean. I told him you used your devilish charm.'

'I wonder how she's doing?'

'The same thought crossed my mind,' said Logan, relieved now that the FBI knew they were safe and that the *Star Supreme* would be under surveillance as she crossed the Atlantic.

Erin arrived with a large tray filled with coffee and sandwiches. As she placed the tray on the table she picked up one of the cups and the smaller of the three plates. 'I'll just take this upstairs to Jane,' she said.

Logan stopped her. 'I'll do it,' he said.

Erin hesitated for a moment, then said, 'Upstairs, third door on the right.'

Logan looked at Scott then said to the Irish girl, 'I think our hero over there needs a bit more of your attention.'

He left with the sandwiches, knocked at the pale blue door and when he got no reply, Logan went in. He placed the coffee and the sandwiches on top of a small cabinet near the single bed. Then he slowly pushed open the bathroom door. Jane was still curled up on the shower floor rocking, sobbing. He picked up a towel and reached in to turn off the water. Logan gently lifted Jane to her feet. As he wrapped a towel around her, he noticed a lattice of small scars gouged in the top of her back.

Above her left shoulder was a bullet hole. These scars were from her past, they had long since healed. Logan was more concerned about the mental scars she was carrying here and now. She sobbed into his shoulder, releasing all her fear, anger and tension. He gently held her as she cried. He kissed her on her temple. Jane pushed herself harder into his body. Her sobs eased.

'What have I done?' she pleaded.

'You saved our lives,' he whispered. He pushed her away and looked into her eyes. 'You saved our lives,' he insisted.

He kissed her on the forehead, brushing her cheek, and gently and slowly kissed her on the mouth. For a moment Jane thought of walking away. She tried to gently pull away from him, but he held her tight. She knew, they both knew, they needed a physical release from the events the last twenty-four hours. She kissed him hard. She led him from the shower to the bed. Jane took control and lay him on his back. He watched her, gently pushing up and down. She moved his hands from her thighs and put them on her breasts.

All thoughts rushed from his head as Jane's passion consumed them both. Their need was sudden and powerful. He moaned gently as she slowly collapsed on top of him. Her anger and pain lost were in her passion. He held her tightly as she cried. He gently kissed away her salty tears. The painkillers kicked in. He closed his eyes, his body was spent. Sleep. They both needed to sleep.

'I've just...'she began to say.

'Shhh,' he said, placing his finger gently on her mouth. 'We'll talk later. Just sleep.'

Jane stirred a few hours later. Her body ached. Gently sliding out of bed to avoid disturbing Logan, she dressed in the bathroom in a top and jeans that Erin had left for her. Making her way to the crew's quarters to get some coffee, she met the winch man.

'I need to get back to Cambridge. Do planes from Shannon fly in to Stansted, or do I have to go to Cork?"

'The next flight out of Cork is at 2.30. I can have a car take you there if you want. You'll have no hassle with a passport. Being from the UK, you don't need one. We have an arrangement with the airline, you can pick up the bill later. I'll give them a quick call.'

'Where's Scott?' she asked.

'He's still in the treatment room, flirting with the medics.'

Jane smiled. 'He can't be too ill, then.'

The winch man's mind was on practicalities. 'If you give me your wet things, I'll get you a black bag and put them in the car,' he said.

As Jane opened the treatment room door, she heard Scott telling a young woman medic how he'd rescued his two companions from the sea. The pair of them suddenly caught sight of Jane in the doorway.

'Is that right? Was this man the hero?' the nurse asked.

'This man needs a lot of TLC, he's a real hero. Could I just have a quick word with him before I go?'

The nurse left them alone.

'How are you feeling?' Jane asked.

'Sore head, fractured collar bone, a few cuts and bruises, but I'll live.'

She could see he was playing down his injuries.

'I've come to say goodbye,' she said.

Scott looked concerned. 'Are we going to see you again, Jane Blackburn?'

'Now let's not get mushy and sentimental. You're far too big a boy for that,' she said, talking to him as if he was a toddler.

'Did Logan give you our cell phone numbers?' Scott asked.

'Well, I...' Scott instantly caught the evasive look on her face.

'Does he know you're leaving?'

'No. It's best he sleeps. He took one hell of a beating. His face…' Jane winced.

'When Logan finds you're gone he'll be like a bear with a sore head.'

'I'm sorry Scott, but my concern is for Anne, Steve Cheney's wife.' She hesitated, realising what she'd just said. 'I mean his widow.'

Scott grabbed a pen from his bedside cabinet, scribbled their phone numbers on a scrap of paper and put it into her hand. She gave him a hug, he winced in agony. She kissed his cheek.

'Ouch.'

She stood back and looked at him. 'Is there anywhere that doesn't bloody hurt?'

He pointed to his mouth. 'There. It doesn't hurt there.'

Jane kissed him on the lips.

'Tell Logan I'm...'

Scott interrupted, 'No goodbyes.'

Erin was waiting by the car. Jane gave her a quick hug. 'Thank you. Thank everybody for me.'

'We've phoned the airline and everything's taken care of.' Erin said.

CHAPTER THIRTY-FIVE

GARY JOHNSON was waiting for her in Arrivals at Stansted, London's third airport.

'How are you feeling?' he asked, taking the black bin bag from her. He was looking at a woman he had known for seven years but barely recognised. She looked bloody awful, Johnson thought.

'You don't want to know.'

'Look, Jane, Benson has told us to take you straight back to the station to give a witness statement.'

'Superintendent Benson can go and...' she stopped herself. Looking into Gary's face she could see he was hurting just as much as she was about Steve's death. She shouldn't take her anger out on him.

'Take me home. I need to get changed. I've got to see Anne. When was she told?'

'Benson and I went to see her at nine o'clock this morning.'

'How was she?'

'Broken.'

'Have they found his body?' Jane asked.

'Not yet. Melanie and Sherlock are at Whitstable talking to fishermen and the Coastguard, trying to calculate where the tide may wash him up.'

'Can I use your mobile phone?' Jane asked. She punched in a number and waited for Detective Constable Chris Holmes to answer.

'Chris. It's Jane. Have you found anything?'

'We've made our way along the Kent coast to Margate. We've talked to a couple of the locals down here and they reckon it could be anything up to three days before the tides give up Steve's body. The tide could take it up or down the coast.'

'Have you alerted the Coastguard?'

'Yes, of course.' It was a very sharp yes.

'I'm sorry Chris. I didn't mean to tell you how to do your job.'

'That's all right, Jane,' he said, his voice softening. 'We're on our way back. They'll call as soon as they find anything. Have you been to see Anne yet?'

'No. I'm on my way there. Give me a ring as soon as you get back to the station. Bye.'

As soon as Jane got home she called her mother and father to tell them the devastating news. As her next of kin, they had already been told she was missing.

'How did Richard take the news?' she asked her father.

'We haven't been able to get hold of him yet,' he said. She could always rely on him to be so calm in a crisis.

'I have to go and see Anne Cheney, Dad. Can you keep trying Richard before he hears this on the news.'

As she stood outside Anne's front door, Jane looked at her watch. It was 5.15pm. She had showered and changed. She almost felt human again. Gary leaned forward and pressed the doorbell. A short, dark-haired woman answered the door.

James, dressed in a Spiderman T-shirt, was holding her hand. 'Who is it, Grandma?' he asked.

Jane looked into the woman's red eyes. Her complexion was pale and drawn. She stared down at the boy. He let go of the old woman's hand and ran into Jane's arms. 'Aunty Jane. Is Daddy with you?'

She hugged the four-year old, 'Daddy's, uh...' She fought back the tears as she searched for help looking at Gary. What was she going to tell the child? Had they told him?

'How do you do? I'm Lorna, Anne's mother. I met Gary earlier.'

Jane introduced herself. 'Where's Anne?' but as she said the words, she saw Steve's widow coming down the stairs.

Taking the boy from Jane, Anne persuaded him to go and finish his supper. Jane promised she'd hug him before she left. Anne took Jane's hand and led her into the living room. The curtains were drawn, Anne turned on the light. Jane could barely look into her friend's face.

'I'm so sorry. This was all my fault.' Jane said.

Gary watched from the doorway as the two women hugged each other tightly, unable to control or contain their tears. It was a good four or five minutes before either of them spoke. Jane gently guided her friend to the sofa and sat down beside her. Anne held Jane's hand between hers. Tears streamed down her cheeks. 'No, Jane. Both Steve and I knew this was a risk of the job.'

How many times in the past had Jane sat down with distraught relatives and explained how their loved ones had died? It was always hardest looking into the faces of mothers who'd have to explain to young children why their father was no longer with them. It was a job no officer relished, but one they all tried to be abstract and professional about, at least while they were in the company of the victim's family. This was different. For the first time in her career she was looking into the face of a police widow.

'Did he suffer?' Anne asked, squeezing Jane's hand tightly. 'Did he suffer in any way?'

'No. He was shot. It was quick.'

'I need to know everything, Jane. I need to understand.'

Jane wiped the tears from her eyes. What was she to do? All relatives want words of comfort.

'He told me to hug you…. to give James a kiss,' Jane lied. 'Has

Sarah Larkin, the Welfare Officer, given you a call?' she asked, hoping she had done enough to ease her friend's grief.

'Yes. She was here this morning.'

'I'll make sure she stays with you until we find Steve's body. We will find him. Sarah will help you make arrangements. I see your mother has moved in.'

Anne smiled. 'I'm not sure whether that's a good thing or a bad thing. But James adores her.'

'I need to go back to the station to sort some things out. I'll call back in again in the morning. We'll make sure a PC stands outside the front door because there's bound to be a lot of Press interest.'

Gary flicked open his mobile as Jane finished speaking and asked the duty sergeant to arrange a guard for the house.

CHAPTER THIRTY-SIX

GARY'S POOL car swung into the station car park entrance to be met by a barrage of flashlights and shouting reporters. They yelled at the car, 'DI Blackburn, are you going to make a statement? Can you tell us how DS Cheney died? Has his body been found?'

The baying pack surrounded the vehicle and followed it into car park. Two police constables manning the gate were swallowed by the tide. More officers ran out of the station, closely followed by the desk sergeant. All Jane could see were the bright lights and a sea of screaming faces.

Gary got out of the car first and fought his way around to her side.

He shouted to the officers in the yard. 'Get that lot out of here now! If they won't go quietly, arrest them.'

Slowly the small force of policemen shoved back the crowd and Gary opened the car door, unceremoniously pushing Jane up the steps and into the station.

'God, it didn't take them long. Are you all right, Jane?' he asked, gasping for breath.

'I'm fine. Let's get this over with.'

She walked quickly past the front desk, along the corridor and up the stairs. She hesitated for a split second outside the CID room door and took a deep breath. With a final glance at Gary, she walked in.

Nothing had changed. Steve was dead and nothing had changed. Jill noticed her first and jumped out of her chair.

'Jane!' she said, as if she'd seen a ghost.

The room fell silent. She looked around, letting her eyes rest on each face. Her gaze eventually fell on Steve's empty desk. She felt her chest tighten. The feelings of helplessness she had tried to wash away in the shower at Shannon came flooding back.

'Jill, could you please make me some coffee?' she asked.

Gary pushed past her, 'Are you all right? Wait here a moment, Jane.'

Closing the blinds, he said, 'It isn't just the local rags we've got out there. You've got the whole damn national Press as well. They've got lenses on those cameras that could pick out a boil on a gnat's arse.'

'Thank you,' she said numbly and sat down.

'Will somebody please tell Benson I'm...' She didn't get to finish her sentence.

'I think he's already here, Jane.'

The Superintendent was striding across the office. He looked at Johnson but spoke to Jane. 'I told your DS to let me know as soon as you were back. I want to speak to you.' As Johnson left the room, Benson slammed the door shut.

Jane said nothing as he exploded in a fury of accusations, every word carefully chosen to hurt and humiliate. She clenched her fists, her whole body, still aching, stiffened with anger.

Eventually, the Superintendent drew breath.

'Have you finished?' Jane asked, holding her anger in check. 'Anne was my priority at that point, not you. Anne is still my priority.'

Benson saved his most cutting jibe to last, 'I'm also informing you that I intend to have DS Johnson brought before a disciplinary committee for direct disobedience of a senior officer's command.'

'Do you have any witnesses to this incident?' Jane asked.

'The whole CID room heard him,' Benson said.

'That wasn't my question, Superintendent,' Jane pressed on. 'Do you have any witnesses? One of your officers is dead, for God's sake. Why are you pursuing this? I can make sure this will not stand up. All I have to do is put Johnson in front of a stress counsellor who will state that due to the loss of a work colleague, it was a momentary lapse in an otherwise exemplary record.'

Benson slowly calmed down.

Jane looked at him, 'I fully appreciate you want to blame me for Steve's death but you're not going to get the opportunity. And you're certainly not going to use my officers as scapegoats' she said. 'Steve and I had no idea what we were stepping into. I was asked to investigate a suspicious death by the Coroner and that's exactly what I did, my job.'

'Your job got DS Cheney killed.'

'And it's your neck you're thinking about. Even your warped sense of right and wrong can't pin Steve's death on me.'

Jane stood up to open her office door. 'I will give my witness statement to DS Johnson. Sir.' she said, waiting by the door for him to leave.

Benson could feel the entire CID room watching as he left. Only the sudden ringing of a phone broke the silence. Through the goldfish bowl walls, her team watched Jane close to tears, struggling to regain her composure. The CID room was silent.

Jane slammed the office door, slumped down in her chair, and for the third time that day let the tears flow. This time they were tears of anger and frustration.

Jill quietly entered the room, 'Your coffee. You look dreadful. You should take a couple of days off.'

'Not until we've found Steve's body. Could you ask Gary to come in?'

Johnson sat down, 'Benson's nothing but a pen-pushing arsehole.'

Jane could see the genuine anger in his face, 'You're not telling me something I don't already know, Gary, but for the sake of your career I wouldn't say that too often.'

'What career? I've stepped on too many toes and the last couple of days has sealed my fate.'

'Benson told me about your little outburst.'

'Yes ma'am,' Gary said with a smile. 'I'm getting almost as outspoken as you are.' He hesitated. 'Look, you have to fill out your witness statement. I think it's best we get it over with. Why don't you dictate it to me, I'll go and get Gibson to witness it, unless you'd prefer someone else.'

'No. Melanie will be fine.'

It took them the best part of two-and-a-half hours to complete her statement. There were over ten pages in Johnson's handwriting. Several times he'd had to stop and let her gather her thoughts and wipe away the tears. With frightening clarity, she gave him a blow-by-blow account of Steve's death and her eventual escape from the ship. Many times in the past, Johnson had watched criminals confess to their crimes. A sense of relief would come over them after they had unburdened themselves with the truth. Somehow, the harder the criminal, the greater was that relief. Jane was undergoing the same process. Now someone else knew the hardships and fear she had experienced. She would sleep soundly tonight.

CHAPTER THIRTY-SEVEN

JANE WOKE on Sunday morning to find the Press camped outside her front door. It didn't take her long to work out she would be safer with her team in the office.

As she walked through the door they were all there finding a hundred and one non-essential jobs just so they could be there. Looking round the office she almost cracked a smile.

'Is this going to be Steve's epitaph? she asked aloud. 'At Last The Bloody Paperwork Got Done.'

Johnson smiled at her black humour.

'Any word on Steve's body, Gary?' she asked.

'No. The Coastguard has brought in extra volunteers and I was told that if I stopped phoning them every few minutes, they might be able to get on with their jobs.'

'I want somebody to make it their job to phone Steve's house every couple of hours to check up on Anne. Also, we'd better put two constables outside her house, there's bound to be even more Press there today.'

Gary could see the professional slowly returning. 'Headquarters are sending down a press officer to help out,' he said.

'Gary, I want it known that anybody issuing freelance statements from our office, however well-meaning, will be carpeted,' Jane said, suddenly realising that the DEA/FBI operation could be in jeopardy, if the contents of her statement leaked out.

Gary followed her into the office. She still looked bloody awful.

'There really isn't a lot you can do here now Jane. Why don't you go home?' Johnson said.

'No, I feel safer here,' Jane said.

Just then Miller burst into the DI's office.

'They've found him. The Coastguard think they've discovered Steve's body.'

'Where?'

'A man walking his dog found him at St Margaret's Bay, a little place just outside Dover.'

'When?'

'Not ten minutes ago. What do you want to do?'

For a moment Jane was numb. Johnson jolted her into action.

'Inspector, what do you want us to do?'

Jane looked up at Miller. 'Phone Kent Police back. Tell them I'll go down to the mortuary at Dover to make a positive ID.'

'Jane,' Johnson protested. 'Do you think that's wise? Any one of us could go down there and do this.'

'No. It has to be me. You can come with me. You drive.'

She turned to Miller. 'You blue light it around to Anne and tell her what's happened before she finds out from the Press. Explain to her that I've gone to check the body is Steve's.'

Then she told Melanie Gibson, 'I want you to inform Benson and his press crew what's going on but not until after we've left the station.'

CHAPTER THIRTY-EIGHT

THEY MANAGED to get out of Cambridge and onto the M11 motorway before the first irate phone call from Benson.

'What the hell do you think you're doing?' he demanded. 'Why wasn't I informed about DS Cheney before you went charging down to Dover? You're in no fit state to be doing this.'

'I thought you'd be too busy organising another press conference.'

Her sarcastic tone didn't go unnoticed.

'I have Gary Johnson with me and we'll inform you as soon as we have a positive identification,' Jane said ending the phone call.

Next, she called the Coroner, Bill Donaldson. He'd just heard the news on the radio that Steve had been killed. It also said a woman police inspector had survived the shooting.

'Jane, are you all right? I'm so sorry about DS Cheney,' Donaldson said. 'If I hadn't asked you to do a favour for me, he'd be alive today. I feel it's all my fault.'

'Look Bill, you were right about Will Davies, it wasn't an overdose. He was murdered. The people who killed him shot Steve Cheney. We know who they are and the FBI will arrest them in the States in a few days time,' Jane explained. 'I'll tell you all about it soon. In the meantime, I'm on my way to identify Steve's body. I'd like the post mortem to be in Cambridge and that means we'll have to apply for the body to be kept in transit, otherwise the police in Kent will end up with the inquiry and Lord knows when we'd get his body back.'

Donaldson cut in, 'I'll call the Kent coroner and put him in the picture. As soon as you've made a formal ID, we'll have DS Cheney sent straight to the morgue at Addenbrooke's here in Cambridge.'

'Thanks, Bill.'

Her next call was to Miller. 'Where are you?' she asked.

'I'm outside Steve's house. I've told Mrs Cheney that you're going down to Kent to take care of the formalities. By the way, the camera crews and Press are already here.'

'Damn,' Jane suddenly panicked. 'They didn't get to tell her, did they?'

'No. They got here before me but the men on the door kept them away, and to be honest, they're behaving themselves.'

'Tell them as soon as we've identified the body, Benson will make a statement. Hopefully that'll send most of them back to the station.'

Jane sat quietly. She was already feeling far too guilty about Steve. She had to do something to help Anne. Jill had been inundated with messages of sympathy from the Press. Many of the journalists who'd called were friends her husband John had made in the media when he'd worked in Fleet Street before he'd become a full-time author. Quite a few of them had attended his funeral but in the years that followed, one by one, they'd lost contact. Now they were eager to get in touch again.

Jane knew how their minds worked. It probably wasn't her welfare that had interested them, but they wanted the story of how Steve was killed. She had to protect Anne from them. As Jane looked through the list Jill had given her, she recognised a name. She dialled the number. The voice on the end of the phone said, 'News International. Can I help you?'

'Phil Grahame, Associate Editor of The Sun,' said Jane.

'Ringing for you.'

A secretary answered the phone in The Sun's huge sixth-floor newsroom.

'I'm sorry, Phil's in editorial conference right now,' she said.

Jane hesitated for a moment, then said, 'I want you to go into that meeting and tell him Detective Inspector Blackburn is on the phone.'

After a couple of minutes a breathless voice said, 'Jane. God, how are you?'

'I'm fine, Phil. You probably already know I'm on the way to identify DS Cheney's body.'

'We know you've left the station and a body has been found near Dover.'

Jane came straight to the point. 'I need a favour. I want you to call around the rest of the nationals and the local freelancers you have on this, plus BBC and ITN. I need you to try to come to some kind of agreement to cut down on the number of journalists outside Anne Cheney's house. I appreciate you have a job to do, but we both know how rare the death of a police officer is, let alone a Detective Sergeant. His widow doesn't need to be in middle of this feeding frenzy and she probably knows less than you do about what's going on.'

Grahame was sympathetic. 'We're trying to be as diplomatic about this as possible, but unfortunately your Superintendent Benson and his ham-fisted press officers are giving us so little information that we..'

'I realise that,' Jane interrupted. 'That's why I'm phoning. Can you make the calls?'

'It's unlikely BBC and ITV news are going to listen to me.'

'We both know they're going to listen to the Editor of The Sun.'

'That's an awfully big favour, Jane.' the newspaper executive said. 'What do we get in return?'

Jane took a deep breath, remembered her warning to her own staff about talking to the papers, and said, 'Eventually, the truth is going to have to be told - and you'll get it. Short of Martians taking over Parliament, it's the best exclusive you're likely have this year.'

'You obviously didn't read last week's front page. They're already here!' Grahame joked, glad he'd got a deal for his paper. 'Consider it done. Can I contact you any time on this number?'

'Yes.'

'Wait a moment. I've just had the latest press statement from your office put into my hand. Christ, they won't even tell us how you were rescued.'

'Speak to your Editor about my request and then phone me back.'

'I don't have to Jane. He's heard every word we've just said. He's already given the OK.'

'Listen, Phil. A huge operation is underway involving other agencies and I don't want to do anything to jeopardise that. Steve's killers will be captured when that operation is concluded in a few days time. But if you want to find out how I was rescued, called the Marine base at Shannon in the Irish Republic. Once you've got that, I'll tell you what you can and can't say.' ·

The Sun man didn't need any more information, 'Thanks, Jane.' The phone went dead.

Gary took his eyes off the road and stared at her, 'When Benson finds out what you've just done he'll put you up before Internal Affairs.'

'If he finds out. Besides, I didn't tell Phil anything The Sun wouldn't have found out themselves, and I did say 'eventually'. You know what'll happen, a few days after the funeral everybody will have forgotten. We'll have the usual huffing and puffing from the MPs about whether to arm the police and then the only other time this will hit the Press is when somebody gets around to having a memorial service, which the PM will attend the day he wants some bad news covered up. Then, it'll take months, if not years, to extradite Steve's killers and then they'll be on remand for the best part of another year before they eventually come to trial.'

As the car descended the steep road into Dover, Jane looked out at the English Channel, still placid in the dusk. Her mind filled with visions of Steve's body lying on the pebbles below the white cliffs that soar above the beach where he was washed ashore. She closed her eyes to clear her mind, to chase away the pictures. But they wouldn't go. She hardly noticed as Gary negotiated the one-way system and pulled up at the police station in the town centre.

Jane instinctively reached for her badge, but it wasn't there. She could never remember at what point she had lost her warrant card. She had presumed it had been disposed of along with Steve's body. Johnson realised she was searching for something she no longer had.

'When I get back to the office tomorrow, I'll sort that out for you,' he said as he palmed his card at the Desk Sergeant.

'Thanks, Gary,' she said.

They were shown to the DI's office. Detective Inspector Ronnie Maxwell stood up from his desk and shook hands with a woman who looked as though she had been to hell and back. She wore no make-up to hide the bruises on her face and neck. The same anxiety that any other member of the public displays when they're about to see the dead body of a loved one was etched on her face. He kept the pleasantries short, then told Jane that a couple of Press men had beaten her to the station.

'They're actually in the station cafeteria.'

Jane looked alarmed.

He smiled to reassure her, 'We figured if we were particularly gracious hosts, you could go and do what you had to do without them even realising you're here. The hospital is only up

the road. Would you like to get this over with now?'
  She nodded.

CHAPTER THIRTY-NINE

IT TOOK less than five minutes to drive to the mortuary at the Buckland Hospital. On the way, Maxwell gave them details of how Steve was found. The body, wrapped in packing tape, would have instantly sunk after it was hurled from the ship. Twice a day tides would have swept him backwards and forwards along the sea bed until he was finally washed up.

'We were asked to do nothing to the body apart from cut away the plastic covering his face so that you could make an identification. Then the body will be sent up to your own pathologist and forensics. Our guys have bagged and kept everything found on and around the body.'

As they approached the door to the mortuary, Maxwell stopped and turned to Jane. 'Because of this, the body has not been touched. It hasn't been cleaned. It's not a pretty sight, I'm afraid.'

Despite the enormous extractor fan working full blast, an overpowering stench invaded their nostrils. Both Jane and Gary wretched. Maxwell gently lifted the white sheet. There he was. The man she had worked with for just over two years. The man she had persuaded to stay in the force. The man who had used his body to shield her from certain death. His face was badly swollen, barely recognisable, but he hadn't been in the water long enough for the sea life to start work devouring the cadaver. The white shirt was torn where he'd been dragged along the seabed. Jane retched and turned her head. She could feel vomit burning the back of her throat. Gary held her tight. The hard-nosed, cynical policeman could see Jane's pain and guilt, mixed with memories of identifying John coming back to her.

Gently he helped her out of the room. When they were back in the corridor, Maxwell asked, 'Are you formally identifying the body as Detective Sergeant Stephen Cheney?'

'Yes. Stephen John Cheney.' said Jane.

Jane sat down on a plastic seat placed against the corridor, stunned and physically drained.

'We'd better phone Anne,' she said, at last.

'Let's just take a couple of minutes first,' Johnson said. 'Why don't we call Miller and ask him to tell Anne. You've done enough for today. He's a good cop and you know he'll be sensitive. There's nothing more you can do now. Forensics and pathology will take over, you know the FBI will do their job. It's time you thought of yourself and took some time off.'

CHAPTER FORTY

HENRY FIELD, the Crown Prosecution solicitor arrived on Jane's doorstep. In each hand he held a bottle of Chianti from the vineyard next door to his holiday home in Tuscany. He saw a look of hesitation on Jane's face. In the eight days since identifying Steve's body, she'd seen a steady stream of visitors. She knew they were all well-meaning but talking of death and loss inevitably lead most of them to unburden all their own sorrow and anxieties onto her. Grief had sat more heavily on Jane's shoulders as each visitor left. Her friend Sally Goodman had stayed for a couple of days but had to go to Milan on business. Richard had come over for the weekend but he was wanted on the yacht. She hadn't been able to sleep and had found comfort driving the MG at high speed in the middle of the night with the top down. She had lost count of how many times she'd started to dial the number Newman had given her but on each occasion she'd stopped herself pressing the last digit. Would Logan have given her a second thought? She kept the number close by at all times, panicked when she thought she had lost it. It had become her comfy blanket but she didn't understand why.

Henry could sense she had reached saturation point for sympathy. 'Look, I'm not here to talk about Steve's death. I've come about work. I thought you'd like to know how my little trip to the CPS offices in London had gone. Oh, and I thought we'd get drunk.'

Jane took a step forward and hugged him. She needed a

distraction and talk of work would give her a few moments relief from her thoughts about Steve. She ushered him into the living room when her phone rang.

'While I answer that, you'll find the corkscrew in the top drawer on the left and the glasses in the cupboard above.'

It was Gary Johnson. 'Just checking in to make sure everything is all right before I head home. I just have one last stop to make on the way.'

'Where?'

'The Cat and Fiddle on Arthur Street.'

'Rough day?' Jane said, mustering a weak attempt at humour.

'I just want to have a quiet word with somebody before Steve's funeral.'

Jane didn't need to ask Gary any details. She knew what it was about.

'Thanks, Gary. Be careful.'

'Do you want me to call in on the way home?'

'No. Henry Field has just dropped by with a couple of bottles of wine. Looks like my night is pretty well taken care of. Thanks all the same.'

Henry had already poured the wine. Jane curled up in the corner of her huge sofa.

'So, what did you find out?' she asked before swirling the delicious red wine around in her glass and taking a huge gulp.

'You were lucky,' said Henry. 'Sylvia was on duty that day.'

'Sylvia? Should I know her?' asked Jane

'No. She's one of the secretaries in the CPS. Nice woman, been chasing me for years. We went to lunch and she told me everything. Turns out that on the morning West's bail application came up, Judge Hammond got a phone call from Sir Phillip Roberts. He's Director of the Judicial Group at the Lord Chancellor's Office.'

'I take it that's unusual.'

'I should say so. That's like the Home Secretary phoning you up and asking how your day's going.'

Jane, with a little help from Henry, did what she'd needed to do for over a week. She got blind drunk.

*

The Cat & Fiddle was a pub on neutral ground. Gary leaned casually against the bar next to Val Smithson. There were no pleasantries. They did not even look at each other. Smithson was a career criminal, introduced to the way of life from an early age by his father, grandfather, brothers and uncles. It was not a question of which one of the Smithson family was in jail, it was a question of how many. In their own way, they had an old-fashioned sense of right and wrong. Part of their operation was prostitution but they despised anybody selling drugs. The family had been known in the past to grass up the drug dealers if they got too close to schools. Gary was on his guard. Although now in his late sixties, carrying a good thirty pounds too much, Smithson had been a street fighter and he could still put young thugs in hospital for not showing proper respect.

'You want a drink? Smithson asked.

'No. You know why I'm here.'

'We were expecting a visit.'

'The funeral is on Wednesday and I want everybody off the streets that day.'

'My boys have made sure everyone understands the rules. No crime, nothing, the day of the copper's funeral.'

'Do they understand the consequences?' Johnson asked.

'Those who didn't, do now."

Smithson tossed a glance over his shoulder into the far corner. Three faces, well-known to Johnson, mainly through petty burglary, sat bearing heavy bruising and freshly stitched wounds from some extremely rough justice.

'Good. As long as we all know where we stand. We reckon there will be at least eight thousand police in Cambridge the day after tomorrow, so we won't exactly be short-handed if anybody is stupid enough to step out of line. This is personal, Smithson. He was a good copper and a good friend.'

'Stop spelling it out. I know where you're coming from.'

For a few moments there was an uncomfortable silence. Smithson looked across at Gary. They had been on opposite sides of the fence all their lives, but Smithson knew that a policeman's death upsets the status quo. It made everybody jumpy and he and his family were desperately trying to keep the lid on an extremely tense situation.

'What do we do with the money?' the villain asked.

Gary looked back at him. 'How big was the collection? No. I don't want to know. Send it to the station anonymously.'

Johnson took one more look at the three thugs in the corner and back to Smithson. Then he left.

CHAPTER FORTY-ONE

GEORGE STREET was a particularly beautiful row of creamy-white Georgian houses. It had been a number of years since well-to-do families lived there. The distinguished buildings were now offices, private doctors' consulting rooms and dental surgeries. Number Five C was where Dr Pauline Webster had her office. A warm smile greeted Jane as she reached the top of the three flights of stairs with its dark wooden rail and deep red carpet. Fiona had been Pauline's receptionist as long as Jane could remember. The two women were partners in work and in life.

'Jane,' Fiona said as she stepped from behind her desk. Giving her a big hug she asked, 'How are you?'

'Fine,' Jane said, 'Until Pauline insisted I came to see her.'

'Psychiatrists are like dentists, you should see them at least once every six months just for a check-up.'

Jane laughed.

'You'd better go in, you know she doesn't like to be kept waiting,' Fiona said, opening the door.

As Jane stepped into the consulting room door all the memories of her first meeting with Pauline came flooding back. The case she was working on was particularly horrific, trying to catch the killer of a mother and her two young children. And right in the middle of it John had died in a car accident after a drunk driver forced him off the road. Pauline was one of the few people who knew the biggest secret of her life, the traumatic reason Jane had left the Navy. The reason that demons she tried to bury deep inside her occasionally rose to the surface. Jane had fallen in love with her commanding officer, Guy Penrose. For months everything had gone well and he was even dropping hints about them getting married. One afternoon he had exploded at Jane beyond all reason, smashing his fist into her face, sending her reeling across the room, banging her head on the radiator, knocking her unconscious. When she finally woke up, they were both stripped naked and he had taken a whip to her back until his sadistic fantasy had been satisfied.

Pauline rose from behind her desk. She was a heavy-set woman in her late forties who had an outwardly brusque manner.

'Take a seat, Jane. Which painting would you like me to hang on the wall?'

As Jane sat down she said, 'No hello, how are you?'

'Darling, I know how you are, or you wouldn't be here.'

'Which painting?' Pauline asked again.

'My favourite,' Jane replied.

Pauline instantly went to a two-feet square oil painting by an Australian artist called Jonathan Moore. It showed a beautiful beach in Australia crowded with families on a warm summer afternoon.

Dr Webster had a theory that if her patients were concentrating on a picture, their subconscious would let go.

She put it up on the wall in front of Jane, then sat down behind her and said quietly, 'Tell me what you see.'

Jane leaned back in a large blue armchair filled with multi-coloured cushions.

'I see Steve's blood all over the sand,' she said.

'Tell me what you see in the painting first,' said Pauline, her voice smooth like honey.

'Steve playing with his son James. Anne is sitting under the yellow and white striped parasol.'

'How long have they been there?'

'All their lives.'

'Who is sitting next to them?'

It was a game of cat and mouse Jane had played so often. Pauline would ask the most incongruous questions. She would dig until she felt she had reached the darkest recesses of your mind. The game played on for another fifteen minutes.

'Hazel,' Pauline said. 'You said the man with the purple shirt has hazel eyes. What do you think his name is?'

'Logan,' she replied instantly.

'Describe him.'

'Mediterranean-looking with hazel eyes.' Jane was now sitting upright in her seat, her face tilted upwards at the painting.

Pauline watched her intensely.

'Have you known him long?' she asked.

'I wanted him. I had to have him,' Jane said.

'Had to have him. What do you mean?'

'It had been so long since I let anybody touch me. I couldn't have stopped myself if I'd wanted to. I had to have him.'

Tears flowed down Jane's face, 'I raped him.'

For a moment Pauline was silent, very carefully choosing her next words.

'Was he willing?'

'Yes'

'Did he push you away?'

'No. He held me even tighter.'

'Did he say no?'

'Never.'

'Did he get an erection?'

'Oh yes.'.

Jane was almost transfixed by the painting. She could see the man in the purple shirt beckoning her to come into the water.

'Did you enjoy being with him?'

Jane hesitated. She placed her hand inside her pocket and held the crumpled piece of paper.

'Yes,' she said. 'Very much.'

'Then how can you say you raped him? It wasn't rape, Jane.'

'I couldn't have stopped myself, if I'd tried.'

'Jane,' said Pauline. 'How many men have you seen since John's death?'

'About half a dozen.'

'And how many men have you had sex with?'

'None.'

Pauline stood up, walked around the desk and faced her. Taking the painting off the wall and turning it so Jane could no longer see it, she stared into those brown eyes.

'You have to get one thing straight in your life, Jane. You cannot go round with this crazy impression that you are Mrs Perfect, righting all the wrongs you find and living the life of a nun.'

Jane stared straight into her face. She had dreamy dark eyes, flecked with green and a pale soft pink complexion.

'Occasionally, darling,' she went on. 'We all fall off the wagon. You just did it a bit more spectacularly than the rest of us.'

'What do you suggest I do?'

'Call him,' said Pauline. 'Invite him around for round two. If you were as good as that, I can't see him saying "no".'

Jane smiled. 'Am I sane?' she asked.

'Define sane,' said Pauline. 'The sanest person I know is doing life with no parole for murdering his entire family.'

CHAPTER FORTY-TWO

LATE AFTERNOON brought a spring shower to Lincoln Park, Washington, D.C. He walked into the Italian restaurant on Grace Street, at the back of the harbour, to escape the rain. It was quiet. Office workers had not yet finished for the day, most tourists had retreated to their hotels. He tucked his hand in his pocket. The precious Blue Heaven was still there. He walked across the room, past empty tables, and sat down at the bar.

'Yes, sir, what can I get you?' the elderly Italian bartender asked.

'Beer.'

He'd have a quick drink, then move on. It was too soon, too quiet.

The man must remember I came in. He must remember I was here. He turned to the barman.

'Have you got the time? I think my watch has stopped.'

'Ten before five, sir,' said the barman who was old enough to be his grandfather.

'It's very quiet in here.'

'Yes, sir. It'll pick up in half an hour or so, when people finish work and call in on the way home.'

That was when he noticed her. He hadn't seen her come in. She sat down on a stool to his left, one away from him. He watched her carefully, studying her reflection in the mirror behind the bar. Was she a professional or not? He couldn't tell. He didn't care. His palms began to sweat, the hairs on the back of his neck bristling with rising excitement. She suddenly looked up and caught him watching her. She was in her early thirties, slim, wearing a blonde wig. Her exaggerated make-up couldn't hide the fact there was no life in her eyes.

'Can I buy you a drink?' he asked.

'Sure you can,' she said, giving him a soulless smile. 'Anything else will cost you a neat, crisp hundred.'

She moved across and filled the empty barstool between them. She smiled. A couple more like this and she'd be able to finish early, for once. The bar tender brought over her cocktail. He listened to her well-rehearsed speech. Her apartment was just around the corner, only five minutes walk. They could have another drink here and then go back to her place. She was businesslike, dictating how the night would proceed. His anger rose. This was his game. He was in charge. She would not tell him how it was going to proceed. He almost walked out, almost said no. Then he put his hand back into his pocket. He stroked the glass phial of Blue Heaven. The desire surged powerfully through him. He knew he wouldn't need to use it, but where was the fun in not letting the genie out of the bottle for the night? If only they knew where he was. If only they knew what he was doing.

Her apartment was small, one living room, a bedroom and tiny kitchen. The bedroom curtains were permanently closed. It was filled with the clutter of her life. Dolls everywhere, sitting on her dressing table, a small chair, and the bed. Their glass eyes never blinking, always watching. She took off her jacket.

'I can get rid of them if you want. Some people don't like them.'

'Doesn't bother me,' he said.

'What's your name?'

'Charles. What do you want me to call you?'

'What would you like to call me, honey?' she asked.

'Jennifer.'

'Then Jennifer it is, Charles. But let's get the awkward business out of the way first.'

He reached into the hip pocket of his chinos and took out a large green wedge. He rolled two fifty dollar bills off the top, handing them to her. She placed them under the skirts of a blue-eyed china doll sitting on her dressing table. The doll sat watching him. Now she was on his time. Now she would do what he wanted, and they weren't here to stop him. That was their fault. They should have watched him more closely. They weren't here and now it was his game.

'What do you like?' she asked.

'I'd like to make you a drink,' he said. 'I'd like to watch you relax first. I want to watch you undress, Jennifer.'

She'd been on the game, one way or another, since she was sixteen and thought she'd seen it all. She had even been hospitalised twice. Considering the hazards of her profession, she thought she'd got away lightly. This was going to be an easy one. All he wanted was to make a couple of drinks and for her to give him a floor-show. Maybe she could roll him over for a bit more of the dough in his back pocket.

'You'll find the drinks in the top kitchen cupboard and some mixers in the fridge, with the ice.'

'Any cola?' he asked.

He found the Coke in the bottom of the fridge door. He mixed two rum and Cokes, with ice. Only one cube of ice in hers, the one he was slowly pouring in the Blue Heaven. His erection was hard. He walked back into the room. She had noticed it as well. He put the doll on the floor and sat in the chair. She had already started to take off her blouse. She let the short, black skirt drop to the floor to reveal her crotchless panties

He handed her the drink, which she placed on the bedside cabinet.

'No. Drink it now, slowly,' he told her. 'Lick your lips.'

He watched her slowly empty the glass. His power was complete. They couldn't stop him. They weren't here to tell him what to do. None of them. This was his world. A world he understood. A world where he was in charge.

'Get down on all fours, on the bed.'

He watched her parade herself on the bed, following her exaggerated movements. She purred like a cat. He undid his fly, releasing his beautiful erect penis. She was getting groggy. He watched her as she struggled and fought to keep alert. The only sensation she could feel was like falling into darkness and the insatiable thirst. He watched her collapse face up on the counterpane. He finished undressing her. He didn't want the tools of her trade touching him. He climbed onto the bed and spread her legs. He grabbed the pillow and placed it over her face. He didn't want to see her face. He wanted to see the women he couldn't have, Jennifer, Claire and Hayley.

He pushed his penis hard inside her. There was no act of passion, no emotion beyond a driving anger at *them*, living his life for him and not allowing him to make his own mistakes. His whole life was planned out. It was all planned but this.

Now he had the power he craved... the power to kill. He had been interrupted with Hayley, but not this time. Nobody would stop him now. It was his time, his thrill.

She wasn't breathing any more. He stood back and looked down on the girl. He pulled up his trousers and did up his fly. He felt no remorse. She was only a prostitute.

'They can arrange anything,' he said to himself. 'Well, let's see how good they are this time.'

He had quelled the demons for now. The genie was back in the bottle.

CHAPTER FORTY-THREE

THE FORCE honoured Anne Cheney's wish that only family should follow the coffin. She had been determined to keep the funeral for her closest loved ones. Everyone else waited in the packed church. It was the church she and Steve had grown to love, where James had been baptised, the church they'd tried to attend each Sunday. An officer stood every few meters along the route from the house to the church. They saluted solemnly as the cortege passed by. Behind the officers stood the public, sometimes five deep, respectfully watching the small procession. Steve's death, as with all police killings in the UK, had touched the nation. The flood of flowers and wreaths that had been sent to the station from all over the country carpeted the grass around the church door.

For Jane, the sweet smell of the flowers brought more painful memories flooding back. She waited with hundreds of officers from stations around Cambridgeshire and across the country. Almost every officer who'd ever worked with Steve was there, plus representatives from forces all over the country. The cortege came into sight, led by six gleaming motorbikes ridden by uniformed policemen. An enormous wreath of lilies and two single red roses sat on the top of the coffin along with Steve's uniform cap. Jane swallowed hard and desperately fought to keep her own emotions in check. She looked around to see her own team, who had asked to line the path between the gate and the church door. Every single one of them wore full dress uniform as a mark of respect, the uniforms they ordinarily fought to get out of.

Gary Johnson led the pallbearers forward as the hearse drew up. Jane should have been sitting in a front pew with the Home Secretary and the Chief Constable. She had deliberately asked for permission to stay with her team.

As Chief Constable Taylor made his way towards the lectern, Jane could see he had discarded most of his own speech and was now carrying the small, yellow cue cards of the eulogy she had written. As Taylor spoke, Jane stared at Cheney's coffin, draped in the Union Flag.

'Today we are here to give praise and thanks to one of our fallen colleagues. Life is divided into those who give and those who take. Steve was one of life's givers... an officer who gave the ultimate gift. A man who sacrificed his life to save a colleague....'

Jane fought back the tears. Today she had to be Detective Inspector Blackburn, not a woman who had just lost a close friend. The woman who owed her life to Steve. She had to be strong for her team. Of all the things she had done in her life, this was one of the hardest. As the Chief spoke of Steve's life, Jane remembered the touching kindness of the public at the loss of one of their policemen. Messages of goodwill had swamped the station. Many of them personal, Mrs Wilson who remembered how Steve had helped her after the burglary, the thousands of pounds sent from all over the country for Steve's widow and son, some of it anonymously. The electrical shop in the High Street had phoned in to offer their help when it was realised that they would have to relay pictures of the funeral to another hall, but Anglia Television had given their help. The press had been as good as their word and Anne had not been harassed. Nobody wanted to say or do anything to upset her. Today, photographers and cameramen were as unobtrusive as possible.

As the congregation rose to sing Steve's favourite hymn, Abide With Me, Jane could see Jill being comforted by Miller. At last Johnson and the five other pallbearers, all representatives from stations where Steve had worked, carried the coffin back out through the door. As the small procession made its way solemnly to the far corner of the graveyard where Steve would be buried in private, Taylor turned to Jane, 'I thought you'd like to know I got a phone call on the way here from the Assistant Director of the FBI in Washington to say that they had picked up Steve's killers and the heroin. He thought Steve's team would want to know that. I thanked him on your behalf.'

Jane's eyes were fixed on the coffin and as she slowly watched it go out of sight, she whispered, 'Goodbye'.

*

Logan was making breakfast when Newman called from the other room. 'Here, quick. Look. It's on CNN.'

'What is?' asked Logan entering the room, where Scott lay on the couch, his shoulder strapped up.

'Steve Cheney's funeral. Look at the long lines of officers that have turned out. The news guy reckons there's over eight thousand mourners, including some big shots from the Government.'

The pair of them watched in silence as the newsreader continued, 'We're now going over to Debra Jednorski for a live report.'

A smartly dressed blonde-haired woman appeared outside a Norman church, 'As you can see behind me, the coffin is making its way across the small churchyard for a private burial. There has been an extremely large turnout as, fortunately, this is a rare event in England for a police officer to die while on duty. Behind me you can see the Home Secretary, Chief Constable Robert Taylor, and Detective Inspector Jane Blackburn, the officer who's life was saved by Detective Sergeant Cheney. He was shot protecting her. Inspector Blackburn then went on to save the lives of two undercover FBI men investigating a massive drug smuggling operation between Afghanistan and the USA...'

The camera panned to two officers with acres of gold braid on their uniforms and then to Jane. She was dressed in her dark uniform with silver buttons. Above her left breast pocket Logan and Newman could make out a row of four medals. Her eyes could just be seen under her uniform hat. She looked gaunt.

'She's not eating. She's lost weight,' Logan said.

'She does look pale,' Newman added. For the first time in five years, he saw a pained, anguished look across on Logan's face. There was nothing either of them could do to help.

'Why don't you phone her?' Scott suggested.

'Because she didn't say goodbye. It doesn't matter.'

He hadn't fooled Newman for a moment. He could see it mattered. It mattered a great deal.

CHAPTER FORTY-FOUR

TOBY HARDING was a blustering, upper-class gossip. In court acting as a defence barrister, he toned down the accent and did his damnedest to keep his clients out of jail. That made him popular with the criminal fraternity. Jane sat down in an expensive leather armchair in his plush office. His clients obviously paid well. She declined his offer of coffee. He expressed his sympathy over 'the Detective Sergeant's death'.

'Steve Cheney,' she corrected. Toby knew Steve's name well enough. They had often crossed swords in court.

'Absolutely appalling business,' he said, without a hint of genuine sympathy. 'It's very rare to have the pleasure of a your company, Jane.'

She butted in, 'You mean apart from the confrontations while I'm in the witness box in a courtroom.'

Jane watched as his soft, pink hands toyed with his Mont Blanc pen.

'We all have a job to do, Jane, however unpleasant,' he said.

'I'm here for some information.'

'You should be at home, taking some time off.'

'I need to finish the last case I was working on.'

'Which one?' Harding asked.

'Charles West, the American diplomat's son we charged with rape.'

'Oh yes,' said Toby. 'The one where his lawyer successfully appealed against the magistrate's decision.'

'I've discovered that on the morning of the hearing the judge was contacted by Sir Phillip Roberts, from the Lord Chancellor's Office.'

Harding rocked back in his seat, revelling in the moment.

'Come on, Toby. You're the biggest gossip in this place. I need to know what's going on.'

'Despite the fact that you're one of this country's best detectives, Inspector Blackburn, you can be quite naïve.'

Jane looked at him indignantly.

'Four years ago, Phillip Roberts spent eighteen months in Washington acting as liaison between the American Justice Department and our own.'

Jane looked at him blankly.

'Your defendant is a diplomat's son.'

'I'm sorry, Toby, but this is going totally over my head.'

'Obviously, darling. Sir Phillip, as he is now, made many contacts while he was in America, despite the fact his posting was cut short.'

'Do you know why?'

'Well, let's just say he and I frequent the same clubs in town.'

Jane still looked blank.

'Gay, dear, gay.'

'That's not illegal in this country. It's not illegal in the USA either.'

'But rumour has it that our Phillip likes them very fresh-faced and young, and had to leave Washington because one of the kids he picked up was under age. He was brought home to save the Americans any embarrassment.'

'So who's been pulling his strings?' Jane wondered aloud.

'Darling, there's only one place you're going to find that out. I think a trip to Washington may be in order.'

Toby Harding stood at his window and watched Jane cross the street below. He held a telephone receiver in his hand.

'Caroline, darling. You must take me to lunch. Have I got

some interesting snippets of information for you?'

Caroline Everett sighed on the other end of the line, 'Toby, I really don't have time for your puerile little games.'

'Meaow, darling. How could you be so nasty to old Toby?'

'Why should I take you to lunch?' she asked.

'Because I've just had a meeting with Detective Inspector Blackburn. Now are you sure you don't have time to take Old Toby to lunch?'

Ms Everett was all ears. It always amused her that he called himself 'Old Toby' when she knew for a fact he was the same age as her.

'For a decent lunch I could give you some information that would probably encourage your clients to pay your bill a little quicker.'

'Where would you like to meet?'

'The Italian, on the corner of Market Square. See you at one.'

CHAPTER FORTY-FIVE

VIRGIN FLIGHT 021 landed at Dulles Airport bang on time. Jane followed the signs for the main terminal and found herself aboard what looked like an oversized railway carriage fitted with four huge tractor wheels. As she waited for the Planemate transporter to fill up with the remaining passengers, she wondered again why she was here in Washington in her own time and without the authority of her senior officers. At the departure gate at Heathrow airport in London her father had asked her if she was sure she wanted to do this.

For a moment Jane had hesitated. 'I need to find out why. It was the last case Steve and I worked on, and for my own sense of tying up these loose ends I have to know, Dad,' she'd told him.

'Sweetheart, we both know there'll be little you can do about this.'

She gave her father another hug and whispered, 'Yes, but at least I'll know why.'

The carriage lurched to a stop to allow a small plane to taxi past. Inside the terminal building, the usual fifteen Immigration desks were open for just ten American passengers and the five hundred overseas visitors had to filter through just eight desks. Jane had already filled in a green immigration card. The immigration officer rattled his keyboard, entering her details.

'You're staying at the Jefferson. Very nice. You must be here on business.'

Jane smiled. 'No. Pleasure, I hope. Just here to meet an old friend and do some shopping.'

He handed back her passport, 'Have a nice day, ma'am.'

In the main arrivals' hall, Darryl Womack wrote BLACKBURN on a piece of card and made his way through the throng of waiting friends and relatives to stand beside the other limo drivers waiting for customers. Darryl felt a tap on the shoulder. Agent Frank Koropecky flashed his badge discreetly.

'Sir, would you come with me please?'

Darryl protested. 'I'm meeting a passenger off this flight.'

The agent was more forceful this time. 'Come with me, now,' he said, leading the driver to one side of the concourse by the arm. The agent gently pushed Darryl through a plain grey door, which hardly anyone ever noticed. Darryl protested even louder. 'Look, I've got this lady to meet.'

He prided himself that in four-and-a-half years, he had never been late for a pick-up.

'Driver's licence or ID. You will appreciate, sir, since September 11 security has become much tighter. We're just making a routine spot check.'

'Yeah, but your spot check could cost me my job.'

'I'd like you to tell me who you are picking up today and where you're taking them?'

Darryl still had the card in his hand. He held it up at the agent. 'An Englishwoman, Jane Blackburn. She's going to the Jefferson.'

Koropecky's partner left the room and spotted FBI Agent Troy Pedersen, who was standing with the drivers. He wore a dark suit and had a similar black Lincoln car parked outside. He held up a card with BLACKBURN, written in neat block letters.

Pedersen's earpiece crackled to life. 'The Jefferson. She's going to the Jefferson.' Pedersen nodded.

Jane's bright red suitcase quickly appeared on baggage carousel six and within minutes she was out in the arrivals hall, scanning the names on the wall of signs in front of her. As she turned to her left, she spied a tall, thirty-year-old man dressed smartly in a dark suit, holding up her name. She caught his eye and he gave her a pleasant smile.

'My name's Blackburn.'

The driver took her case and enquired, 'The Jefferson, ma'am?'

'Yes.'

'The car's this way.'

As they made their way to the car park, Jane stood still for a second to get her bearings. The lanky blond-haired driver waited. Koropecky and his partner Alex Thistleton watched her from a car parked several cars behind the black Lincoln.

'Are you all right, ma'am?' Pedersen asked.

'Yes. Thank you. Just taking in some fresh air after sitting on a plane for seven-and-a-half hours.'

'Aeroplane smells. Never did like them myself ma'am.'

He unlocked the car and opened the back door for his passenger, while he placed her suitcase in the boot. Jane deliberately slid along the seat so she wasn't sitting directly behind the driver. The car eased slowly out of the car park, through the toll and onto the main highway towards Washington.

As they made their way quietly along the Hirst Brault Expressway, Jane began to relax. She had never been able to sleep on planes. What on earth did she think she was doing, that would make one jot of difference to getting that little bastard back into the UK for trial? As she closed her eyes, Steve's face appeared before her. Her eyes welled with tears.

The driver spoke up, 'You here on business, ma'am?'

'No.'

Jane didn't mean to be rude, she just wasn't in the mood to for conversation. She took her sunglasses out of her handbag, put them on and rested head on her hand, staring out of the window. They passed beautiful clapboard homes, all painted in light pastel colours, like rows of dolls houses.

'You from the UK, ma'am?' the driver asked.

'Yes.'

'The Jefferson is quite a beautiful hotel. Have you been there before?'

'No,' Jane said, almost curtly.

'If you're here sightseeing, ma'am, I can recommend the Lincoln Memorial, and of course, there's the White House.'

Jane didn't answer him. From behind her dark glasses she watched his face in the rear view mirror. Either this driver was extremely thick-skinned or he was deliberately being nosy.

Three cars behind the black Lincoln, Koropecky and Thistleton listened in to the conversation.

'She obviously doesn't want to talk. Why the hell doesn't he just shut up? Have you worked with Pedersen before?' Thistleton asked.

'No. He's fresh out of training school at Quantico.'

'Who briefed him?'

'I did. He was told to drive the car and say nothing unless he was spoken to. He's too keen.'

'So who's he trying to impress?'

Jane's voice suddenly crackled into their ear-pieces.

'So, where are you from?' she asked the driver. She listened hard to his accent, which seemed to be a strange mix, but underlying it all Jane could hear a definite Texas drawl.

'Connecticut, ma'am'

'Have you lived there all you life?'

'Yes, ma'am, until I moved to Washington to find work.'

'And how's the limousine business?'

'Kept very busy ma'am, night and day.'

In the time that Jane had been watching his face in the rear-view mirror, she realised he had checked it no less than eleven times. They hadn't changed lanes on the straight highway. He might just have been looking at her, but the hairs on the back of Jane's neck tingled. Caution. He'd lied.

The hotel entrance was discreet. Only a small dark green canopy over the front of a revolving door and a liveried doorman standing next to a small brass plaque announced the Jefferson Hotel. The driver opened the car door for her and took her case out of the boot. She reached into her handbag and took out a ten-dollar bill then got out of the car. The driver gave the case to the doorman and handed Jane her coat. She placed it over her arm and gave the banknote to the fresh-faced driver. Jane looked straight into his grey eyes. For a fleeting moment she thought she saw his discomfort. He thanked her for the tip as she turned to walk into the hotel.

Kirsty Davis, Assistant Desk Manager, a pretty young girl with auburn hair and a mile-wide smile, greeted her, 'You're in room 509, ma'am. Fifth floor. The dining room and bar are just behind you. We have conference room facilities if you should need them.'

The large grandfather clock in the white marble-floored lobby told her it was 5.35pm. England was five hours ahead and Jane's body was already telling her it was time for bed. She asked Kirsty for a pocket tourist guidebook of Washington.

A bellhop put the key in the door of room 509 and waited for Jane to enter. It was a smart room with pale walls, dark wood furniture and a large, king-sized bed. A small round table and two comfortable chairs sat under the window. The bellhop pointed out the mini-bar, how the air conditioner worked and left her suitcase in the large walk-in closet. He waited expectantly until Jane tipped him.

She allowed her head to clear, took a shower and changed before picking up the phone and calling an old friend, Dave

McIntyre, now editor of the Washington Post. Dave had been a pal of John's. They'd met when they were young reporters covering the Yorkshire Ripper serial killings in northern England.

She got through straight away. 'I'm in Washington for a couple of weeks and I was wondering if you were free to show a stranger around your home town and grab a bite to eat?'

'Jane, it's great to hear from you. I can't believe you're here. So what finally lured you to our neck of the woods? Where are you staying? How long are you here?'

She laughed. It was great to hear his friendly voice after so long. 'Ever the reporter, Dave. I guess the trip is an unplanned but very welcome break after a disastrous few months at work. I'm staying at the Jefferson for now. After that, who knows.'

'Great, you're just a few blocks from me. I really can't believe you're so close. Listen, I'd love to have dinner but you've caught me on a really bad night. I've got to go to a function I just can't get out of, but seeing as you're so close, how about dropping around to my office at about seven o'clock. We could fit in a quick drink before I head off and use the time to sort out our next dinner date. Sound okay?'

'Sounds like a plan. Where are your offices?'

'I'm on 15th Street North West. You can't miss it. Tell the security guard at the door you're meeting me and she'll point you in the right direction.'

Three FBI agents sat almost opposite the Jefferson, their white, unmarked car parked in a narrow alleyway next to the Gold Insurance headquarters.

Pedersen, sat in the back seat, broke the silence. 'She isn't going to do anything tonight. We might as well hand this over to the night watch. I mean, she'll be tired and jet lagged from the flight. Where's she gonna go?'

Koropecky and Thistleton shot each other a weary look.

Thistleton turned in his seat to look at Pedersen. 'And that's your expert opinion with how many years experience in the Bureau?'

Angered by the jibe, Pedersen barked back, 'I was just making polite conversation with the lady. It would have looked odd if I'd just sat there and not said anything.'

Thistleton's voice rose, 'You were told to keep quiet.'

'Nothing I said gave me away. She didn't have a clue.'

'You don't know that. You've been out of Quantico five minutes...'

Koropecky stopped them. 'Shut up! Look.'

They watched Jane walk down the road opposite them. They sat still and let her get fifty yards ahead.

'Thistleton, you follow her on foot. Pedersen, you drive the car. I'll grab Kilburn from the van and we'll go and search her room,' said Koropecky.

CHAPTER FORTY-SIX

BY THE TIME Koropecky reached the hotel entrance, agent Francie Kilburn was already waiting on the corner. She slipped into his hand a small box, no bigger than a packet of mints.

'You've got two cameras and two bugs. It's up to you where you put the bugs, but I suggest you keep the cameras up high.'

'We don't even know what room she's in.'

'I'll have it for you in a minute. I'm gonna use the credit card scam.'

'Fine.'

The tall agent, wearing a blue blouse, smart trousers and court shoes, strode into the Jefferson's hushed lobby while Koropecky hung about on the street. Kilburn flashed her badge at the young receptionist.

'We believe one of your guests has been using a hooky credit card at several stores. Can I see your registration cards please? I want to see if the handwriting matches on any of them.'

Kirsty asked the agent to step around the desk into the back office and handed her a sheaf of about 50 white registration cards.

Kilburn scanned them until she came to the name Blackburn. The English cop was in room 509.

'Nope. None of these. The con artist must have lied about where she was staying. I'll go back to the store and ask a few more questions.'

Kirsty looked at her and frowned. 'Very civil-minded of an FBI agent to be making enquiries about a false credit card,' she said.

'One of life's little coincidences, Kirsty,' said Kilburn, smiling sweetly. 'I just happened to be nearby when the store called 911.'

'Sorry I couldn't help,' the receptionist said.

Koropecky was stood on the street corner reading a newspaper in the evening sun when Kilburn walked past and whispered, 'Room 509.' Frank Koropecky, dressed like a bank manager, wandered into the lobby and took the lift to the fifth floor. Within seconds, he'd picked the lock and was inside the room.

He took a small digital camera from his pocket and photographed the room and the en-suite from all angles. Then he opened the small box and took out the first of the two tiny video cameras. He picked up his cell phone and a number he'd dialled so often it was pre-programmed.

'Where do you want me to put them?'

'Curtain rail, in the folds at the top,' said Kilburn.

Koropecky took a jacket and scarf from the back of the dressing table chair and placed them on the bed. He moved the chair back to the window and stood on it. Reaching up with his right hand, he placed the camera in the folds at the very top of the cloth pelmet.

'What can you see?' he asked.

'We have a clear view of the entrance door, the bathroom door, and basically the entire room.'

'Do you want me to put the other one in?'

'Yeh, just in case the first one goes down. You know how temperamental these damned things are.'

'And the bugs?'

'First one in her phone, the second in the bathroom.'

Five minutes later, Koropecky made the call again. 'Are we up and working?' he asked.

'Yep,' said Kilburn on the other end of the phone. Koropecky put back the chair and checked the digital picture he'd taken to make sure he'd hung the jacket and scarf in the exact spot. After double-checking all the pictures against the room he left, convinced she would never know he'd been there.

The grey van, which had at one time belonged to a telephone company, was parked at the back of the hotel. Everyone passed the rusting truck sat on four balding tyres and never realised it housed thousands of pounds worth of state-of-the-art surveillance equipment. Koropecky tapped on the back, opened the door, climbed in and slumped into a chair. Kilburn looked at him. 'Did you search her luggage?' she asked.

'Yeah, she's carrying nothing. Just like a normal tourist, unless there's something in her purse. She's certainly not carrying any identification to say who she is. Where is she now?'

'Thistleton has followed her to the Washington Post Building. She's just gone in.'

CHAPTER FORTY-SEVEN

IT AMUSED Jane to see no fewer than twenty-five newspaper vending machines outside the Washington Post building, all of them selling rival newspapers. Editors are the same the world over, she thought, they'll do anything to annoy each other, no matter how petty.

She strode up the steps, past a large red and black, now-obsolete printing press. Original printing plates were mounted on the wall above. One announced John F Kennedy's assassination, another told of Eisenhower's invasion of Europe. She turned left and into the lobby where she was met by a middle-aged African American security guard, Elspeth. As Jane looked at a stand displaying award-winning photographs, Elspeth called McIntyre's office.

She replaced the receiver. 'Mr McIntyre's office is on the sixth floor. The elevator will take you straight to Mr McIntyre's secretary's office. Have a nice day.'

Jane smiled. It was after seven in the evening and there wasn't much of the day left.

As the lift door opened, a woman about her own height was waiting. She was probably twenty-four years old and dressed in a light summer fawn coat. She smiled, 'Mrs Blackburn?'

'Yes.'

'Mr McIntyre's office is just there on the left. He's expecting you,' she said, waving her arm vaguely in the direction of the office as she hastily leapt into the lift.

Jane walked past a wall covered in over-blown pages from

the Post, knocked on The Editor's door and opened it. As she poked her head around, she saw Dave was deep in conversation on the phone. Without pause in his discussion, he waved her in and pointed to the chair opposite him. He then jabbed his finger towards a small drinks cabinet in the far corner of the room. She looked around. Dave was sitting behind an enormous antique desk. She took off her jacket and placed it and her handbag on the chair. She made her way across the thick pile carpet towards the drinks cabinet. One of the walls was covered with photographs of Dave with dignitaries. The President and the First Lady, Clint Eastwood, Barbra Streisand. Some faces weren't so recognisable to a Brit. Right in the middle was a photograph of Dave with his arm around a wheelchair-bound girl, aged about ten. She'd been given an old-fashioned green plate man's visor. A sign on the desk beside her announced she was Editor For The Day.

Dave finished his conversation, leapt out of his huge leather chair and hugged her. He kissed her warmly on both cheeks. Jane pointed to the photograph of the little girl. 'Editor For The Day?' she asked.

'She needed a bone marrow transplant. It was a publicity stunt to get her some help. She died about three weeks later. Drink?'

'I'm sorry. I didn't realise...'

Dave interrupted her train, 'Hey, it was just a story.'

She looked at him questioningly. 'Then why is her photograph given pride of place on the wall if she was just a story?' Despite the hard front he put up, Dave was a softie at heart. 'I'll have a gin and tonic please, no ice,' she said.

'So, what brings you to Washington?' He turned to prepare the drinks. Jane watched the little man bustling at high speed. He was 5'8" at the most, with blue eyes and thinning blond hair cropped into a power-cut. He looked dapper in his tailor-made shirt and suit. There had been an outcry when he became the first Englishman to be made editor of the Washington Post, the mighty paper that had brought down President Nixon.

'I don't think you've put on any weight at all since I last saw you,' Jane said.

He handed her a glass. 'Ellen hired me my own personal trainer. She's determined that I eat the right foods and get enough exercise. She doesn't want to add me to the statistics of those who never make it to retirement. This job is stressful enough without me destroying my health.'

'How's she enjoying Washington's social life?'

'Loving every minute of it. She's on nearly as many charity committees as the First Lady. I think that they assume that she can get things done because of her English accent.'

Jane raised her glass. 'To Ellen and her charities.'

She could feel the drink warming her. 'Still find time to try for children?' she asked.

'We've had so many tests done now that we both thought it was time to give up and accept the inevitable.'

Jane watched as he swirled his ice around in his whisky.

'Any time that you want to borrow Richard, you can have him. He may be a little too old to take to the park and feed ice-cream these days but he plays a mean game of tennis. You'd better not go sailing with him, though. He turns into Captain Bligh.'

Dave chuckled. 'You still haven't answered my question. Why are you here? We've been following the news. Your partner's funeral made a three-minute slot on CNN.'

Jane sank into her chair. 'If I'm being honest with myself, Dave, I think he's the reason I'm here. We were working on a case together. A young man called Charles West. We're almost sure he's guilty of two rapes, possibly a third. One of the girls slipped into a coma and never came out. She died a few weeks later. Just as we get him nicely locked up on remand, in walks Daddy, a diplomat called Sterling West. He gets the magistrate's decision overturned and wham, our suspect's gone.'

A concerned look crossed Dave's face. He slowly shook his head and said, 'I know Sterling West, Jane. He's at the US Embassy in London. Comes from a very powerful family. Sterling's father-in-law is in the House of Representatives, Congressman for Georgia. Charles Monroe. I know you're not a lady who appreciates games so I'm going to tell you straight, nobody crosses that family and gets away unscathed.'

Jane sat in silence as this latest piece information sank in. It took her a few moments to recover her train of thought.

'So who's pulling the strings, the father or the grandfather?'

'What strings?' Dave asked.

She explained how West had been placed on bail despite their warnings about him being a flight risk.

'Surprise, surprise, within twenty-four hours he's back here in the States. I also discovered that Sir Phillip Roberts contacted our judge on the morning before the appeal was heard.'

'Now isn't that interesting,' said Dave. 'Sir Phillip was out here a while ago, part of some joint initiative between the Justice Department and the UK to discuss anomalies between the two systems. It was chaired by Congressman Monroe. Oh, what a tangled web. There were lots of rumours about why Roberts suddenly disappeared.'

Jane interrupted. 'I was told it was because he picked up an under-age kid in a gay bar.'

'We heard that too, but couldn't prove anything. The kid involved suddenly went back to college with all his tuition paid from the Monroe Educational Foundation.'

'I guess that answers our question then. It's obviously the grandfather who's calling the shots,' said Jane.

'Congressman Monroe is a man who gets what he wants and

my guess is that would extend to sweeping his grandson's little indiscretions under the carpet.'

'Look,' said Jane. 'I'm on a fortnight's holiday so I thought I'd waste some of my time finding out about this kid's family so I know who I'm up against. I've got to try to get him extradited back to England.'

'Finding out about the family isn't going to be hard. You only have to walk around the streets of Washington to stumble over buildings or streets named after them. Pinning them down is going to be a different story. The family have never quite made it to the top of the ladder though.'

Jane looked at Dave with a puzzled expression. 'The top of the ladder?'

'The White House, the ultimate prize. My guess is that's the reason this kid is being protected. Monroe has two daughters, Beth and Grace. Beth's son, Adam, was being groomed by the grandfather to run for President, but the boy died in boating accident three years ago. He was in his second year at Yale, the only member of the family to get in without the help of a cheque book. A 'straight A' student. Looks as if Grace's son, Charles, doesn't quite fill his cousin's shoes. Have you told anybody else what you're up to?'

'No. I thought I'd spend the next couple of days finding out a bit more about Charles West.'

Shrugging her shoulders, she looked at Dave, 'I can see the cogs in your mind whirring into overdrive. Don't print anything until I spend a few more days digging and can prove the interference from this end. Then you'll have your exclusive.'

'I've got a couple of journalists and a photographer you can borrow.'

Jane shook her head. 'Journalists and photographers are the biggest gossips in town. I've never yet met one that could keep a secret. However, I could do with spending some time in your cuttings library.'

'I can do better than that,' said Dave. 'In the middle of next week I'm having dinner with someone at the Attorney General's office. Why don't you come along and meet him? At the very least you'll know where you stand.'

'Thanks, 'Jane said. 'I could also do with the loan of a mobile phone. Mine doesn't work in this country.'

'Here have this one,' he said as he pulled a phone from his desk draw. 'I've got a dozen of these things hanging around. I'll also give you my cell number so that you can get in touch with me any time. Listen, would you like to come around to dinner with Ellen and me tomorrow?'

'Can I take a rain check on that and get back to you. I've got a couple of FBI agents I need to see tomorrow.'

Dave's ears pricked up. He was a man who still enjoyed the thrill of the chase, tracking down the bad guy. 'So, the FBI are involved in this case, as well?' he said.

Jane smiled. 'You don't miss a trick do you? At what point did I say the FBI were involved? They're just two friends I'm here to see.'

Dave looked at his watch and realised time had raced by. 'Jane, I'm sorry to have to do this to you but I'm late. Ellen has arranged a dinner to support her latest cause and I've really got to go.'

Jane rose and reached for her jacket off the back of the chair.

'My driver is downstairs. Can he drop you off anywhere?' Dave asked.

'No thanks, it's still early and I'd prefer to walk.'

CHAPTER FORTY-EIGHT

JANE STOPPED on the corner of 15th and M Street North West. She rummaged in her handbag and pulled out a crumpled piece of paper. She clutched the paper and her borrowed cell phone in her left hand and with her right index finger she punched a string of numbers.

'Hi Logan. It's Jane.'

The line was silent for only a second, but long enough to fill her with a sudden panic that he didn't recall her name or perhaps didn't want to remember. Maybe she had been under a misapprehension about how close they had become. She held her breath.

It had been over a month since he had heard her voice. All thoughts of anger and what he'd wanted to say to her for leaving before he woke up at Shannon were gone. The speech he had rehearsed in his mind nearly every day was forgotten.

'Jane, how are you?'

A warm feeling of relief washed over her. She had wanted to dial his number so many times but he was so far away what could he do? She'd tried to push him out of her mind, putting all her energy into trying to recover and helping Anne. This man had completely unnerved her. She had been affected by him in a way that no one else had in over four years. She was rescued from having to answer him before she could recover.

'Jane, I know this is going to sound like an excuse but I really wanted to call you. I just wasn't sure where we stood after our last encounter and I guess I lost my....'

'I know. It's okay, I understand. Listen, I'm actually in Washington at the moment. I'm over just visiting an old friend. I was wondering if you wanted to grab a bite to eat tonight, to catch up and well, I don't know really. Just talk.'

'Sure. Where are you staying?'

'I've got a room at the Jefferson.'

Logan gave a low whistle. 'Very nice. You've come up in the world Inspector Blackburn. Pay rise or blowing the budget?' he said with a laugh. 'Listen, if you're not above slumming it with a lowly FBI man, I know a great little restaurant not far from your hotel. How about I meet you in the lobby in about fifteen minutes. I was about to finish up for the day anyway.'

'Make that twenty minutes and you've got a date.'

As Jane got out of the lift she saw him admiring the grandfather clock in the lobby. She hardly recognised him. The wild-haired 'Spaniard' was gone. Instead she was looking at a smart man, six feet two tall. His athletic body apparent under the well-tailored lightweight two-piece suit, white shirt and red tie. His dark hair had been trimmed. He was going slightly grey. Not bad for a bloke in his mid-forties, she thought. She coughed politely and he swung around on his heels. His hazel eyes danced as he looked at her. He was relieved the gaunt look he'd seen at the funeral, that had caused him so much pain to watch, had gone. The bruises had disappeared too. She looked trim in summer slacks and her favourite tailored Jaeger jacket.

Jane wasn't quite sure what to expect. A polite kiss on the cheek? He opened his arms hugged her and held her the same way he had at Shannon. He kissed her gently on the lips.

'I take it I'm forgiven for running away,' she said looking up into his eyes.

He squeezed her a little more tightly. 'Forgiven and forgotten,' he said.

If you were to ask Jane today where the restaurant was and

what she had eaten she would not be able to tell you. It was one of those dinner dates where the only thing that matters is the person sitting opposite you. They seemed to slip effortlessly into each other's company.

'How's Scott?' she asked

'Oh, strong as an ox. It would have been easier to tie down a Rottweiler. He starts back at work on Monday. On light duties, of course. That means if he's a good boy I'll let him drive the car.'

Jane laughed.

'But how are you Jane? How did it all go back in England?' he asked.

Her smile vanished. 'I coped,' she sighed. 'The only person that really mattered was Steve's widow, Anne. Everybody else…'

She didn't finish her sentence. Logan could see she was struggling and didn't really want to talk about it.

'Here I have the luxury of pushing it to the back of my mind. So, if you don't mind…' Jane continued.

Logan let it drop. 'What are we doing tomorrow?'

'I don't know. Do you want to show me the sights?'

'I'm yours for the whole day.' Jane smiled and raised her eyebrow just as Logan's cell phone rang.

'Hi Logan. It's your father,' said the voice at the other end.

Logan was puzzled. It certainly wasn't his father speaking.

'Dad?' he said hesitantly.

'Very casually, look over at the bar,' the voice said.

Still confused, Logan looked over Jane's shoulder. He spotted fellow agent Alex Thistleton, sitting on a stool, holding a mobile to his ear.

'Keep quiet and listen,' Thistleton hissed. 'Your lady's being babysat. You've got instructions to give Tenant a call. He'll fill you in.'

Logan involuntarily glanced at Jane and shifted uncomfortably in his seat. He had only a split-second to decide to keep up the pretence.

'Dad, Dad, you're breaking up. There's a bad signal. I'm going to hang up and try calling you again outside the restaurant in a couple of minutes,' he said, hoping he'd convinced Jane.

'Bye, son,' Thistleton said sarcastically. Logan could see him grinning in the distance.

CHAPTER FORTY-NINE

LOGAN LOOKED at Jane apologetically, 'Excuse me for a minute. I've got to give Dad a call. Um…bad reception.'

Thistleton stayed at his bar stool. Logan blanked him as he went outside to call Tenant.

'Chris, it's Logan. What the hell is going on? Thistleton has just gate-crashed my dinner, telling me some story about Jane Blackburn being babysat.'

'The Bureau has been following Mrs Blackburn since she arrived in Washington, keeping track of her movements. Looks like it would have been quicker just to call you.'

Logan ignored the remark, 'What's she done? You seem to forget this woman saved the lives of two FBI agents. How does that make her a national threat? You should be giving her a medal, not tailing her!'

'Obviously she hasn't told you why she's here. We think Detective Blackburn is running an independent investigation here in Washington where she has no jurisdiction. We've got a camera in her room and a phone tap. How well do you know her?'

'I've known her for a while now. She's, well, a close friend. The woman saved my life, what do you expect?'

'Okay, until we find out what she is up to I want you to spend more time with your *friend*. I don't want her finding out she's being followed?'

The way his boss emphasised the word friend angered Logan even more.

'Am I at least allowed to ask who you think she is investigating?'

There was silence for a while. Eventually Tenant said, 'Congressman Monroe. That's all you need to know. Keep a close eye on her over the next few days. She's already been to see Dave McIntyre at the Washington Post. We don't know the connection there yet but we need to keep an eye on her, see what she gets up to.'

Logan was worried about the conflict of interest. Tenant could hear the aggression in Logan's voice, 'Why not just ask her what's going on?'

'You're assuming she'll tell us.'

'You're assuming she *won't*.'

Tenant's voice became hard. 'Logan, I don't give a damn about whether this project offends your delicate sensibilities or gets in the way of your love life. Besides, you're hardly in a position to be making any demands. You've got a job to do and I expect it to be done. I don't need to tell you that you can't afford to mess up.'

Logan hung up, outraged at being pulled in to a case that was being carried out as a personal favour to a congressman. His desk was piled high with work, all of them deserving cases. What was he going to say to her? If they were not careful Monroe could stamp on them both, crushing their careers forever, without even missing a stride. Just get through the meal, Logan thought, then run this whole thing past Scott.

Jane saw instantly something was wrong. His whole demeanour had changed. She'd got the distinct impression that the call had been about her and Logan's behaviour when he returned to the table seemed to confirm it. He shifted uncomfortably in his seat, nervously looking over her right shoulder. She was burning with curiosity but at the same time his behaviour unnerved her. She decided to say nothing.

The phone call hung like a black cloud between them. They continued with the small talk but their conversation was awkward. It was clear Logan didn't want to discuss whatever was bothering him. What had the phone call been about? Did he have a girlfriend and he was too embarrassed to tell her. Surely it couldn't have anything to do with Monroe. There was no way Logan could have known about the West case. It must be girlfriend trouble.

On the flight over, Jane had debated whether to tell Logan the real reason she was in Washington. As the evening wore on she decided to tell him nothing. Not because she didn't trust him but because if she was going to ruin a career on this one it had better be her own and not somebody else's.

They finished dinner and returned to the hotel. Jane wasn't sure whether she should invite him up to her room. Earlier in the evening she wouldn't have hesitated but the invisible wall between them was still there. Jane decided she may be imagining it, she would have to tackle him now. She asked him in but hadn't prepared herself for his answer.

'Look, you must be jet lagged. Why don't you get a full night's sleep and I'll join you for breakfast in the morning, say, eight o'clock in the restaurant?'

Jane knew he was talking sense but the nagging doubt was still there. Her worry was almost laid to rest when he held her once again and gently kissed her good night.

Logan was torn between his heart and his work. He couldn't deny he felt something for Jane that he hadn't experienced in a long time. But at the same time he couldn't afford to jeopardise another investigation. He had to keep a distance now. He feared Jane already suspected something was going on. When she'd asked him up, he'd hesitated. He knew it would be safer for Jane if he were to keep an eye on her, rather than another crew of agents. He also knew they would be watching his every move. Then he had remembered the cameras they had installed in her room. He decided not to accept her invitation.

As Jane left him in the entrance lobby, her eyes betrayed disappointment and confusion. A sudden and powerful urge to watch over her and protect her caught him off guard. He knew she could look after herself better than almost anyone he had ever met but she was on unfamiliar turf here, a different set of rules applied. The thought of the FBI keeping a constant watch of her every move made him extremely uneasy. As long as there was anyone watching Jane he would need to be a part of it, looking out for her. She had got herself mixed up with some powerful players and he couldn't be sure of how far they would go. It had taken all his willpower to walk away.

CHAPTER FIFTY

SHELLY AND Tonya were tired. The restaurant in Lincoln Park had been busy all night. The loner had come in late and sat at a table at the back of the restaurant. The two waitresses had made a joke of it. Which of us do you think he'll take home? They both knew he was out of their league. He looked like a rich college kid in his hand-made loafers, chinos and Oxford shirt. Still they'd been attentive. If nothing else, they were damn good waitresses.

Charles West watched them clearing up. In his head he played his own private game. Eeney, meeney, miney, mo, he quietly sang to himself. He reached into his pocket and felt for the familiar cool, smooth glass tube. Whichever of them comes to me next will be the one. She'll be tonight's lucky princess. The blonde one walked over and asked if there was anything else he wanted.

'Yes.' he said, giving her his best dazzling smile. 'You.'

She didn't hesitate. 'I finish my shift in half an hour. We could have a drink.'

'Then Shelly,' he said, reading the tag on her tight, white blouse, 'If you get me the check. I'll sit at the bar and wait.'

As he wandered to the bar he watched Shelly's tight bottom as she moved about the room.

The barman placed a whisky and soda in front of him.

'I asked for rum and Coke.'

'No, sir. You asked for whisky and soda.'

West raised his voice. 'I never drink whisky and soda. Why

would I ask for a drink that I don't like?'

The barman frowned. He glanced over at Shelly, who was just finishing tidying up the last table, and rolled his eyes. He was good at his job. He could almost second-guess what people would ask for before they sat down. He rarely got it wrong. The wastage would come out of his salary and he cursed under his breath as he re-mixed the drink.

West had the two witnesses he needed. Shelly appeared in her coat. 'You're in luck. I'm ready to leave now.'

The barman placed the rum and Coke on the bar. West looked at the drink, stood up and walked away.

'Hey, your drink!' the barman called out after him.

Charles West took a twenty-dollar bill out of his pocket and tossed it onto the bar, 'You have it.'

He hooked his arm round Shelly's trim waist and they strolled out into the car park.

'What should we do, now?' Shelly asked.

'I thought we'd have a couple of drinks, a movie and maybe a motel?'

'Hey, I'm not that easy,' she laughed.

'All right, three drinks, a movie and a motel.'

She let out a high-pitched, screeching giggle, which grated on his every nerve, but he was becoming aroused.

CHAPTER FIFTY-ONE

LOGAN opened his phone and pressed speed dial one. Scott answered almost immediately.

'Hi, it's me,' he said to a sleepy yawn.

'It's late, Logan, I'm in bed…'

'Alone?'

'What do you think? My head still feels like crushed eggs. So what's up?'

'Jane's in town, I'm…'

'That's fantastic! She phoned then?' Scott interrupted. 'See, I told you she would.'

'It's not that simple. She's being babysat. Tenant has her under round-the-clock surveillance.'

'Why? Tenant knows who she is. He's read our reports.'

'My guess is Monroe has pulled in an IOU.'

'Congressman Monroe?'

'What Jane has done to upset him?' Scott asked.

'I don't know. Tenant probably doesn't know either. He told me just to stay with her.'

'Some people have all the luck, Logan.'

'Maybe so, but it's gonna get messy.'

'Look, friend, if Monroe's involved it's already messy. What harm can Jane do him? He's throwing his weight around because he can, so why not hang on. Maybe she's just waiting for the right moment to tell you what's going on.'

'You think?'

'Yes, I think. Call me tomorrow evening if, and it's a big if, she hasn't confided in you we can always make our own checks. Start with the London office.'

Suddenly a woman's voice interrupted. 'Scottieee, come back to bed, darlin'.'

'I thought you said you were alone.'

'I never said I was alone. Some physios make house calls. Phone me. Bye'

Logan then scrolled through 'Calls Received' on his cell phone until he spotted the number. He hit redial. Thistleton answered.

'Where are you?' Logan demanded.

'Take a right outside the hotel entrance, and right again. The van's in the alley.'

It took Logan less than a minute to find the beaten-up van. As he opened the side door and stepped into the back, he was staring at a black and white TV picture of Jane's room. Thistleton was eating a sandwich. Koropecky had headphones on and was making notes. Kilburn greeted him.

She was hard-bitten, from the Bronx, and gave as good as she got.

'Gentleman, move over. The lothario is here.'

Logan let the jibe pass. 'Tenant said it was just a watching brief. How many cameras have you got in her room?'

Thistleton put down his sandwich, 'Two. Telephone's bugged and there's a listener in her bathroom. She's obviously picked up a mobile from somewhere. McIntyre probably gave it to her.'

All the time Thistleton never took his eyes from the TV monitor. Jane was slowly getting undressed. She had already taken off her shoes and her trousers.

Logan's heart missed a beat. 'The easiest and most efficient way of dealing with this is for you guys to pack up and I'll keep a watch on her myself,' he said.

'Easier and efficient for who?' Kilburn snapped. 'Us or your love life?'

Jane was taking off her blouse.

'All right,' Thistleton said, still staring at the screen. 'But I'm warning you Logan, you'd better make sure you don't mess up because it's my ass on the line, too.'

'I'll okay it with Tenant in the morning. I'll babysit her myself.'

He could see that they were still not convinced.

Jane slipped off her bra.

'Look. You lot said that you wanted to meet the woman who had saved Newman and me. Well you're looking at her.'

That grabbed Thistleton's attention away from the screen. They all looked at Logan and then at the woman on the monitor.

Jane took off her panties and walked into the bathroom. Kilburn flicked a switch and the monitor went dead.

CHAPTER FIFTY-TWO

HE PARKED the silver Mercedes SL outside a cheap motel just off the Beltway.

'Wait here,' he told her.

Shelly sank down into the cream leather seat. She had never been in a Merc before. Wait until I tell Tonya tomorrow, she thought. She won't believe me.

He returned two minutes later with a key to a room at the furthest end of the courtyard, nearly fifty yards away from the reception. She shivered in the cool night breeze while he unlocked the door.

'I'll mix you my favourite drink. You'll soon forget about the cold,' he said pushing open the door. The alcohol was in a brown paper bag tucked in the crook of his left arm.

The room was sparse, a double bed covered in a cheap candlewick bedspread, a small table, television and a shower room. He thought it was shabby. She said it was fine.

She made herself comfortable, laying on the bed watching TV while he mixed the drinks in the shower room. He poured the alcohol and mixer into two glasses then reached into his pocket for the Blue Heaven. Panic hit him like a bolt of lightning. It was gone. He dashed to the door.

'What's wrong?' she asked.

'Nothing, I've, er, forgotten something. I'll just check the car.'

There was that annoying giggle again.

'Don't worry. I've got some in my purse,' she said, laughing out loud.

222

For a second his heart stopped. 'What? Some what?'

'Condoms, silly'

A broad smile crossed his face, 'Make yourself comfortable. I'll be back in a minute.'

He almost sprinted to the car. It must have fallen out of his pocket as he sat down. He couldn't find the small phial anywhere. He moved the driver's seat as far back as it would go and ran his hand underneath. His hands were sweating now and his shirt clammy. There it was. The glass phial of blue liquid was safe again. He stood up and locked the car.

She had already started on her drink. This one would be more difficult. He wasn't paying for her time. He would have to be more gentle, coax her.

'Hey, this is good. What is it?' She held up her glass.

'Rum and Coke. When you've finished that one, let me pour you another.'

'If I drink any more of these, I won't be capable of anything.'

That's the idea, darling.

He felt the power rising inside him. He could see Jennifer's face. He started to undo Shelly's blouse, but she waved the empty glass under his nose.

'Let's have another one of these first.'

'It'll be my pleasure.'

He stood just out of her sight at the shower room sink and mixed the drink, pouring in the Blue Heaven. He handed her the glass. She was already getting drunk. It wouldn't take long.

Shelly felt thirsty. She was falling, falling into a big, black void. He stretched her out on the bed and undressed her. Cheap perfume assaulted his nostrils but at least he didn't have to listen to that awful, high-pitched laughter any more. He flipped her over, undid her bra, and then rolled her back. He took off her pants and there she lay, naked. He ran his hand through her blonde pubic hairs. Shelly didn't move. He undid his belt and took out his beautiful erect penis. The sex was like clockwork, devoid of passion. He reached for the pillow and put it over her face. He wouldn't make the mistake he made in England, leaving his hand marks on her neck. As he ejaculated he could feel her body as she gasped her last breath.

His power was at its peak. Nobody could stop him now. He would be with his grandfather all weekend. On Monday he was on his own again. He would look for somebody new.

The killing would go on.

CHAPTER FIFTY-THREE

IT WAS three thirty in the morning when Jane stirred and realised she had fallen asleep on top of the bed covers. She took off her dressing gown, climbed between the sheets and watched CNN before dozing off. She woke with a start at eight o'clock. She showered, dressed quickly and took a last look in the mirror. Smart but functional, just right for a day's sightseeing.

Jane stepped out of the elevator and turned left along the marble-floored lobby towards the dining room.

'Good morning,' called a voice from behind her. Logan, dressed in chinos and polo shirt was sitting on a plush sofa underneath a magnificent teardrop chandelier.

'You're early,' Jane said, ignoring the fact she was late. 'If I'm going for a full day's sightseeing, I'm having breakfast first.'

'Good. I thought I'd join you.'

'You could have joined me last night.'

The restaurant bore all the hallmarks of a classic gentlemen's club. As they sat down in well-upholstered leather chairs, two Mexican waiters appeared. Jane chuckled as one, in his middle fifties and sporting a greying moustache, poured her orange juice.

'What's amused you so much?' Logan asked.

'The elder waiter bears a remarkable resemblance to my Chief Constable, Bob Taylor. I didn't realise he needed the overtime!'

Jane glanced down the menu. The Jefferson breakfast sounded

wonderful, but she decided on the Belgian waffle instead. As they waited, Jane removed the pocket tourist guide from her handbag.

'Most of it seems to be within walking distance.'

Logan smiled. 'You Brits really do love your walking.'

Jane's finger ran over the city centre map. 'I wouldn't mind a look at the White House. Then maybe we could walk on to the Washington Monument. The Lincoln Memorial and the Reflecting Pool. Sound good?'

Jane tucked into a waffle the size of a dinner plate, covered in fresh fruit with a sprinkling of icing sugar, and a whole sauce bowl full of maple syrup. Logan's plate was laden with bacon, eggs and potatoes.

'You'll soon walk all this food off if that's your route for today,' said Logan.

Jane fell silent for almost five minutes.

'A little hungry?' he enquired.

'Ravenous. I was awake at four courtesy of jet lag, I dozed off again and woke up with hunger pangs. This is a real treat for me. My Saturdays are normally taken up with filling the fridge and the cupboards with food after Richard has done his usual raid.' Jane took another gulp of coffee. 'By the time I get home, I normally find Dad tinkering with the old MG. My weeks are probably like yours, so hectic that I enjoy doing nothing on the weekends. Sometimes I get dragged into a bit of sailing with Richard...'

'There's that Richard guy, again. Your latest boyfriend, husband?'

Jane took another bite of waffle. She had to take a napkin to her chin to stop the maple syrup running down. She never lost eye contact with Logan, savouring the moment. He had a slightly pained look. She placed the napkin back on her lap and very slowly and deliberately finished her mouthful before she spoke.

'Richard is my eighteen-year-old son.'

Logan tried to hide his relief, but it didn't work. There was a question he didn't want to know the answer to.

'Married?' he asked looking at the wedding band on her left hand.

'Widowed. John died in a car accident nearly four years ago.'

Logan hesitated. 'Sorry. I didn't realise...'

Jane cut in. 'It was a long time ago.'

'You must have married young to have an eighteen year old son,' he said.

It amused Jane to see Logan go into detective mode.

'Richard wasn't John's son. I had Richard while I was still at university. With a great deal of help from Mum and Dad, I finished my degree. Mum just about brought Richard up so I could do something I'd always wanted to do - follow in Dad's footsteps and join the Royal Navy.'

Jane gazed down at the remains of the waffle, wondering why she was telling him her life story. People she had worked with for years didn't know this much about her past.

'What made you leave the Navy?'

She called to the waiter. 'I'd like to sign for breakfast please?'

The Mexican in the long white apron nodded and disappeared. She still hadn't answered his question.

'I felt like a career change,' she said, at last.

She had lied and Logan knew it. The waiter tactfully placed the bill between them. Jane picked up the pen and signed her name, giving a generous tip.

Logan watched Jane chatting to the waiter. He could see her mood lift. It didn't take Einstein to realise he'd hit a raw nerve with the Navy. He decided that the day would be just them, enjoying a day's sightseeing. No FBI, no Detective Inspector.

As they walked out of the hotel, the doorman raised his hand to hail a cab.

'No thank you.' Jane said. 'We'll walk.'

Logan and the doorman shot each other a glance. He smiled weakly, 'British,' he said. The doorman, nodding knowingly.

They took a right, headed south down 16th Street, passing the back entrance to the National Geographic Building. At ten fifteen in the morning the temperature was already in the low seventies.

'Have you ever been to the US before?' Logan asked.

'New York a couple of times, and Florida once on holiday, but John and I were always great lovers of...' Jane stopped herself.

Instead, she said. 'That's the fourth police car we've seen and we've only walked three blocks.'

'The Washington Capitol square mile,' Logan began, trying to figure out why she hadn't finished her sentence, 'is the most heavily-policed area in the United States of America. There are over five thousand officers from different police forces. We've even got Park Police here, and mixed in with all of this is the FBI and the Secret Service.'

'Good grief. What do you all find to do?' she asked.

CHAPTER FIFTY-FOUR

THRONGS OF tourists snaked along the fence in front of the White House, all of them desperately trying to take photographs. Jane stopped to take in the view. 'Not very big, is it? It's just like a country house,' she said.

'What do you mean not very big?' Logan said indignantly.

'It has to be one of the world's most recognised buildings, but it really isn't that big.'

'So you're not impressed.' said Logan.

Jane smiled at his expression of mock hurt.

'Size isn't everything,' he said.

Jane burst out laughing, 'Only men ever say that.'

She was still chuckling when she turned to read one of the notice boards erected next to a makeshift tent that has stood outside the White House for twenty-one years, as a protest against nuclear weapons. Scanning her eye across the bottom of the board, she read the statistics about how many women had aborted children or gone on to have foetal abnormalities as a result of the atomic bombs dropped on Hiroshima and Nagasaki. The noise behind them grew louder as a group of school children suddenly appeared. Four teachers desperately tried to keep control, clucking around them like hens. A lone protestor, a woman in her early sixties, with badly weather-beaten face and hands, spoke to the youngsters.

'She must be intelligent,' Jane said.

'What makes you say that? She's been out here for over twenty years in all weathers. She can't be that intelligent.'

'Because that's the third lot of tourists that she's spoken to, and she always talks to them in their native tongue.'

Logan gently pulled on Jane's hand to move her away. She became aware that he was still holding her hand and, for some strange reason, began to feel self-conscious.

'The crowds have thinned out a bit,' she said. 'Quickly, stand in front of the White House and I'll take your picture.'

'You're the tourist here. You go and stand over there and I'll take yours.'

She straightened her hair and took off her sunglasses. Logan put her tiny 'point and shoot' camera to his face. He centred Jane slightly to the left of the frame and stared at her hard through the lens. She stood out among the tourists. She had managed to dress casually, but at the same time still smartly. All the time she had been on her guard with him, telling him just enough without giving too much of her story away. She called out to him, 'Come on, Annie Leibovitz. This is taking too long.'

He clicked the camera and gave it back to her.

They walked on. She took her own photos of the Washington Monument, a large obelisk shape stood on a mound, surrounded by 50 flags. A long, tree-lined mall led up to the Capitol building. Logan stood behind her, so close that she could feel his breath as he spoke.

'Is that building big enough for you?'

'Now that's quite spectacular.'

'The powerhouse of the free world,' he said with pride.

Jane turned and looked at him. She took off her glasses and winced at the sun. 'Only an extremely patriotic American would say that.'

A flash of annoyance crossed his face fleetingly. 'You obviously don't think so.'

'It depends on the calibre of the men and women who serve there. It always has.'

She suddenly broke out into a smile, and gently kissed him on the cheek. 'And here endeth today's lesson.'

He slid his arm around her waist. They stood at the corner of the Reflective Pool, looking towards the Lincoln Memorial. A dog ran into the water, sending half a dozen ducks into the air in fright.

'The pool is exactly 2,000 feet long. On still nights, from the Lincoln Memorial, the entire length of the Washington Monument is reflected perfectly.'

Jane looked at Logan admiringly. 'I didn't realise you knew so much. That's impressive.'

Logan waved Jane's guidebook in front of her. 'Nope. What's more impressive is that I learned to read in first grade.'

Jane laughed and tapped him on the arm. Logan fell back on the grass, as if he had been laid out by a heavyweight boxer. A couple of passing tourists stared at them. Jane tried not to blush. She turned sharply and walked away. Logan quickly scrambled to his feet and caught her up.

'Sorry.' He shrugged his shoulders slightly in apology.

She smiled and shook her head. 'How did you ever get teamed up with Newman?'

'Why?'

'Because when somebody new comes onto my team and they turn out to be a bit of a clown, we always make sure they're paired up with someone who's a bit more steady. You and Newman seem to be on the same wavelength.'

'Hey, I'm the steadying influence of our partnership.'

Jane looked surprised.

'I am. I'm the brains.'

It was cool inside the Lincoln Memorial. Nobody seemed to be in much of a hurry to go back into the sunshine and the memorial was getting more and more crowded. At last Jane said, 'I could kill a cup of tea.'

'This way, madam. A short walk behind us is an excellent little restaurant.'

Walking around the back of the Lincoln Memorial, they passed four large bronze statues of horses. Down Rock Creek and into Potomac Parkway, which ran along the Georgetown Channel. The water looked cool. A handful of single scullers gently rowed up and down. A girls' rowing eight was followed by two men in a small motor boat, yelling at them to keep out of the way of a tourist launch, the Matthew Hayes,

Jane's heart sank when they stopped outside a restaurant on the Quayside. A host of royal blue parasols shaded diners from the midday sun.

'This is one of the best restaurants in Washington,' Logan said proudly.

'I'm sure it is but just look at the queue of people waiting.'

Logan glanced across to see at least twenty people waiting patiently in line.

'Wait here,' he said.

Logan fought his way through the restaurant to the far end of the bar where a portly man with thick dark hair was checking the cash in the till.

'If you've got time to sit and count it, you're not making enough.'

The manager, Marcello, looked up and smiled, 'Logan, my friend. I haven't seen you for some time.'

The two men greeted each other warmly.

'What have you been up to?'

'Ah, you know. There's always bad guys to be caught. I'm entertaining a lady and I need a table. I appreciate you're busy, but I could do with the favour.'

'Hey, Logan, anything for you. You know that. Would you like a table outside?'

'Yes, that would be fine. Any chance of one of the tables near the water?'

'No problem. So who are you with?'

Through the glass wall, Logan pointed out Jane standing on her own by the water's edge.

'You're with her?' he asked incredulously.

Logan looked at him, 'What do you mean?'

'Well, she's a little classier than your usual dates.'

'Come on,' Logan laughed. 'I'll introduce you.'

Waiters and waitresses hurried in and out of a glass door, laden with trays of drinks and food. The decking between the restaurant and the river edge was packed with walkers and cyclists enjoying the pleasant Saturday afternoon.

Jane heard her name being called and turned around. Logan was standing with a man in his mid-forties. He was round and had a soft face.

'This is Marcello. He runs the restaurant. If we give him five minutes we can have one of the tables on the edge.'

Jane held out her hand and he shook it quite firmly.

'That's very kind, but I'm getting quite warm. Is the restaurant air-conditioned? Could we move inside for a while?' she asked.

'Hey, no problem. Anything the lady wants.'

Jane took a long, slow sip of chilled white wine. The waitress also brought two tall glasses and filled them with ice and water. Jane asked her to recommend a dish. The girl pointed to the bottom of the menu, Toni & Joe's World Famous Crab Cakes.

'I'll have those,' Jane said, closing her menu. Logan ordered the seafood soup.

'How did you get us a table? There's a queue of people a mile long out there,' she asked, impressed at his powers of persuasion.

'Scott and I were working on a case about five years ago. The perps cut up rough and took two hostages after a failed bank robbery. Marcello was one of the hostages we rescued.'

It amused Jane that he still saw life in boxes, the good guys and the bad guys.

Talking of Newman reminded Jane that she hadn't found out all the details of how Steve's killers had been captured.

'The *Star Supreme* docked in New York but the heroin was offloaded to see where it would end up and the DEA spent the next three days tracking it to Knoxville, Tennessee.'

'How did Captain Robertson explain you and Scott not being on the crew manifest?'

'He said we'd got drunk in England and that the ship had left without us.'

'What about the four Italians?'

'They were held over in port on some trumped-up immigration problems until we had all the heroin and then the whole lot of them were arrested. I understand your Home Office, through the British Embassy, has already made the first approach about having them extradited to stand charges for the death of your partner.'

He watched as Jane's face formed a frown. 'Yes, but for three young girls they let...' She stopped herself. But Logan tried to push on the conversation.

'You're not happy with some of their decisions?' he asked.

'Are you always happy with your senior officers' decisions?' she snapped. It was more of a statement - she wasn't looking for an answer.

Jane excused herself and went to the bathroom. She splashed her face with water and reminded herself that it was not Logan she was fighting. By the time she returned, Logan was already tucking into the most amazing bowlful of seafood with clams the size of the palm of your hand, mussels, prawns and fish in a delicious-smelling spicy sauce.

Jane's glass had also been refilled. Two small, round crab

cakes were sitting next to large, spiral French fries and salad. Jane tucked in.

'I was hungry. It's hard work being a tourist you know,' she said at last.

Logan laughed. Something he'd said about the Diplomatic Service had obviously upset her but for now he would just enjoy the meal and let it drop.

She fell silent for a moment, then looked him straight in the eye. 'There's something I need answered,' she said.

'What's that?' he asked.

She swallowed hard. 'When I read the autopsy report on Steve, he had three bullets in him. Two from the back but the third entered him from the front. I couldn't account for it in my statement.'

He held her gaze. Her eyes had a pained look every time her dead partner's name was mentioned. Maybe knowing the truth would make her open up a bit more, he thought.

He took a deep breath, 'We were told to kill you. I had to think fast. I put the other bullet into him, making it look like I'd shot you. A quick kick with my boot made your body twitch. It gave us time, Jane. You must understand that. He was already dead.'

Before Jane could reply, Marcello wandered over. She complimented him on his world-famous crab cakes. Jane felt unsteady as she stood up. Marcello caught her.

'You've only had two glasses of wine, Jane.' he said.

She smiled weakly. 'I suffer terribly from jet lag.'

Logan could see it was more than jet lag. 'Maybe you should go back to your hotel,' he said.

'No. I'll be fine. I really did want to see inside the Capitol Building.'

'Then let's catch a cab,' Logan insisted.

As she walked towards the taxi, her light-headed feeling

began to subside.

Logan shook Marcello's hand. 'She really doesn't fit your normal mould of girlfriends, Logan. She's quite independent, isn't she?'

Logan patted him on the back and smiled. 'Trust me, you have no idea.'

CHAPTER FIFTY-FIVE

THE ETHIOPIAN taxi driver dropped them off at a roundabout next to a statue of Civil War hero General Grant. As Logan paid the fare, Jane looked up at the Capitol Building's huge dome, painted white and reflecting like marble in the mid-afternoon sun. There was not a breath of wind and the American flag hung limply above the entrance, as if it, too, was wilting in the heat. The two sets of granite steps that rose up in front of her were totally deserted.

'People used to be allowed up there before 9/11,' Logan explained.

They took a left and slowly walked up a steep path around the back of the building to an enormous tarmac area where crowds of visitors gathered in the heat, some taking photographs and others standing in awe. A queue had formed outside a Portakabin to her left. Every few minutes three or four policemen ushered small groups of sightseers across the road and into the building.

Logan took Jane's arm, 'Come on.'

He flashed his FBI badge at one of the officers who waved them on. They attached themselves to the back of one of the touring groups.

Inside, their party split into groups of eight. Their tour guide was a slim, eighteen-year-old brunette who never dropped her smile.

'My name is Becky,' the girl in a red jacket announced, her smile fixed. She began by telling them how in 1793 George

Washington and a gang of local stonemasons laid the foundation stone for the United States Capitol. They celebrated by tucking in to a 500lb ox.

'It took a hundred years to become the building you see today,' said Becky leading off.

Logan watched Jane with amusement. At no point did she seem to take any notice of the girl, who was proudly giving the speech she had made a thousand times before. Jane was constantly looking behind her, at the walls and ceilings they had just left. As Becky pointed out something fascinating on the ceiling, Jane seemed to be looking at the floor. While the group was asked to look at something on the south wall, Jane would be looking at the north wall. As they stepped into the Rotunda, Becky explained it was loosely based on the Pantheon in Rome. Huge paintings depicting scenes from American history, including the embarkation of the Pilgrim Fathers, the Declaration of Independence and George Washington at Yorktown hung around the walls. But Jane hadn't taken her eyes off the beautiful fresco on the domed ceiling nearly two hundred feet above them.

'At least nine presidents now lie in state here,' said Becky. Jane suddenly felt woozy. Logan grabbed her as she began to sway.

'It really is time you had a lie down,' he said.

A heavy lady, sporting two cameras around her neck and looking like a professional tourist, overheard his comment and obviously misunderstood. Jane smiled as Logan shrugged weakly.

'Let's just finish the tour and then we'll go back to the hotel,' Jane protested.

The overweight tourist gave Logan a foul look. He ignored her.

At the end of the tour, Becky asked where they were from.

The professional tourist announced loudly and proudly, 'Wisconsin'.

'Your Congressman is Andrew Mitchell. He's been here four terms and sits on the Select Committee for Intelligence.'

'Very impressive,' said Mrs Two Cameras from Wisconsin, grinning from ear to ear.

A tall man in his late sixties was from Tennessee.

'One of your more senior congressmen is Mrs Margaret Walker-Smith. She's been a Congresswoman now for thirty-two years. At the moment she is Chair of the Appropriations Committee,' said Becky who had obviously memorised the entire 535 Members of Congress.

Jane spoke up, 'Congressman Monroe?'

Becky's smile was even wider than normal, 'Congressman Monroe is one of the easiest ma'am. He heads the Committee on Standards of Official Conduct and has done for the last three Congresses.' He was, she explained, one of the House's elder statesmen and spent a lot of time on charitable causes. Logan watched Jane intensely.

'Thank you once again, and on your way out you'll see a kiosk selling books on the Capitol Building and how Congress works. You'll be able to get more information there.'

Jane fought to stay awake in the taxi on the way back to the hotel. She steadied herself in the lift and when she entered the room she kicked off her shoes. She sighed at the pleasure of walking on deep pile carpet. She wandered into the bathroom. The cool marble floor helped her aching feet. She turned on the shower then put her head back into the bedroom.

'Can you amuse yourself for five minutes while I have a shower?'

Logan was glad of the excuse to scan the room. There were no tell-tale marks where the cameras had been. While they were out the van crew had obviously let themselves in and cleared away the bugging gear.

Satisfied, he picked up the Washington Post - delivered to every room in the hotel each morning - and sat at the small table by the window. Jane stripped and stepped into the shower, the cool water a relief from the heat of the day.

In a white towelling bathrobe, Jane wandered back into the bedroom.

'Women have always been good at that,' Logan said admiringly.

'What?' Jane asked.

'Wearing a bathrobe that's miles too big and looking devilishly sexy.'

Jane flopped on to the double bed, 'This devilishly sexy woman is too blasted knackered to even raise her head off this pillow.'

Logan sat down next to her on the bed.

'Would you like me to massage your shoulders?' he asked kissing the back of her neck.

'That would be nice. There's a tube of body lotion next to the sink in the bathroom.'

When he returned, Jane had loosened her bathrobe but was still lying on her front. He gently pulled on the end of the sleeves and the robe rode down, exposing her back.

The five scars criss-crossing her back he'd seen at Shannon were clearly visible. Each flesh-coloured scar was about the length of his first finger. He put cream into his hands, rubbed them together and placed his palms on her shoulders.

Jane held her breath. She knew what the next question was going to be.

'How did you get those?' he asked quietly.

'They're what ended my career in the Navy.'

'Are you going to explain that?'

'I made the mistake of having an affair with a senior officer. It wasn't until we were both on a course in Portsmouth that I discovered what he was really like.'

Logan listened intently.

'He liked extremely rough sex. He ended up putting me in hospital for nearly three weeks. When I was well enough to talk, a delegation from the Navy appeared and I was offered,' Jane spat out the word, 'the opportunity of being medically discharged.'

'Didn't you protest?'

'If I hadn't taken the "opportunity" of leaving, they could have doctored my file enough to make it difficult for me to walk away with a clean record. I was young.'

'And the guy?'

Jane could hear the anger in Logan's voice. His fingers probed her back.

'Still in the Navy. Commander of a ship somewhere.'

Logan bent down and kissed her neck.

'That doesn't explain this one,' he said, placing his fingertip on a small round scar on the top of her left shoulder.

'First rule of policing...' Jane said, her voice tailed off.

Logan finished her sentence, 'Is never get involved in domestics.'

'Correct,' said Jane. Her skin tingled as his hands moved from her shoulder and down her spine.

'You're very good at that. You've done it before,' she murmured.

'Who shot who? Did the wife shoot the husband or the husband shoot the wife?'

'Wrong on both accounts. The twelve-year-old son tried to shoot himself and I...' Jane never finished her words as she fell asleep.

Logan gently pulled the bathrobe over her shoulders and tucked her in.

CHAPTER FIFTY-SIX

AS JANE slept, Logan sneaked into the bathroom, closed the door behind him and made a call on his cell phone.

'Hi Dad. I'm really sorry but I can't make it to your birthday tomorrow. I've been given a last minute assignment that I just can't get out of.'

'It had better be nothing short of a threat to our national security to keep you away tomorrow or you'll be out of the will,' Logan senior joked.

'That threat doesn't hold so much sway these days, Dad. You forget, I know how much you're worth! Anyway, I really can't get out of this one. I'm on a babysitting assignment for the next few days, maybe a week. Just a watching brief at the moment but it's round the clock. But I have to say, I've enjoyed my day sightseeing.'

'Who is she?'

'I don't remember saying it was a female.'

'I know you too well. Who is she?'

'She's an English policewoman.'

For some reason Logan had never got round to telling his father about how he and Newman had been saved from the Atlantic Ocean.

'She doesn't sound like too much of a security threat to me. What's she done?' the old man asked.

'It appears she's annoyed some people in high places. Let's just say the Congressman of Georgia isn't a happy man.'

'Why don't you bring her along tomorrow?' his father asked, sounding much more insistent now. 'That way she'd still be under your watchful eye and can't get up to any mischief.'

'It's a bit late in the day to try and swing something like that.'

'Why not? You went sightseeing today. What's the difference, as long as you're keeping an eye on her?'

'I guess so, but I'm sure she has better things to do with her time than attend someone else's family gathering. Besides, I don't fancy spending the entire day fending off comments from nosy family members who are far too quick to jump to the wrong conclusion!'

'I never said a thing!'

'You didn't have to. I can almost hear your old mind ticking away. I know what you're thinking and it isn't like that. Forget it, Dad.'

'Of course, son,' Logan could just see his father smiling on the other end of the line. 'I promise I won't say a word, but she must come. Flatter an eighty-year-old man's birthday wish and bring her along. I want to talk to her about policing in England. It's always fascinated me. Besides, I can bore her with all my old war stories and save you and your brothers from having to listen to the old man going on again. Consider it my gift, because if I know my youngest son he was going to front up tomorrow armed with nothing more than excuses about why he hasn't brought a present!'

Logan could hear the affectionate humour in his father's voice and immediately felt a pang of guilt. It dawned on him he hadn't given a second thought to a present.

'All right, I'll see what I can do,' Logan said finally. 'But if I hear so much as one word from you...'

Logan kicked off his shoes and stretched out on the bed beside Jane. Keeping the volume down low to avoid waking her, he surfed the TV's 60 channels until he found a baseball game. He rose, took a beer from the mini-bar and settled back down.

It was a good two hours before Jane stirred. In that half-awake, half-asleep state, seeing Logan there actually made her jump. She watched the baseball game for a few moments.

'Are you game for round two?' she asked.

Logan slowly turned his head and looked into her eyes. 'You wanna pass that by me again?'

'My friend Pauline said you'd probably be up for round two.'

'You told her everything?' he said with a grin.

'I told her about Shannon.'

'So what next, he asked.'

'Strip,' she said smiling.

Logan slowly unbuttoned his polo shirt and pulled it over his head. Bending down, he took his socks off one at a time. He turned his back on Jane and undid his belt, flung it in the air, it flew over her head and landed behind her. He then turned undid the top button, unzipped his fly and slowly, very slowly, took down his trousers. As he stood in his boxer shorts, the sheer anticipation of touching Jane for the second time had already aroused him.

'Come on,' she goaded, 'All the way. The Full Monty.'

'You take them off, ' he whispered.

Jane needed no encouragement. Kneeling on the bed in front of him, she ran her hand down his back, took hold of the top of his boxer shorts and pulled them down. Logan stepped out of them.

She leaned up and gently kissed him on his chest, on his throat and just before she kissed him on the mouth, she said, 'Now that was worth the wait.'

He could not hold himself back any longer. Folding his arms around her, he pushed her back onto the bed, kissed her neck and let his tongue run around her left nipple and then her right.

As his tongue ran down her stomach to just above her pubic hairline, Jane's thoughts raced. You were right, Pauline, I shouldn't have waited for round two. He gently pushed her legs apart and ran his tongue from inside her thigh upwards and just as Jane was become lost in the ecstasy, he stopped and moved over to the other thigh.

As he slowly moved back up her body, he slid himself inside her and Jane was lost in a passion she thought she'd never experience again.

CHAPTER FIFTY-SEVEN

JANE WASN'T entirely sure why she relented and accepted the invitation to Logan's father's birthday. She had known Logan for such a short time, yet there she was in his car heading north on Route 95 towards Baltimore. She so desperately wanted to tell him everything but something still held her back. She turned on the radio to break the silence and help her think. Her mind focused on Charles West and his smug lawyer. She sank back into her seat as the events of the past month came flooding back.

Logan watched Jane lost in her thoughts, almost brooding. He couldn't put his finger on what it was about Jane that kept her firmly in his thoughts. This woman had certainly opened doors into the dark recesses of his mind. Doors he had deliberately kept closed because of his job

'Hello. Are you with us?' he asked, breaking the silence at long last.

Jane was jolted out of her thoughts, 'Sorry. I was just thinking...' she trailed off.

The movie in her mind had replayed again. Every time she tried to relax she would close her eyes and see her bloodstained partner's body lying there, looking into her face, his eyes burning into her. She felt a stabbing pain, as sharp as a knife and she still felt that pain, every time she thought of it. Instead of easing, these flashbacks had come much more often lately. She had not had a good night's sleep since that day. Not until now. Not until she was with Logan. She felt safe with him, but she would never escape her own burning guilt. In her heart she knew the real reason why she was driven to chase Charles West. She was using West to help her come to terms with her guilt.

'Sorry, I was just thinking. I'm not a hundred per cent sure why I'm here. Surely your father's birthday is a family affair?'

'It's simple. I haven't bought Dad a present. He knows that. I was hoping that you could flash him a dazzling smile and keep him entertained with that cute little accent of yours and I might just get away with it.'

Jane smiled.

'What?' he asked.

'Maybe I could tell him just how good his son is in bed.'

Logan beamed at the compliment. 'Compared with how many?' he teased.

Jane almost didn't tell him and instantly wished she hadn't.

'Four.'

'Four?' Logan scoffed. 'You're in your late thirties and you've only had four lovers?'

'It's not the quantity, it's the quality,' she smirked.

'Yeah!' replied Logan. 'And only women say that!'

'Touché.'

They were still laughing about it when moments later he swung the car into the driveway in front of a pretty white clapboard house.

'Are you sure you're all right?' he asked before opening the car door.

She smiled, 'Yes. Thanks.'

Jane stood in the driveway, admiring a well-kept garden. All the house needed was roses around the door to make it look as if it had come straight off the lid of a chocolate box.

'Your father's a keen gardener,' she said.

'Yeh. Since he retired, he's taken up one or two hobbies.'

He looked up at the sound of an approaching car, 'Here's Ted.'

Jane watched a huge maroon Chrysler convertible pull into the drive behind them. It had all the grace and elegance of a 1938 movie. She expected Spencer Tracey and Katherine Hepburn to step out. It had magnificent white-wall tyres and enough chrome on it to keep an army of valets polishing for hours. She admired the varnished wood around the rear door panels and back fender. The hood had been neatly tucked away to reveal beautiful matching leather upholstery with dark green piping. Distracted by the car, she barely noticed the man and woman, their two sons and young daughter getting out.

Logan greeted his brother and sister-in-law. Jane looked up from examining the gleaming dials on the dashboard to see a woman standing beside her laden with a large, white box. She was 5'5", slim, with auburn hair, wearing a pale blue summer dress.

'Hi, I'm Maree,' she said, smiling. 'That's my husband Teddy, Rock's oldest brother.'

'I'm Jane,' she replied and shook Maree's free hand. But Maree could see the confused look on Jane's face.

'No,' she said. 'I'm with Logan.'

'Yes,' Maree said. 'Rock.'

A devilish grin came over Jane's face. 'Logan's first name is Rock?'

'Yes, after Rock Hudson. Their mother had a thing about the actor while she was carrying him.'

But Maree was more curious about Jane's English accent and looked angrily at Teddy for not warning her that Logan would be bringing another of his long string of dates. Maree was too polite to ask any questions and didn't want to appear nosy but it was an effort to stop herself.

'Those two rascals over there are my sons, Ben and Teddy

Junior, and that's my daughter Katie.'

On hearing her name, Katie wandered over and clung to her mother's leg, gazing up at Jane. Ben gave her a cursory glance as he passed, slouching his way up to the front door.

'Please excuse Ben. He's going through an "I'm seventeen, I know everything and I'm above all this" phase.'

Jane laughed. 'Don't worry. I have an 18-year-old son myself. I know that phase.'

Maree was barely able to hide her surprise. Logan was handsome with a classic all-American square jaw and had never had a problem attracting women. Until now they had all been the same: too young; too pre-occupied with their flawless looks and had little in the way of intelligence.

The conversation reached one of those uncomfortable pauses when new acquaintances are unsure of what to say next.

'You have a beautiful car,' said Jane, slowly making her way towards it to take an even closer look.

'My husband would love to hear you say that. It's his pride and joy. I'm not sure who he loves more sometimes,' said Maree with a dismissive laugh. But Jane couldn't shake the feeling that there was more to that comment than she would care to admit to a stranger.

Teddy noticed Jane admiring his car and wandered over, never wanting to miss an opportunity to indulge in his second greatest passion. Maree had always reminded him that she had better stay his first.

'You like my car? Fiftieth birthday present to myself. It's a...' Jane interrupted. 'Chrysler Town and Country Convertible. Did you restore it yourself?'

Teddy looked at her with admiration.

'In England it would be classed as show condition. She continued bombarding Logan's brother with questions. How long had he owned the car? Who had helped him restore it?

Teddy glanced up at Logan, one eyebrow raised. Logan shrugged and grinned in amusement. He was also surprised at her knowledge of classic cars but he knew enough by now to expect the unexpected. There was so much more to this lady than met the eye and he suspected he hadn't even begun to scratch the surface.

'I own a 1936 MGTA myself,' she told Teddy. 'You've got a very valuable piece of machinery on your hands. You're a lucky man.'

'Really valuable?' Maree said, her interest suddenly excited. 'Exactly how much are we talking here? Teddy refuses to tell me how much it cost him.'

'Oh yes, it must be worth...'

Teddy quickly slipped his arm around Jane's waist, a guilty look on his face. He guided her towards the house deliberately avoiding the subject. 'I think it's time you met Dad,' he said.

Teddy glanced sheepishly at his wife. It was a game they had played for almost four years. She would try to find out how much the car cost and enjoy watching him evade the subject.

As they passed Logan, Teddy whispered loudly, 'I think I'm in love'.

Logan heard Jane laughing as she walked through the front door.

CHAPTER FIFTY-EIGHT

INSIDE THE house Jane met Logan's other brother, Matthew, his wife Ellen and their two children, Jake, a gangly eighteen-year-old and Sarah who was sixteen. As Jane made small talk with Ellen and Matt, Katie, who was no more than six, appeared and stood beside her.

'Where do you live?' she asked confidently.

'Cambridge. It's a town a long way from here, in England.'

'Are you one of Uncle Logan's girlfriends?'

Jane floundered momentarily. She had forgotten just how forthright children can be at that age. She quickly recovered and asked, 'Has there been many, sweetheart?' Jane smirked at Logan. Matt and Ellen were obviously finding the conversation entertaining. Logan looked decidedly uncomfortable.

'Oh yes,' said Katie, showing off two gaps in her front teeth. 'Daddy says he has a collection but Mummy doesn't like them. She said the red-headed one ate like a bird and annoyed her.'

Jane laughed, as much at the look on Logan's face as what his niece had said. Logan blushed and seemed lost for words, a position she suspected he rarely found himself in. Matt was in stitches. Maree, who had come over to check on her daughter, overheard the end of the conversation and threw her hands up in mock horror.

She turned to Katie, 'I think that's enough for one day, darling. We don't want to scare Jane away.'

As Maree shepherded her daughter into the kitchen an old man with thick white hair appeared. He was five feet ten, his body showed some frailty but he looked lively. Logan hugged his father, there was clearly a bond between them.

'Dad, this is Jane. Jane, my father, Ed.'

The old man's greeting was friendly but he didn't hold her gaze and he didn't prolong the conversation. There were no questions about who she was, where she was from. Nothing. It was almost as if the audience was over. Just at that moment Ellen and Maree pulled her to one side to meet the rest of the family. They walked to the kitchen along a hallway hung with pictures of young men in police uniforms. Some of the photos were quite old. Logan had never mentioned what his father's occupation had been, but she suspected he was one of the men in uniform. As she gazed at the monochrome faces, she went over their conversation again in her head but she still could not work out what she had done to offend the old man. Had he misread her relationship with Logan, seen her as a threat to the bond with his son? Did he think she was stepping in the shoes of a favoured ex- girlfriend? Or was she just seen as an intruder, a stranger at his family gathering?

She didn't have long to dwell on it. The kitchen bustled with activity and the chatter of relatives clearly pleased to be in each other's company. She was aware of Logan hovering close by, not letting her out of his sight. It annoyed her that he feared she might say or do the wrong thing, something that might embarrass him in front of his family. She was suddenly stung by the thought that his worry had already been borne out. She had managed to alienate his father. Logan had seemed reluctant when he asked her to come along in the first place. If he had been so worried about her and did not want her there, then why had he asked her to go in the first place?

She wandered out into the garden, where two elderly gentlemen offered to show her around the garden. They were members of Ed's bowling team. As they ambled around the flowerbeds, she had caught Ed looking at her. Surreptitious glances when he thought she wasn't looking. It was like watching her son Richard agonise over how to ask her for the next big favour. While Logan's father seemed to be avoiding her, she couldn't shake the feeling that he wanted to speak to her. There was something. She'd wait, pick her moment and find out. Jane excused her self from the conversation and made her way to the bathroom.

When she'd gone, Logan caught his two brothers and their wives discussing Jane. This was exactly what he had wanted to avoid. He knew one of their favourite pastimes was gathering in a little group to discuss the latest woman in his life. Remarkably, this time they were all positive. It was Maree, as ever, who came to the point.

'Well I like her, and I hope she's around a little longer than the rest.'

Logan smiled. So do I, he thought.

As Jane passed an open bedroom door she came across Ben mesmerised by a Play Station game. She stopped to watch him, distracted by the memory of her son going through the same sulky phase and locking himself away for hours to play computer games. Ben was still there when she returned from the bathroom.

'Is it a good game?' she enquired.

Ben gave her a look that said loud and clear he did not appreciate being interrupted. He grunted a 'yeah' and returned his attention to the game. His mood hadn't improved. She was struck by a sudden thought.

'What won't your parents let you do?' she asked, sitting down on the edge of the bed.

'I don't understand what you mean.'

'There are only three reasons why boys your age sulk - friends, girls or parents, and my money's on parents. Am I right?'

Anger flared on his face. Jane realised she had referred to him as a boy but was looking at a young man. With a sinking feeling, it dawned on her she'd done exactly what it was his parents had probably been guilty of, seeing a child and not the young man he had become.

Great work, Jane, she thought to herself with annoyance. First the grandfather and now the grandson. How many more members of the family can you alienate in one day? She pressed on. 'So, tell me, what won't they let you do?'

The boy put the video game handset down and spoke without looking at her. 'My friends are organising a skiing trip in Canada over the Christmas break. I'm not allowed to go.'

'Then it's time you got a grip and showed your parents that you're a young man. If you want your mum and dad to stop treating you like a child, then you should stop behaving like one. Stop wasting time moping and give your parents a plan to try and win them around. What were your last school results like?'

Ben didn't want to seem interested in what Jane had to say, but he couldn't hide the fact that he was curious about what 'plan' she might come up with to help him out.

'Bs and Cs. So what?'

'Then it shouldn't take too much effort to change them into As & Bs. Trust me, if anything is going to win over parents, it's good grades.'

He shrugged dismissively, mumbling 'Yeah, whatever,' but Jane instantly saw through his indifference. She'd had too much practise with her own son. She fought to suppress a smile and left to join the family.

She found Logan on the back porch. 'So, you've survived the first few hours of a Logan family gathering seemingly unscathed,' he said, giving her a smile. 'We're usually wheeling newcomers out in a straight-jacket by this stage. I'm impressed!'

'Cut it out, Rock. You have a lovely family,' Jane grinned. 'How many of your friends know your real name?' she teased.

'Most of them.'

'So, Rock, are you enjoying your afternoon?'

He grabbed her by the waist and held her tight.

'Logan!' she protested. 'People are watching.'

It was his turn to enjoy the teasing. As she tried to escape from his arms, he held her closer.

'You never answered my question. Compared to your vast experience of four lovers, just how good am I?' he mocked.

Jane blushed as she wriggled free. 'I'm a bit worried that I may have said something to offend you father, though,' she said.

Logan looked concerned. He had obviously noticed his father's distance as well.

'Yeah, I'm sorry about the way Dad has been behaving. I don't understand. He insisted I brought you along today. I didn't think you'd want to come.'

Now Jane was certain she hadn't imagined it. His father really did want to speak to her, but was reluctant to make the first approach. She was going to have to initiate the conversation herself.

'What does your father like to drink?'

'He's on medication. Ellen and Maree don't really like him to drink alcohol. He'll have tea, no milk.'

'I didn't ask what he was allowed to drink. I asked what he liked to drink.'

Logan gave a conspiratorial grin. 'They'd never forgive me if I told you his favourite drink was whisky on the rocks, so I'm not going to.'

'Thanks,' she said. 'Logan.'

'Yes,' he replied.

She smiled and winked at him mischievously. She fixed two

drinks in teacups and headed to where Ed was sat at the bottom of the garden.

She stopped in front of the old man. He looked up and she noticed he had the same beautiful hazel eyes as his son.

'I've brought you a drink.'

He looked at the teacup and said, 'There's only so much tea a man can drink in any one day. I love my daughters-in-law but they are going to drive me to an early grave with their healthy living. Please take it back.'

Jane smiled, 'Prohibition's over, Ed.'

As she handed him the cup, he could smell the bourbon.

He took a sip and looked up at her with a grin as he felt the warmth of the whisky in his throat.

'You know, Ellen and Maree have removed people from the house for lesser crimes,' he said with an embarrassed chuckle.

'I know but I won't tell if you don't.'

'Are all English policewomen this devious?' Ed asked.

'It's part of the job,' she said pulling up a chair in front of the old man. Jane took a deep breath and explained that she hoped she hadn't intruded on a family gathering and certainly hadn't meant to tread on any toes.

'You must have liked his previous girlfriend very much.'

The old man frowned. 'What are you talking about?'

'I just thought…'

'No, no. You don't understand.'

The conversation seemed to be going in circles. She jumped in. 'Logan and I are just good friends.'

'Just friends, eh? So both you and Logan are sticking to that story,' he said smiling.

'Yes. I'm just in Washington for a while to see some friends and I thought I'd meet up with Logan while I was here, just to say "hi". Actually, I was the one he was having dinner with on Friday night when you phoned him.'

Ed looked confused, 'But I didn't call him on...'

He stopped, concerned at what he had just said. It took Jane a couple of seconds to comprehend what the old man had just told her. Suddenly it all made sense. The call had been about her. She was under surveillance and Logan was part of it. Her heart sank. She tried desperately to hide her deep disappointment but her face gave her away.

'I can see I've said something I shouldn't have,' said the old man. Logan will never forgive me. He was worried about bringing you here in the first place.'

Jane desperately tried to recover her composure. 'You haven't told me anything that I didn't already suspect,' she said, putting the old man's mind at rest. She hesitated for a moment and then went on. 'Ed, why have you spent the last three hours avoiding me when you asked for me to come here?'

The old man took another sip of his whisky.

'I'm sorry if it seems I've been avoiding you. I wasn't sure if I should talk to you while my son is keeping an eye on you.'

CHAPTER FIFTY-NINE

THE OLD man looked at her. 'Did you know I'm a retired lieutenant? I had thirty years on the force before going on to work for an insurance company as fraud investigator. First, why don't you tell me the real reason you're here in Washington, Jane? Then I'll tell you a story I think you'll be very interested in.'

She was intrigued but she didn't know why she should tell him something she hadn't even told his son. As she looked into those hazel eyes, she found herself starting to explain.

Ed listened while she told him about the date rape case she was investigating.

'He raped three girls. Gave one of them too much of the drug, she slipped into a coma and died,' she said. 'In my book it's murder. But he's getting away with it.' She felt better already.

'I don't understand why that brings you to the US.'

'The man is American and he jumped bail. I've found out he's now living here in Washington with his grandfather, a congressman called Monroe.'

A combination of shock and anger masked Ed's face.

'What I don't understand fully,' she continued, not sure if Ed was still listening, 'is why he started raping girls. There must be something else,' Jane stopped. The old man looked like he'd seen a ghost.

'Are you all right?' she asked.

'It's time I told somebody,' he began slowly. 'I haven't talked to anyone about this in over fifty years. I've had to bury it deep inside me to save all this,' he said pointing towards his children and his grandchildren. 'My hatred and bitterness would have destroyed us all.'

Now Jane listened. Ed explained how he had fought across Europe with the 1st Airborne in World War II and on being demobbed he and his buddy Al had joined the police in their hometown, New Haven, Connecticut.

Four years later, on a cold November night, he found himself walking briskly down Elm Street towards the poorly lit campus of Branford College. He pulled his coat collar up around his chin to block out the freezing wind.

Half an hour earlier, he had woken Richard Coleman, Master of Yale University. He had been Master for only six months and this was the first serious incident involving the police. The colour drained from the Master's already gaunt face when the young officer told him why he was there.

Declining the Master's offer to accompany him, Ed had made his way to the Memorial Gate, under Harkness Tower, and walked through to Branford Court. Al was waiting, his warm breath crystallising in the cold air under the light of the street lamp. He rubbed his hands together in a futile attempt to keep them warm.

Side by side, the two officers made their way across the courtyard. They were both uneasy. Rape cases were always hard to deal with and when the prime suspect was the son of a State Governor, every step would be under scrutiny. They were silent as they approached the dormitory, each knowing that this would be the last moment of peace they would have on the case, the calm before the storm.

A student, seven years younger and three inches taller than Ed, answered the door. He had thick, dark hair and the broad shoulders of a football player. The two policemen held up their shields. The young man squared-up to the two officers. Anger turned his grey eyes the colour of gun metal as he challenged them, 'Yes. So what do you want?'

'You are under arrest for the rape of Juliana Den Ouden,' said Ed, watching the suspect intently. For a second those eyes betrayed another emotion, fear. He quickly composed himself and the mask of arrogance returned. Ed was certain, this was their man.

'I'm sorry Ed, but I don't understand. Maybe, I'm just having a thick day but…' Jane didn't finish her sentence. It suddenly dawned on her just who he was talking about.

'Monroe,' she said.

'Charles Samuel Monroe,' Logan's father said, staring into a dark corner of his past.

He spoke softly, 'We took him back to the station for questioning. He didn't deny meeting Julia at an ice cream parlour on the waterfront or taking her to his room. He just kept saying, "Prove it". He kept telling us the girl had been willing. I knew she wasn't willing. The look of utter devastation on her face, the emptiness in her eyes, said she wasn't. She was a nice, cute kid who had been forced into something so degrading she would live in shame for the rest of her life. We put Monroe down in the holding cell, with the winos, the drunks, the pushers and the prostitutes to loosen his tongue.'

Ed looked at Jane, his eyes betraying the bitterness he had harboured for half a century, 'It was Al who made the connection with the other girls. It was the ice cream parlour. They'd all been regulars there. Two of girls had been raped by a dark-haired stranger who leapt out at them as they walked home from the ice cream bar. Six months before, a 17-year-old girl was found dead in the bushes near the rail track. She had been raped and strangled. Her killer had never been found. One of the waitresses had put together a good artist's impression of a man who had left at the same time as two of the girls.

'I was one hundred per cent sure Monroe was the man in the artist's impression. I'm convinced he was the killer but nobody had even questioned him. That night I put a file together on all the cases and took it to the nightshift Captain. Next morning, instead of interviewing Monroe, I found myself hauled in to the Captain's office. The boy's father who was the Governor of Connecticut and his uncle, the mayor of New Haven and a lawyer, were there. They insisted there was no evidence against the boy. When I reminded the Captain we had the waitress's statement, I was told she had withdrawn her evidence. They insisted it was best for all concerned to let the matter drop.

'We all knew what they were saying. Drop the case, or you lose your job. The Captain protested at first. We all protested, but it was no good. The Chief of Police was going to lose his job, so the case against Monroe went no further.

'I watched the father and uncle lead Monroe out of the station. He was ushered into an expensive Mercedes. The lawyer turned and with a sly grin, said "Always a pleasure doing business with you guys." As the car pulled away, Monroe looked at me out of the back window and gave an arrogant smile. I would remember that face.'

More to himself than to Jane he said, 'Funny how the world works, history repeating itself.'

She understood his frustration and sense of powerlessness.

Ed went on, 'I was furious and started arguing with my boss. They had set a guilty man free. Surely they could see that? I was told to leave the matter alone. The paperwork would be destroyed. There would never be a conviction. "Think of your wife and your new son. For their sake, let it rest", they said. As I began to gather together all the documents implicating Monroe - dates, times, anything that could possibly have brought him to justice - all I could think about was his victims. Only five weeks later Juliana Den Ouden's father was killed in a so-called car accident. He had already talked to anyone who would listen but I discovered from his widow he had made an appointment to meet some out-of-state lawyers to take on the case. Three days before that meeting he was dead. It was all neatly swept under the rug. Monroe would never suffer the consequences of his actions. The girls he had raped would be condemned to a life of mistrust and fear. The family of the dead girl would never see justice done. Only one person would thrive.

'All the documents were in a blue file but instead of destroying them, I put the folder into my bag and took it home.'

He looked at Jane. 'I told the Captain I'd burnt the file but I've still got it, here in the house.'

The old man called Maree over and asked her to bring him a blue folder from the bottom drawer of the desk in his study.

'Three families were crushed and it haunts me to this day,' Ed continued as Maree left. 'Many years later I made some enquiries about what happened to the two surviving victims. One committed suicide a few years after the attack. The other one drank herself to an early grave. I've long given up hope of Monroe ever paying for what he did but you may have better luck. I hope it helps. You're only the second person I've ever told.'

'Whoever it was couldn't help you?' asked Jane.

'No. He was only fourteen days old at the time. The only other person I've ever told was my son Teddy. I had to talk to somebody and he couldn't interrupt me.'

CHAPTER SIXTY

A SHADOW lifted off Ed's face. At long last he had been able to share his secret with someone who would understand.

'Who's helping you out in Washington?' he asked.

'The Editor of the Washington Post is an old friend. He's trying to help me get the ear of someone who might be able to help once I've got to the bottom of what's going on.'

'You mix in some high circles Miss Blackburn. I'm very impressed. I sincerely hope that this file proves to be enough to let you succeed where I failed.'

Maree returned with a battered blue wallet folder. As Ed handed it over, Jane read the words MONROE: CHARLES SAMUEL in faded black ink.

'Mrs', she corrected him as Maree made her way back to the house. 'I'm like you, widowed. There's still one thing I don't understand about this case. I now know Monroe interfered with the course of justice but I still don't understand the boy, Charles West. He doesn't fit the profile of a rapist.'

'What do you mean?' Ed asked, looking puzzled.

'Rape has always been about power. What has changed a fairly ordinary student and turned him into a rapist? There has to be something else.' Jane said. She stood up and began pacing up and down in front of the old man. 'You know the profile of a typical rapist. You tell me.'

Three decades had passed since Ed had been a lieutenant, but he had forgotten little about policing. 'It could have started for any number of reasons: Abuse; overbearing parents; a feeling of inadequacy. This was his power kick, everyone knows Monroe wants this boy to one day become President. Maybe Charles West doesn't want to follow the path his grandfather has set for him. It could be a way of trying to sabotage his grandfather's ambitions for him.'

'You could just be right,' she said. Jane thought for a moment, 'If I was trying to find out something about the kid in his home town, where would you suggest I started?' she asked.

'My cup is empty. I could do with a little more 'tea' to help me think,' he said with a sly grin. That's where Logan gets his lop-sided grin, she thought.

'Sneaking one cup of bourbon down here is one thing. Two is an entirely different matter. Your medication doesn't allow for two. I don't want to kill the guest of honour at my first Logan family gathering.'

The old man screwed his face into a pained expression.

'So where do you suggest we start?'

'We?' he asked, incredulous.

Jane sat back down in her chair. 'I'm a stranger around here. I don't understand how your system works and I've got your son watching my every move. There is now a "we" in this case.'

Ed protested, 'Most of the people I knew on the force have long since retired themselves or have died of heart attacks by now.'

'Rubbish, once a copper, always a copper. Even in retirement your badge would open doors. Make some phone calls.'

The old man smiled. It was definitely an order. She was obviously used to issuing orders but for the first time in a long time, he was looking forward to a Monday morning and the thrill of the case. He watched her, the afternoon sunlight shining on her dark hair.

'I know what my son sees in you,' he said. 'By the way, I think I should put your mind at rest. You're not stepping on anyone's toes here. Logan is renowned for a string of disastrous relationships.' Ed laughed and shook his head, momentarily caught up in the memory of a few of his youngest son's more notable girlfriends. 'I don't think I could recall a single one of their faces. They all passed in one long stream. I have a feeling, Jane, I won't be forgetting your face in a hurry.'

She smiled, 'Why don't we meet up tomorrow morning? I'm staying at the Jefferson on 16th Street.' Jane felt uncomfortable asking the next question, 'Look, I don't want to be ageist here, but...'

Ed shot her a hard stare. 'Young lady, I am perfectly capable of driving down to your hotel,' he said firmly.

She looked apologetic, 'I'm sorry. I didn't mean to..' He held up his hand and shrugged it off. 'Did you have anything else planned?'

'Only dancing. We all meet up at a dancing club on Monday afternoons.'

Jane smiled. 'I miss that. My husband, John, could dance really well.'

She held out her hand and helped him from his chair. He took a step forward and put his arms around her. Slowly, to the imaginary beat of a Latin rhythm, they danced around the garden. She had told somebody the full story at last. It was probably the wrong Logan but she liked Ed. She understood him. She watched his face. He was just an older version of his son. Was Logan getting too close? Concentrate on West and Monroe, she told herself. You must focus.

Then came the statement she had been waiting for since she had first met Ed. 'My son's not such a bad boy, you know.'

Since John's death, she'd lost count of how many times people had said something like that to her. She smiled. Only a father could call a forty-five-year old man 'a boy'.

'Who are you, the Schaukelhorn?' she asked, putting on a

lilting Irish accent.

Ed looked bemused. 'A what?'

'An Irish matchmaker, sometimes known as a marriage broker. Your son has had a string of casual relationships, some of which, according to my sources, ended quite abruptly. Not the best track record I'd say.'

'You don't want to believe everything my grandaughter tells you. I wasn't trying to..'

'No,' Jane interrupted. 'Nobody ever does. I've sat through enough poorly-disguised dinner parties where well-meaning friends made me look desperate to be remarried. Besides, my source was a little more reliable than Katie.'

Ed looked at her. 'Scott. So you've met Logan's partner. He's a great kid.' It was obvious to Jane that Logan hadn't told his family about the incident on the *Supreme Star*. He probably didn't want to worry them. Like most cops, he kept his work in a separate compartment of his life.

'Anyway, I'm not ready for…' she stopped herself. Why was she having this conversation at all? Over the last four years, she'd felt as if she had had to justify every day she was still single.

Ed pressed on. 'You're still wearing your wedding ring.'

'You still wear yours,' she retorted, a little abruptly.

'I have to,' he whispered conspiratorially, whisking her across the imaginary dance floor. 'Do you know how desirable eighty-year-old men are in this country? There are twenty-two widows for every widower. I'm quite a catch.'

Jane laughed. 'I have a home, a life and a job in England. Logan's life is here.'

'When are you going to tell him what's going on?'

Jane sighed, 'I don't know. Let's just find out a bit more information tomorrow, then we'll present our case to Logan. If the FBI are watching me, then Monroe is more powerful than I realised. Until I know everything. It's best I don't ruin his career as well. So tomorrow we will do a bit more digging.'

'There's that "we" again.'

Logan and Teddy watched Jane and their father dancing around the lawn.

'Are you going to explain that?' Teddy asked.

'I haven't been able to explain Jane Blackburn since she saved my life, rescuing me out of the Atlantic.'

Open-mouthed, Teddy stared at Logan and then at Jane.

CHAPTER SIXTY-ONE

AS THEY left the party, Jane was so caught up in her thoughts that without realising it she climbed into the driver's seat. It amused Logan but he could see that she was a million miles away. He simply handed her the keys without questioning it. As she drove onto the turnpike he stole a glance at her. He had been watching her all day and wondered at how effortlessly she had seemed to mingle among his relatives, charming them all. The whole family had warmed to her straight away. She had even managed to bring his father around. From an almost embarrassingly distant reception, she had won him over and by the end of the day he seemed particularly taken with her.

He had watched his father and Jane sitting together at the bottom of the garden, only half listening to his nephew Ben who was telling him something about skiing and his grades. He had seen the old man hand her a blue folder.

Logan had spent the afternoon racked with curiosity about what they had discussed and what the folder contained. He hoped Jane would tell him about it on the way to the hotel, but she was totally silent. Curiosity burned inside him like an ember. After all they had been through, she still wouldn't tell him. A combination of frustration and anger prompted him to break their silence.

'What was in the folder?' he asked as the car pulled up outside the hotel.

Her answer came as a shock, 'Why are you babysitting me? I've been watched since the moment I stepped off the plane. You even switched drivers. Are you going to tell me what the hell is going on?'

Logan looked at her. His mouth opened but nothing came out.

'If you're not going to answer my question, why should I answer yours,' she said climbing out of the car and slamming the door as she left.

As they walked into the lobby in silence, the receptionist handed Jane her key and a note. She turned to Logan. 'Good night,' she said without proffering even a peck on the cheek. He went to say something but his cell phone rang. In the second or two it took him to answer it, she was gone.

It was Tenant. 'So, how did you and our English policewoman get on? How much of Washington did you actually manage to see at the taxpayers' expense?'

'Why the sarcasm?' Logan asked, still smarting over his angry exchange with Jane. She was right. The way the Bureau had treated her was shocking. Tenant's call was adding to his embarrassment.

'Because I was at home today enjoying a peaceful afternoon, only to have it interrupted by Congressman Monroe,' Tenant said tetchily. 'I need to tell him something.'

Logan wanted to tell his boss to stick his assignment where the sun don't shine. Instead he asked, 'Have you managed to find out why Monroe wanted her followed in the first place?'

'No.'

'Then it looks like neither of us is much further forward.'

'If you don't get me some answers quick we're going to have to bring her in for questioning.'

'No, wait. Give us another couple of days. Scott and I will hit the phones in the morning...'

The line went dead. Logan knew he would have to give Tenant something to placate Monroe. He wandered over to the reception desk and took out his badge from his pocket. The receptionist read his name above the FBI badge and smiled, 'How can I help you, sir?'

'The note you've just handed to Mrs Blackburn, do you keep copies or can you tell me what it said?'

'I'm sorry, we don't keep copies, sir, but it was from a Mr McIntyre asking her to phone him at the office about meetings with a couple of people.'

Logan looked at her in surprise, 'You have an excellent memory.'

'Not really, sir. It's just been a slow day for messages.'

Logan speed-dialled Scott's home number.

'How did you're weekend go?' Scott inquired.

'Let me sum it up for you. Jane's not speaking to me. She's discovered we're watching her, Tenant has been bombarded with calls from Monroe and now he has put the phone down on me because I can't give him any answers.'

'It's just as well you're not in the Diplomatic Service, Logan.'

'Yeah, tell me about it. We've got to hit the phones in the morning. Get in very early so we can make the most of the time difference. Bye.'

Logan walked across the tiled lobby into a small bar. Sunday evenings were always relatively quiet. The barman, dressed smartly in blue and white striped vest, black trousers, and a long white apron, looked very busy doing nothing. Logan perched himself on a stool at the bar and asked him for a beer. He thought out aloud, 'How does she know Dave McIntyre?'

The young bar tender placed the drink in front of him. He said, 'Sorry, sir, perhaps if you give me the whole question I'll understand the answer. You know barmen make better confessionals than your local priest.'

The bar tender had lost count of how many times he had helped strangers concoct excuses or listened to their worries, mainly to do with women and money. He watched the stranger stare at nothing.

At last Logan looked up from his beer and spoke, 'Son, I don't know what she's up to or where she's coming from. I don't understand how she knows him or why she's seeing him tomorrow.' He lifted his glass and took a long swig.

'If it was my wife sir, hell, I'd want to know,' said the barman. Logan spluttered, sending beer down his chin and onto his shirt. The barman handed him a napkin.

Logan finished his drink, placed a five-dollar note on the bar, and looked straight at the barman.

'That's the most annoying part. I'm not even married to her.'

CHAPTER SIXTY-TWO

LOGAN DID not join Jane for breakfast. As she dined alone, she scanned the Washington Post. Most Monday morning papers tended to be full of nothing more than re-written copy from the Sunday papers, but on an inside page, half way down, a small five-paragraph article caught Jane's eye:

IS DATE-RAPE KILLER IN DC?

DC police are investigating the death of a young woman in her early twenties found dead in a motel room at Hillcrest Heights in the early hours of Saturday morning.

Second District detectives will not yet confirm a possible link between this death and the case of Laura Brimson, the call girl whose body was found fifteen days ago in her home.

Sources have confirmed that both women had been given the date-rape drug GHB, commonly referred to as 'Blue Heaven'.

Police are advising women in D.C. to be aware that this drug is once again circulating.

A force spokesman said: "Females should not accept drinks from strangers or leave drinks unattended."

She stared at the article in disbelief. Her stomach did a somersault. The coincidence was too great. She wanted to be sick. Two more girls were dead and she could have stopped it. Jane looked at her watch. Five past nine.

She folded the newspaper and strode out of the restaurant. The waiter called out after her. 'Is everything all right, ma'am? You haven't finished your breakfast.'

'Fine.' Jane said absent-mindedly as she returned and signed the chit.

She picked up the telephone receiver in her room and dialled Logan's cell phone.

'Good morning,' Logan said, almost sheepishly. 'About yesterday...'

Jane cut him short. 'It's forgotten. It doesn't matter. This thing has gone past that. I need to talk to you. Now.'

Ed was already waiting in the entrance lobby when she stepped out of the lift. The old man looked dapper in a sports coat and grey slacks.

'Hi. I've left my car at the front of the hotel. I didn't think we'd be waiting long.'

'Fine,' she said pushing the Post into his hand. 'Read this.'

Ed perched a pair of half-moon, gold-rimmed glasses on the end of his nose and brought the article into focus. After a minute or so, he looked up.

'You think this is West?'

'No, Ed. I know it's West. You don't think it's a coincidence that there have been two murders in Washington, both using Blue Heaven, one of them almost within days of him returning to the country? It's time we all stop pratting around. We need to talk to someone from that police department, see what we can find out.'

'Second District Station,' Ed said, flicking through he mental address book. 'The son of an old colleague of mine is a Lieutenant there. Carter. I'll give him a call and see if we can meet him this morning.'

'The Monroe family are extremely powerful. How much help do you think he'll give us?' Jane asked.

'They may be powerful, but power doesn't win many friends.'

She opened her handbag and gave Ed the cell phone she had borrowed from McIntyre.

By the time Logan and Newman wandered into the lobby, Ed was on the phone speaking to Carter.

Jane hugged Scott.

'It's so good to see you,' he said, bear-hugging her back, then kissing her tenderly. He too looked good now he'd shaved and the bruises had gone.

'How are you?' she asked.

'A lot better for seeing you.'

'When you two have finished,' interrupted Logan. 'What the hell's Dad doing here? And who's he talking to?'

'I'm sorry,' Jane apologised. 'I shouldn't have kept this from you…'

Ed butted in. The Lieutenant would be in his office all morning.

Quickly, Jane told the two FBI men how she believed a rapist who had attacked women back home in Cambridge was now killing here in Washington.

'We're going to see a Lieutenant Carter at Second District.'

Logan and Newman followed them to the Second District station. As his father's old Ford Sedan pulled away from the kerb outside the Jefferson, in the car behind Logan dialled Tenant.

His boss's mood hadn't improved overnight. 'So what's new?' he asked grumpily.

'Jane did a bit of sightseeing over the weekend and the only time Monroe's name was mentioned was when we were in the Capitol Building and she asked one of the guides what committees he sat on. At the moment, she's more concerned about the deaths of two date-rape victims she read about in the Washington Post this morning.'

'I don't want her interfering in any investigations in this country,' Tenant said.

'She's only here for a fortnight. What harm could she do? We'll tag along and keep an eye on her.'

Logan wasn't sure why, but he neglected to mention Jane's forthcoming meeting with McIntyre.

'Right. Keep me informed,' Tenant said. Perhaps the news about McIntyre would keep him happy later in the day.

Tenant rocked back in his chair. He still couldn't work out why Monroe had called him three times at home over the weekend. Maybe this latest bit of information would get the Congressman off his back. If Inspector Blackburn was now distracted by some other investigation, she might leave Monroe alone now. He hoped so. The sooner this ended the better. He hated tying up men on a personal goose chase.

He picked up the phone.

CHAPTER SIXTY-THREE

ED APPROACHED the front desk inside the concrete station house, home to Second District, Washington PD. He asked the sergeant, a woman in her early thirties with short, blonde hair, to let Lieutenant Carter know that Ed Logan was here to meet him. Not long after, a tall, dark-haired man walked towards them, dressed in a well-tailored suit, which showed off his broad shoulders. Ed stepped forward to greet him and they shook hands.

'Lieutenant Logan, retired,' said Carter warmly, 'How are you? It's good to meet you at last. My father spoke warmly of you.'

'Well. Nice to see you, thanks for meeting us at such short notice. This is Detective Inspector Jane Blackburn from Cambridge, England.'

Carter looked at Jane with admiration. 'You've come along way to track down some information in this world of e-mails, faxes and cell phones.' He shook Jane's hand firmly and didn't let go.

'Sometimes you get more information with the personal touch,' she said and smiled.

'I couldn't agree more.'

There was a polite cough from behind them.

'Oh, sorry, this is my son, Special Agent Logan and his partner Scott Newman,' Ed said.

She watched Carter's body language change from open to defensive in a split-second. The detective turned to Ed accusingly. 'I thought you wanted an informal chat. I didn't realise the FBI were here to take over.'

Newman looked at him, 'Well if you don't think you're running the case properly then perhaps we should.'

Jane watched the two men behave like playground gangs defending their turf until she'd had enough of their childish posturing.

'Gentlemen, please. We don't have time for you two to have a pissing competition.'

Both men could hear the exasperation in her voice.

'You must have somewhere we could sit down and have a conversation,' she said to Carter. 'I know I can help on the two murders you're working on.'

The Lieutenant could see the sincerity in her face. He pointed to a door at the far end of the corridor behind the desk. 'Let's go in here,' Carter said.

The room was laid out like a small lecture theatre, with half a dozen rows of chairs, each with a small desk attached to the arm. The chairs faced a large white board and an oversized television screen.

'If we could all take a seat.'

Jane took a deep breath and paced the floor as she told them how Charles West had been arrested in England for the rape of three girls, involving the use of the date-rape drug GHB.

She was in her stride now. 'His attacks got progressively worse. We discovered that the drug was home made and one of his victims slipped into a coma and died. His third victim should have died. He tried to strangle her but was disturbed during the rape.'

Jane now had Carter's full attention. The Lieutenant spoke up. 'That ties in with our other inquiries,' he said.

'What enquiries?'

'Spring last year we got a phone call from a detective from the

Third District making general inquiries about four guys from Yale University who had been discovered making the drug GHB. We were called because your kid, West, was one of them. His parents live in Georgetown. From what I understand of that case, nothing was ever proven about him using it. His family kept it quiet and had him shipped out of the country.'

'Yes,' said Jane sarcastically. 'Straight on to my patch. The reason I'm here in Washington is because West's grandfather is Congressman Charles Monroe. The Chairman of your House Ethics Committee had West shipped out of the UK and back here after we made our arrest. Since he arrived back in Washington two girls have died after taking Blue Heaven. I think you'll find the drug was home-made.'

Logan looked stunned as the enormity of what she was saying dawned on him.

Jane pressed on. 'What I don't understand is why. Why did he suddenly become a rapist?'

'I could run his name through the computer and see what else comes up,' Carter said.

'You could try Yale as well. His family have all gone there,' said Ed.

Carter picked up the phone and asked his secretary to send down the files on the two victims.

'Also, tell Brad to call Yale University Police Department to see what they have on a Charles West,' Carter said. 'Get them to fax over a mug shot of him ASAP. The University should have one on file. He would've been a student there about a year ago, perhaps year and a half.'

As they waited, Jane caught Logan watching her. His expression was definitely mixed. She was not sure if it was anger or just plain frustration.

'Why didn't you say anything?' he said.

'I just...' She stopped herself.

Logan could see in her eyes the torture she had put herself through. All he wanted to do was hold her and tell her she should have trusted him. But if the roles had been reversed, what would he have done? If nothing else, Jane was a professional. It's time she met Tenant, he thought.

Jane laid both files out on the desk in front of her. She forced herself to look closely at the photographs of both women, naked and spread-eagled. Defiled. Their faces blue. She carefully thumbed through the witness statements, comparing one to the other.

'That's odd,' she said.

'What?' asked Carter.

'In Laura Brimson's case you have the bartender giving a rough ID of a guy who had asked him the time. In the second one, Shelly Sanders, not only do you have the bar tender remembering him, but he ended up almost picking a fight with the barman. Why would somebody who is knowingly on the prowl deliberately draw such attention to himself?'

Scott butted in. 'Because he's an arrogant little bastard who knows grandpa will clear up the mess.'

Jane looked up at Carter and across at Logan. 'Or,' she said. 'A psychologist would probably say he is deliberately selecting more witnesses as the attacks get progressively more vicious, as if he's deliberately making sure his grandfather can't clear up the mess.'

'So' Ed asked, 'Where do we go from here?'

Logan stood up. 'I'm taking Jane to see Tenant and Scott is going with you back to your car.'

Ed could see his son was in no mood for a discussion.

'Who's Tenant?' Jane asked.

'He's somebody we should have spoken to much earlier.'

Carter, who could see his case being taken away from him, said, 'As soon as the mug shot comes through, I'll send a couple of detectives down to see if we can get an ID from the witnesses and we'll talk about picking up West this afternoon. I take it you'd like to be there, Inspector.'

Jane wrote her mobile telephone number down and handed it to him.

'I'll let you know how it goes,' Carter promised as Jane turned to leave.

CHAPTER SIXTY-FOUR

TENANT WAS in a meeting. Jane and Logan waited in a small reception area and drank coffee. Jane felt as though she was being dragged into the headmistress's office. The reception area was smart, like a corporate headquarters, certainly a long way removed from the cramped Cambridge police station. Logan had remained silent during the short journey to the FBI's Washington Field Office on 4th Street North West. From the moment she'd explained the link between West and Monroe, his whole demeanour had changed. There was no doubt about it, Logan was livid. Was he angry with her for not telling him the truth?

Jane's phone rang, shattering the silence.

Lieutenant Carter bubbled with energy, 'Just thought you'd like to know, both barmen identified West from the photo. The Assistant Co-ordinator of Investigative Services at Yale University PD has also confirmed West was part of a group questioned for making GHB. There were also allegations of indecent assault, but both girls withdrew the accusations not long after being contacted by a lawyer from Washington. Soon after that, West was apparently offered a scholarship to study at Cambridge. Convenient. We're just on our way to pick him up. Want to join us? This is your case as well, you know.'

Jane really did appreciate the gesture but one look at Logan told her he was in no mood to go anywhere.

'I've been asked to meet this guy Tenant,' she said as the reception area door opened. 'I think he's just walked in. I'll catch up with you when you've got him back at the station. I wouldn't mind watching the interview.'

Jane could see Logan talking to a man in his early fifties who could have been mistaken for a bank manager.

She continued talking to Carter, 'Not wishing to teach my grandmother to suck eggs, I'll give you a tip.'

Laughter burst through from the other end of the phone.

'I'm not sure what that means,' Carter said. 'But I think I get the gist.'

Jane pressed on, 'Find a young, pretty female to interview him, and if you really want to annoy him, mention his father. We discovered this back in England.'

'Thanks,' he said, and was gone.

Jane placed the phone back in her pocket. The "banker" she presumed was Tenant walked towards her. He didn't bother introducing himself.

'Come with me,' he said.

His office matched the rest of the building. It was an impressive room with a large desk and a comfortable leather sofa. Everything neat and ordered. Her own goldfish bowl back in Cambridge, piled high with papers, would barely cover Tenant's desk.

'Take a seat, Ms Blackburn,' he said, pointing towards the low-slung sofa.

Jane said no, 'If you don't mind, I'll stand.' She wasn't going to fall for that old trick and let him look down on her.

Logan watched Jane deliberately lean against the wall and push her hands deep inside her pockets.

'It seems you know a lot more than us…'

Jane interrupted Tenant, 'I doubt that.'

Logan wanted to reassure her, but thought it best to keep quiet for the moment.

'If you would just let me finish my sentence, Ms Blackburn.'

'Mrs. My name is Mrs Blackburn. Detective Inspector Blackburn, if you want to use my full title.'

'A rank that wields no power in this country,' Tenant snapped back.

He could see she was not somebody to be intimidated, regardless of his rank or the fact she was on unfamiliar territory. He pressed on, 'If you had come to us in the first place and told us your concerns about West, perhaps we could have kept a closer eye on him.'

Jane stared straight at Tenant. 'You mean instead of you having to waste time and resources following me.'

At last Logan spoke up, 'Jane, I'm sorry. We honestly didn't realise what this kid had been up to.'

'Stop calling him a kid. He's nineteen, nearly twenty. That's an adult in anybody's book,' she snapped.

The two men watched her. Jane thought the looks on their faces said they both thought she was still smarting from the recent death of her partner and this had obviously become a crusade.

'Charles West is being picked up now. I've just had a call from Lieutenant Carter. He was ID'd positively by two barmen, so at least that brings it closer to an end. Although that's cold comfort for two more families.'

Logan could see her anger and frustration. Her phone rang. She ignored the pair of them and answered the call.

'So, give me some good news,' she said brusquely.

'I can't.' Carter sounded deflated. 'Apparently he's on a yacht. Been there since last week, which puts him out of reach. He couldn't have been around for the second murder. Congressman Monroe told us the boat left Friday afternoon. Jane, it was a well rehearsed alibi.'

Her heart sank. 'How did Monroe know?' she asked. She looked up and fixed her eyes squarely on Tenant. 'I think I can answer my own question,' she told Carter. 'I know you're as pissed off as I am, but please do me one last favour. Find out the name of the boat and where it is. Just remember people can be flown in and off these boats by helicopter anywhere in the world. That's how they move some of these crews around.'

'So what are you saying? Carter asked. 'He joined the boat long after it left port?'

'Yes. My own son has crewed on a couple of ocean-going yachts and been brought in by helicopter. Monroe's not stupid. Think about what he said, "the boat left on Friday" not his grandson.'

She turned off the phone, still looking at Tenant. 'West's gone. How much did you tell Monroe?'

For a moment, Tenant looked uncomfortable.

He recovered and said, 'If you'd told us what was going on, he would never have found out.'

'And if you hadn't treated me like the criminal, I would have been more open. I was on to you from the airport,' she said, turning what had been a mere suspicion into a hard fact. Neither of them corrected her. By now Jane was leaning over Tenant's desk staring down the FBI man.

Logan tried to calm her. 'Jane, please. There's nothing any of us can do about this until he's back in the country. There's no point in shouting at each other.'

Tenant interrupted. 'And by then his family will have hired so many lawyers it will make the OJ Simpson trial look like a picnic. Nobody will be able to get close enough to get a DNA sample, and if we don't have that, everything else is just speculation.'

CHAPTER SIXTY-FIVE

IT WAS as if a 500-watt halogen light switched itself on in Jane's head. Her whole attitude suddenly changed.

'What time is it?' she demanded.

'Three fifteen,' Logan replied.

She looked at him. 'Plus five hours makes that eight fifteen in the evening. Give me a phone. I need to make an international call.'

'Jane, what's all this about?' Logan asked. But Tenant stopped him. She was like a woman possessed. She would not let go. Logan was right.

He turned the telephone on his desk towards her. 'Press zero,' he said. 'Then press nine for an international call.' Tenant was beginning to wish a few more of his staff had her passion and instinct for their work.

Jane grabbed her handbag, flipped through a small notebook, picked up the phone and punched in a fourteen-digit number.

The voice at the other end of the phone was its usual grumpy self. 'CID room. Detective Sergeant Johnson speaking.'

'Gary. It's Jane. What are you still doing in the office?'

'Somebody has to hold the fort while you're on your jolly in America.'

'They must be desperate if they picked on you,' said Jane with laughter in her voice.

'Almost funny, Detective Inspector.'

Her tone changed. 'Gary, I want you to do me a favour. The DNA sample we took from Charles West. I need the results e-mailed to a lab in Washington.'

'Why?' Johnson asked, looking at his watch.

'There have been two murders here in Washington and I think Charles West is the killer.'

Gary hesitated. 'You were meant to be on holiday...'

'I know but I needed to bring this case to a close. Unfortunately the bird has flown the coop yet again, but at least when he gets back this time, we'll all be waiting for him.'

Tenant and Logan were looking at her in astonishment.

Jane cupped her hand over the receiver. 'I have a DNA sample gentlemen,' she said in triumph. Logan smiled. God, he thought, she's good.

She asked Tenant for an e-mail address where Gary could send the DNA results from the sample of West's hair that Melanie Gibson had taken in Cambridge. She gave Johnson the details and hung up.

Jane sat down on the sofa and told Tenant the whole story.

'But I don't understand how he got out on bail,' Tenant said at last.

'I think Monroe had a contact in our Lord Chancellor's Office who was able to pull strings with the judge in our case.'

Tenant looked at her with sympathy. 'You must understand, Jane, I had no idea doing a favour for Congressman Monroe would interfere with natural justice. He's been like a spider in a web, pulling all the strings.'

'Now explain to me how Monroe's getting away with this,' Jane insisted.

'Since 9/11, the FBI has had to court all the friends it could in Congress, even if that means doing the odd "favour" for a politician,' Tenant explained.

'Well, it's time it stopped,' she snapped. 'The FBI has nothing to apologise for. Politicians are the same the world over. They will use any situation to their own advantage.'

Tenant told her of Monroe's life in politics. '"His" Ethics Committee had been a large stick to beat every one with. Every time just as Capitol Hill thought they were about to get rid of him, another politician would be exposed in the Press over yet another scandal. There would be yet another public outcry and off Monroe would go campaigning to right wrongs, or so we thought.'

Jane watched his face. His eyes were a washed-out grey and she was beginning to see she was as much caught up in his system as she was in hers.

'Monroe has made many enemies, knowing he cannot be touched he has blown out of all proportion minor misdemeanours, finishing the political careers of many good men and women who dared to stand up to him.'

'The Levy Case,' Logan interrupted him.

'A good man,' Tenant explained, 'Even for a Republican. Lou Levy did nothing more than slightly exaggerate a motor insurance claim after a minor shunt twenty-seven years ago. He caught the eye of the President who liked his energy and enthusiasm but he also made the mistake of crossing Monroe. His career was in ruins. So you've got to understand, Jane, we will now spend as much time as we can talking to as many people as we can. But until we have some firm evidence about Monroe's interference with the course of justice, there's not a lot more we can do.'

'Now what?' Logan said finally.

'We wait,' Tenant insisted. 'For West to come back into this country. Logan can give your friend Lieutenant Carter a call and find out the boat's itinerary to see if it will dock at any friendly ports where the FBI have offices. It's just a matter of time.'

Jane sat back in her chair and eyed the pair of them up. Just one more dig before she let go, she thought. It was Dave

McIntyre she had to trust now. She still hadn't told them about Monroe's past. Why? It was so long ago, what could any of them do any way. Dave was an old friend and a good friend. She would ask his advice first and perhaps tell them tomorrow.

Jane's stomach growled. 'You're right,' she said, jumping to her feet. 'There's nothing more we can do until West gets back in the country. Let's eat.'

CHAPTER SIXTY-SIX

JANE RETURNED to her room at the Jefferson. She hung her jacket on the back of the chair, kicked off her shoes and redialled McIntyre's number on her mobile phone. After a couple of rings, an answerphone kicked in. A polite female voice chirped up.

'You have reached the message bank of Dave McIntyre. Please leave a short message after the beep.'

'Dave, this is Jane. It's eight o'clock Monday evening. It's important you get back to me. I'm in room 509. Speak to you soon.'

She went to the bathroom and turned on the shower. She stood looking at herself in the mirror. Taking out her ear-rings, her thoughts raced.

'That bastard Monroe.' She let Tenant's words about the Congressman wash through her mind. 'After all he's said, all his preaching, he has the dirtiest secret of all. Come on Dave, phone back.'

She caught sight of herself in the mirror. 'Jane Blackburn, you're talking to yourself. That's the first sign of madness.'

Her clothes fell to the bathroom floor. She climbed into the shower, letting the water pound her from all sides. The day's events floated around in her mind but her thoughts kept coming back to Logan, who was working late in his office, ploughing his way through a backlog of case notes. They would meet again tomorrow. She couldn't wait to be with him.

As she stepped out of the shower, the phone rang.

It was Dave. 'Jane, I'm in the middle of a dinner party. I've snuck to the toilet to give you a call...'

Jane interrupted him 'You're in the toilet? What are you doing in there?'

'What do you think I'm doing?'

'Woah, too much information there. Spare me the details.'

'You said it was important. I can give you two minutes.'

'Our congressman has a very nasty secret. Back in 1950, while at Yale University, he was arrested over a possible murder and three rapes. Before any further questioning and before he could be charged, his uncle, the Mayor of New Haven, and his father, the Governor of Connecticut, had the investigation stopped. Seems he just walked away and the policemen who arrested him were ordered to "forget" what they knew.'

'Christ, Jane, how did you find this out? You're going to put me out of a job. So Mr Monroe is not so lily white after all.'

'That's not all,' she said. 'I reckon his grandson, Charles West, is responsible for murdering two girls here in Washington. You know, the date-rape deaths you had in your paper this morning. Given time, I think I can also prove that Monroe has deliberately lied to give his grandson an alibi. You said we were going to meet somebody on Wednesday.'

'Oh, forget that,' McIntyre said. 'This is too big. Meet me at a restaurant called Signatures on Pennsylvania Avenue at 12.30 tomorrow lunchtime. You mustn't be late. Make sure you've got ID on you and dress smartly.'

'What do you mean dress smartly?' Jane asked indignantly. 'I always dress smartly.'

'Jane, I've got to go. I can hear Ellen calling. She'll murder me if she sees me on this phone.'

Still smarting over his order to dress up, Jane said, 'Who are we meeting, Dave? The President?'

'Nearly. Bye sweetheart.'

She could hear Dave chuckling as the phone went dead.

Jane flung open her wardrobe doors. She hadn't packed really smart. She hadn't expected to attend any meetings. Besides smart to Dave was Washington chic, not what passed for chic in Cambridge. She decided to go shopping in the morning. She reached into the mini bar and took out the half bottle of white wine. She poured a glass and, laying on the bed, started re-reading Ed Logan's file. The last four pages were his own conclusions, obviously written days after Monroe's release. She could sense the bitterness hidden between the lines. She knew that gnawing feeling of powerlessness. The glass slipped out of her hand and hit the floor, as the wine and tiredness consumed her.

CHAPTER SIXTY-SEVEN

A FIVE-MILE, early-morning jog cleared Logan's head after his late night in the office. He stood in the shower and let his brain race. There was nothing more Jane or any of them could do until West was back on either American or British soil. He had made up his mind. He was going to spend more time with Jane. He had a couple of weeks vacation coming and they were going to spend it together. They both needed time to get to know each other.

'Yes.' he said, looking in the mirror at a half-shaven face. 'You're going to find out what really makes that woman tick.'

He glanced down at his watch. It was nine thirty already. He called Jane's mobile. It was turned off. Then he tried the hotel.

'Good morning. Jefferson Hotel. How may I help you?' chirped a female voice.

'Put me through to Mrs Blackburn, please. Room 509.'

After several rings, she came back to him and said, 'Sorry sir, there's no reply.'

'Could you put me through to reception?'

'Reception. How can I help you, sir?'

Logan recognised the voice of the smiling young woman he had spoken to on Sunday evening.

'This is Agent Logan here, FBI. I spoke to you the other night.'

'Yes sir, I remember.'

'Mrs Blackburn isn't in her room. Do you know if she's still in the hotel?'

'No sir, she's already left. She came down and had an early

breakfast, asked about hairdressers and where she could buy a smart suit. I told her about a couple of shops just off Vermont Avenue, but she'll be back at the hotel by eleven because she's booked for a hair appointment.'

Logan was worried. What are you up to now Jane? he thought.

As if she'd read his mind, the receptionist said, 'I think she's looking forward to her lunch date, sir.'

Logan was confused. They hadn't made any arrangements. He decided to play along.

'Yes, I'm supposed to be meeting her there. Did she book a car?'

'No, sir. When I explained to her how close Signatures is to the hotel, she said she'd walk.'

He hung up and slumped in his chair. So Jane, what is so important that you're having your hair done, buying clothes and visiting one of Washington's most prestigious restaurants? Christ, even the President is on the waiting list. He took a sip of his coffee. Five days with the woman and he knew nothing about her. All he'd done to help her and she's still keeping secrets. Why didn't she trust him? It was time to find out, and besides, Logan rather fancied an expensive lunch on the Bureau.

*

Dave McIntyre had arrived early at his office. His news editors had brought him up-to-date with the top stories that had broken overnight. He'd heard them all on TV and radio before he left home. There were a couple of exclusives brewing but nothing that would compare to what he'd heard last night. It was too soon to tell anyone but when the Post did break the story it would be top of everyone's news list in the USA, let alone DC.

He asked his PA to get Sara Barry's office.

A couple of minutes later he was speaking to her.

'This is very pleasant, Dave, but we'll be seeing you in three hours. Can't it wait?'

'I know, but I'd like to add a name to the list for today's lunch. Jane Blackburn.'

'You newsmen are always leaving it to the eleventh hour. The rest of us do work on a schedule, you know. Can you vouch for her?' Sara sighed.

'Yes. I've known her for over ten years. She's an English policewoman.'

'Okay, I'll add her to the list. There isn't time for the usual checks so she'll need to take ID, but if they'll let you through Dave, they'll let anyone in.'

'Sarcasm is the lowest form of wit,' McIntyre laughed, pleased that he had got his own way yet again.

CHAPTER SIXTY-EIGHT

TWELVE TEN PM. Jane looked at her watch yet again. Time dragged. She had a final check in the mirror. She was wearing the sage green suit with an A-line skirt and a short-cut jacket that she had bought in Vermont Avenue. She wore a soft cream silk blouse underneath. With all that had happened over the last two months, Jane had lost weight. She'd applied just enough make-up without overdoing it. She slipped on her new Jimmy Choo shoes and added the finishing touch, a pair of single pearl ear-rings. She was quite satisfied with the results.

'So Dave McIntyre, is that smart enough for you?'

She placed Ed's faded blue file in a small black attache case, which she had managed to find in the hotel boutique, along with her English police warrant card, passport and driver's licence. She took another glance at her watch and left.

As she walked out into 16th Street the doorman stepped out to hail her a cab.

Jane stopped him. 'No, thank you. Can you tell me where I'll find Signatures restaurant?'

'Down 17th Street and along Pennsylvania Avenue.'

*

Logan palmed his badge at the Secret Servicemen standing at the entrance to the restaurant. One of them spoke through a headphone mic to supervisors in a van in a nearby side street.

'I've got an FBI man here who says he's here to meet a lady called Blackburn. She's on my list but he isn't.'

Logan waited uncomfortably. Eventually, the security man handed his badge back and waved him through.

The maitre d' approached.

'Can I help you, sir?' he asked.

'I'm early. The people I'm having lunch with haven't arrived yet. I'll just wait at the bar,' Logan said. Without waiting for a reply, he walked over to the bar, positioned the stool to get the clearest view of the room, and waited.

*

McIntyre arrived just before twelve thirty. Security knew him and he recognised their faces. As he entered the restaurant, he caught the maitre d's eye. The two men were the same height, but Dave had kept trim and fit while the maitre d' had obviously indulged in some of his chef's finest cooking.

Dave held out his hand. 'Bill. How are you?' he said warmly.

'It's good to see you Mr McIntyre. How's your beautiful wife?'

'You'll see her in a week. I had to bribe her with a romantic dinner for two because she's not here for today's lunch. How are the preparations going?'

'Well, Sara has already checked over the room.'

'I'm waiting for a lady to arrive, Jane Blackburn. Is she here yet?'

The maitre d' checked his list. 'Not to my knowledge sir, but as soon as she comes in I'll show her to your table.'

*

Signatures is on the ground floor of a smart Fifties-style stone building, dark green shades overhang the entrance. Jane looked down at a map of the world engraved into the pavement as a woman security officer ran a portable scanner over her. One of the two security men blocking the door handed back her police badge.

'So, Detective Inspector Jane Blackburn,' he said, in a very poor imitation of an English accent, 'what is a British police officer doing in Washington DC?'

Jane decided against a flippant remark. Humour had obviously by-passed these two.

Instead she said, 'I'm here to meet Dave McIntyre, Editor of the Washington Post.'

The other service agent checked her off the list and let her pass.

As she stepped inside the air-conditioned cool of the restaurant, she scanned the room. It was busy, half the tables filled with businessmen in smart suits, all seemingly immersed in the importance in their own discussions. A well-groomed woman, about 5'1", with manicured nails, approached. Her badge said she was Amanda, the reservations manager.

'My name is Jane Blackburn. I'm here to see Mr McIntyre.'

'Mr McIntyre has already arrived ma'am. If you'll just follow me.'

The restaurant was on two levels. The large L-shaped bar ran along the lower level on her right, down a couple of steps. On the pale blue and yellow walls hung framed signatures and memorabilia belonging to the rich and famous. They were all for sale. She noticed a poem written by the painter Van Gogh for fifty-nine-and-a-half thousand dollars. A signed photograph of Charles and Diana on a formal state visit was a mere three-and-a-half thousand dollars.

As Jane followed Amanda across the dark blue patterned carpet, she passed a large glass cabinet containing a rocking chair. One of twelve chairs specially made for John F Kennedy to help ease his bad back. A snip at half a million dollars.

Dave was sitting at a table at the far end of the room. He rose from his chair and they greeted each other fondly.

'I could do with a rocking chair. Now that I'm an accredited journalist, can I add this to my expense account?' Jane joked.

'Even I wouldn't sign that expenses sheet.'

'So, smart enough for you?' Jane teased as she sat back and relaxed in the cool air-conditioning. She smiled and warmed at the compliment Dave passed but it was Logan she could feel. Good grief, girl, she thought, you really have let that man get right under your skin.

Tucked out of the way by the bar, Logan had noticed Jane as she entered the restaurant. He'd watched her walk across the room where she greeted Dave McIntyre warmly, too warmly. He ran his eye the full length of her body. She was dressed to perfection, not a hair out of place. She easily fitted in with the restaurant clientele in a way he didn't. He was sure she hadn't noticed him.

Jane turned to Dave, 'I know security in Washington has been tight since September 11th, but you didn't tell me that I'd be frisked at door of the restaurant by Washington's answer to the Gestapo. So, who are we here to meet?'

'Did you remember to bring the file?' he asked, evading her question.

'Yes, but you still haven't told me who we're here to meet. Is he important?'

Dave was quiet while a waiter placed a glass of white wine in front of Jane.

'Yes, so important that she warrants all this security.'

'So who is she?'

Dave smiled. 'She sleeps with the President.'

CHAPTER SIXTY-NINE

THE ROOM fell silent. Jane was stunned and before she could recover her composure, Dave rose to his feet. He walked over to the restaurant entrance to meet a striking blonde. She was beautifully groomed, wore a pale blue shift dress with a matching jacket and carried a small cornflower blue handbag. The First Lady of America had the attention of every pair of eyes in the room.

His greeting was a little more formal than he'd been with Jane, 'Forgive me ma'am, I've delayed lunch for five minutes. There's somebody I'd like you to meet.'

'This must be important to you, Dave. I already owe you so much for your valuable help with my War On Want project, I can't possibly refuse,' she smiled.

Her bodyguard warned her that this extra meeting was not on the itinerary. She reminded him that the whole restaurant had been checked and double-checked and it would be fine. Jane watched as Dave guided the First Lady to their table. She walked across the room with the poise and elegance of Grace Kelly. She was one of the most photographed and written about public figures in the world. Confidence oozed from every well-toned muscle in her body. She was an ex-attorney although, unlike Hillary Clinton before her, she had a more traditional approach to the role of First Lady.

Jane rose from her chair as they approached.

Dave spoke first, 'Jane, I'd like to introduce you to Mrs Elizabeth Dacre, the First Lady. Ma'am, this is Detective

Inspector Jane Blackburn.'

They shook hands but Jane was almost speechless. 'Ma'am, I..' she stumbled. The First Lady could sense her awkwardness.

'Please, call me Elizabeth,' she said. 'Should we sit down?'

The maitre d' hovered and enquired if the President's wife would like a drink.

'No thank you, Bill. I'll wait until lunch. Could you please give us a couple of minutes?'

'Yes, ma'am.'

Jane's composure and confidence returned slowly. She noticed how the First Lady seemed almost oblivious to the rest of the room. The businessmen resumed their conversations and the hum of the restaurant returned.

Elizabeth Dacre was a natural at putting people at their ease.

'So, Jane, how is it you know a scoundrel like Dave?' she asked.

Jane smiled and shot a glance at McIntyre. 'I've heard Dave called a lot of things, some extremely nasty, but "scoundrel" is definitely a new one.'

The Post Editor came to the point. 'Jane has been working on a case which I think would interest you greatly. It concerns an old friend of ours.'

'Oh, really? Who's that?'

'Congressman Monroe.'

The smile disappeared from the First Lady's face.

Jane took a sip from her glass. Something had obviously passed between Elizabeth and Dave. There was sarcasm in Dave's voice but she knew she didn't have time to find out why. She took a deep breath and started to tell Elizabeth her story. She explained how Charles West had been arrested in Cambridge for the rape of Hayley Bannerman and how they'd discovered the link to Jennifer Clarke's death. DNA samples and the way West had interfered with a witness should have guaranteed he stayed on remand until trial.

Elizabeth interrupted, 'How does this relate to Monroe?'

'Congressman Monroe is his grandfather. Charles West is being touted by Monroe as a future Presidential candidate. I'm convinced Monroe put in a call to the Lord Chancellor's Office in London, who in turn had a quiet word with the judge in the West case, and had his grandson released on bail. Within twenty-four hours of his release he was back here. I decided to take a short break after the death of my partner to find out more about West's family.'

'I saw a police funeral on CNN,' the First Lady said.

'Yes. We were on a different investigation. The death of a young man on a ship. We didn't realise at the time there were a couple of undercover FBI agents on board.'

Elizabeth looked surprised. 'The FBI killed the boy?'

'No. They'd infiltrated a drug trafficking cartel. The drug runners killed the boy and shot my sergeant, Steve Cheney. The FBI agents managed to rescue me. Their names are Logan and Newman.'

Jane pressed on. 'Yesterday I read a small article in the Washington Post about the deaths of two women. They'd both been given the same date-rape drug that was used on the girls in England. I'm sure Monroe's grandson is the killer. He has got progressively worse. When he was at Yale there were allegations of sexual assault. He first made the date-rape drug at Yale. All the time his father and grandfather have been hiding and covering up what he did. I believe killing is the only thing that gives him a sense of power over his grandfather.

'Then I discovered that history was repeating itself. I was asked to go to Logan's father's eightieth birthday party. His father gave me a present.'

Jane leaned down and removed the blue file from her case and placed it on the small table.

'Logan's father, Ed, had been a policeman back in Yale in 1950, when Congressman Monroe was a student.'

Jane now had Elizabeth's undivided attention.

'Ed was part of a team investigating the murder and the rape of three girls. They connected the crimes to Monroe. They arrested him but before they could question him, in rolled his father, who was the Governor of Connecticut, and his uncle who was the Mayor of New Haven. All charges were dropped. Ed was ordered to "lose" the file.'

'But he kept it,' finished Elizabeth, desperately trying to take in the enormity of what Jane was telling her. Here was Charles Monroe, Chairman of the Committee on Standards of Official Conduct, a killer pulling strings like the grandest of puppeteers to keep his own grandson one step ahead of the law.

'I don't understand why you've both brought this to me,' the First Lady said, finally.

'I couldn't think of anyone in a better position to bring this to the President's attention,' Dave said.

Elizabeth looked at Dave and then back at Jane, her tone slightly changed.

'I'm sorry, Jane, but I'm not a political wife. I have made it a personal policy not to interfere in politics.'

Elizabeth watched the fight slowly drain out of Jane. This English policewoman obviously felt passionately about the case. She had risked so much to bring it to her attention. But if Monroe was a killer, it was so long ago, how could anyone prove it. Where was the proof that the Congressman had pulled strings to get his grandson flown out of the United Kingdom. Those beautiful brown eyes have obviously seen so much pain, Elizabeth thought. Studying her face, she saw a smart lady, tough, too. She admired that.

Jane stared into her wine glass lost in her thoughts. Her case had gone all the way to the White House and she was still getting nowhere.

Elizabeth broke the silence, 'You must have got to know Logan well if you ended up meeting his family.'

'Yes,' said Jane, breaking from her brooding. 'We became good friends when we were waiting to be rescued in the Atlantic off Ireland.'

Elizabeth looked at Jane, her eyes wide open in amazement.

'I was eventually discovered on the ship. The two FBI men, Logan and his partner Scott Newman, were nearly killed because they had saved my life. The drug gang tied them up and pushed them off the ship to drown. I jumped in to help them.'

'You jumped off a ship?' the First Lady exclaimed. McIntyre could feel another scoop coming.

'It wasn't a difficult choice to make. If I'd stayed on the ship, they would have killed me, Logan and Newman would have drowned.'

'So how long did you spend in the water?'

'Several hours. We were taken back to a Marine base at Shannon in the Irish Republic...' Jane went quiet. She was lost in her thoughts again. It was all in vain. She needn't have bothered. What was the point of carrying on? Most of this happened in the UK, why should she help? Logan, please come and hold me.

'Jane?' Dave said, but she didn't answer.

Elizabeth raised her hand to stop him interrupting and leaned forward in her seat. In a low whisper she asked, 'Was he good?'

Jane flushed and looked straight into the First Lady's cool blue eyes. This woman was obviously extremely bright and very intuitive, she thought.

'Breathtaking. Absolutely breathtaking,' Jane whispered, forgetting she was speaking to the wife of the most powerful man in the world.

Elizabeth's smile broadened as Jane continued conspiratorially, 'You should try one. Secret Service, CIA, FBI, you're surrounded by an alphabet soup of potential candidates.'

Elizabeth gave a mock shocked expression. The two women laughed.

'Where do you think I should start?'

'That's easy,' said Jane. 'Sitting three tables to my left are a group of men who don't particularly fit the political scene. Look over my right shoulder. The one with the mop of dark hair and opal green eyes.'

Both women turned to face him.

'Very nice,' the First Lady murmured. The man with green eyes, who looked up under their gaze and flashed them a devilish grin. They both instantly turned away, grinning and enjoying the joke.

'How could you resist that?' said Jane. 'Do you know him?'

Elizabeth replied, 'Oh yes, that's...'

McIntyre interrupted. 'Monroe!' he said in a loud whisper.

'It can't be,' said Jane. 'He's too young. I've seen a photo of him...' She never finished her sentence.

'No. Coming through the door!'

CHAPTER SEVENTY

CHARLES MONROE worked the restaurant with a perfection that comes from four decades of schmoozing his way to the top. Knowing Elizabeth Dacre would be there, he had deliberately arranged a lunch meeting in this restaurant to impress his three companions. Supremely confident and relaxed, he shared a joke with the maitre d' then made his way over to the First Lady, leaving his lunch guests at the bar. On the way, he pressed the flesh, a smile here, a pat on the back there. At seventy-two years old he still stood six feet one. A fine head of white hair framed a face deeply tanned from weekends at the family holiday home in the Hamptons, winter breaks in Aspen and the Bahamas. He was wearing a three thousand dollar suit of the finest lightweight Yorkshire worsted. As he approached, McIntyre bent down, picked up Jane's attache case and placed it on the table on top of the blue folder. Jane was transfixed by him. Elizabeth tried to hold Jane's gaze but her vision was tunnelled. She saw nothing but Monroe.

The Congressman greeted the First Lady, 'You're looking as elegant as ever today, ma'am,' he said holding out a tanned hand, which revealed a diamond-encrusted cufflink.

Elizabeth smiled, 'As charming as ever, Congressman Monroe.'

'Meeting with editors,' he said looking at McIntyre, 'Which worthy charity needs publicity this time ma'am?' His patronising tone did not go unnoticed.

'Occasionally one has to climb into the lions' den. Of course, you know Dave McIntyre of The Post.'

The two men greeted each other and shook hands. It was clear there was no love lost between them.

'I'd like you to meet, Jane, a friend of mine. I'm helping her and Mr McIntyre out with a small problem.'

Monroe shook Jane's hand briefly and dismissively, not even making eye contact. Men like Monroe had very simple criteria for judging people. You were either useful to them or not useful, and Jane was immediately placed in the "not useful" category.

He turned to Elizabeth, 'A small problem ma'am? I flatter myself that I have a little influence around here. Perhaps I can help you out?'

Jane could not believe what Elizabeth was doing. Surely after all his family's victims had been through, she was not going to help him.

'Please take a seat, Congressman, we would very much appreciate your input,' the First Lady said.

Monroe's vanity made him pull up a chair. Elizabeth moved forward in her seat. She locked him with her blue eyes. Like everyone who looked into them, Monroe felt he was the only person in the room.

'You know I don't like to interfere in politics, Charles. You don't mind if I call you Charles do you? But it appears that we may have a scandal on our hands.'

'Would it affect the President, ma'am?' Monroe enquired.

'Yes, I'm afraid so.'

'Then I'm assuming the person involved holds high office in the administration.'

'Correct.'

'Is he a member of the Senate or the House of Representatives?'

'The House of Reps.' Jane watched Elizabeth fly-fishing, gently teasing out her line to attract and draw in her victim. It slowly dawned on her just what Elizabeth was up to.

'The reason I don't want to interfere, Charles, is that I know that disclosure would upset this man's whole family and, like any scandal, will damage the presidency.'

'As you know ma'am, I'm Chairman of the Committee on Standards of Official Conduct and I like to run a clean ship. If this person's behaviour will reflect badly on the presidency or Congress, then he should be brought before the Committee. I'm assuming here, ma'am, that it's a male?'

'Yes.'

Monroe took his eyes away from the First Lady and glanced at McIntyre.

'What have you dug up this time, McIntyre? How much do the Press already know of this potential scandal?'

'Is there something I should know, Congressman Monroe?' McIntyre asked, staring straight at him.

'Is there anything that goes on in this city you don't know about?' Monroe asked accusingly.

Dave's poker face gave nothing away, 'There are still skeletons that even I can't find.'

'Charles,' Elizabeth continued. 'I've discovered that this man is abusing his position by interfering in other government departments, possibly even using blackmail to achieve his aims. I do hope blackmail isn't too strong a term.'

'I'm afraid that hardly narrows the field ma'am,' Monroe said.

'Not everyone abuses their power to this extreme, Charles. The first was an abuse of power, the second an abuse of trust of his office. But of course, Charles, one of these felonies did happen quite some time ago.'

Monroe didn't flinch, 'My advice is still the same, ma'am.'

Elizabeth interrupted, 'Are you sure, Charles? He was a very young man when his...'

But Monroe persisted, 'At the very least he should be brought before Congress to answer for his actions. However, a little more information would help me to point you in the right way to proceed with your problem. A name perhaps?'

Jane's eyes flicked between Monroe and Elizabeth. She hardly dared breathe as the First Lady reached forward and pulled the blue file out from underneath the briefcase.

'In 1950, the Governor of Connecticut and the Mayor of New Haven squashed an investigation into the rape and murder of one girl and the rape of two other young girls, devastating the lives of three families.'

CHAPTER SEVENTY-ONE

ELIZABETH DACRE'S legally-trained mind was a like a rapier. The colour drained from Monroe's face as the reality of what he had said dawned on him. In his arrogance to play games with the First Lady he had condemned himself over and again. His breathing was shallow as he desperately fought to regain his composure.

His eyes fixed on Elizabeth, he said, 'This supposed incident happened over fifty years ago. There's no proof.'

The rapier made another cut, 'I find it interesting that you claim there is no proof rather than denying your involvement. But of course it didn't stop there, did it? You went on to interfere in your own grandson's life, sending him to England after covering up his crimes at Yale. Then after his arrest in Cambridge, you abused your power to get the boy back to the United States so he would not stand trial. It will not take long to establish the lengths to which you've interfered with the investigation into your grandson's actions.'

The First Lady continued, her eyes boring into Monroe, 'You probably thought you had nicely taken care of "the problem" until the deaths of the two young women in Washington. Just yesterday as the police were about to arrest your grandson for questioning regarding the deaths of those two girls, you interfered again. Your grandson disappeared to escape justice. Who fed you the information this time?'

Jane knew the answer, but remained silent as Elizabeth continued, 'If your family had not interfered with justice in

1950, three families in England would not now be going through hell. You are absolutely right, Congressman Monroe. The whole matter should be brought before Congress and, of course, I will fully brief the President.'

Monroe turned to McIntyre, anger welling inside him, His fists clenched as he stared, intense hatred etched in his face.

'You can't prove anything,' he spat at McIntyre.

Elizabeth placed the blue Connecticut Police Department folder in front of Monroe so he could clearly see his name on the cover.

'You don't understand, Monroe. It wasn't Dave who brought this to my attention. It was Jane. I apologise for not giving you her full title. This is Detective Inspector Jane Blackburn of the Cambridge Police, England.'

Monroe looked at Jane. He was in shock. This little person, this nothing, this powerless little minnow was to blame. He slowly rose to his feet. So did Logan, still at the bar and watching the whole episode, although he couldn't hear what was being said.

Jane didn't move.

'Why?' Monroe pleaded.

'Spare me from your own pity, Monroe. I was the one who had to look into the haunted eyes of Claire Reece and Hayley Bannerman, the girls your grandson raped. I was the one who held Jennifer Clarke's mother when they turned off her daughter's life-support machine. I was the one who listened to Officer Logan, now retired. He was one of the officers who arrested you that night and was ordered to drop the case for the sake of his family.'

Jane could see Monroe's face desperately searching his memory. Like a cornered animal, he had one last bite.

'You have no proof he killed anyone here in Washington. If Charles gets back in this country, I'll hire the best lawyers in the land to defend him. You will never win.'

'You couldn't be further from the truth,' Jane said. 'You know that while in England I took a DNA sample from your grandson, that's why you got him out of the country. The results of that same sample are now with Lieutenant Carter of Washington Second District being matched to the two DNA samples taken from the dead women here.'

'Evidence you cannot use in this country, you stupid woman.'

McIntyre leapt to Jane's defence. 'Wrong. When you sit on your powerful committees, Monroe, you should pay more attention. You were the chair of a steering committee six years ago which ironed out some of the inconsistencies between the US and UK judicial systems. The most important of these allowed forensic evidence collected in one country to be admissible in court in the other.'

'But,' Jane continued, staggered at McIntyre's revelation, 'The real irony of this whole thing is that your grandson is as much of a victim here as these women. Any criminal profiler will tell you that he deliberately and progressively got worse to get away from the relentless pressure you and your family have placed on him. A pressure which manifested itself in these appalling attacks, a pressure you knew all too well back in 1950. You must have realised what was happening but your blind ambition pushed him harder and ever harder.'

Elizabeth now watched Jane. She was good, keeping her intense anger under control.

Monroe, his face flushed, looked at Jane, 'Your accusations against me are unsubstantiated. You have no witness to prove that I interfered with natural justice.'

Jane had the rapier now and struck the final blow.

'I have a witness. Your grandson. When he realises that you can no longer harm him, you can no longer torture him, he will talk and condemn you for what you have done.'

The Congressman buckled like a fighter on the ropes, staring at defeat. He put his hands on the table to steady himself. He suddenly looked old.

'What are my options?' he asked Elizabeth.

'None.'

Monroe didn't look back as he walked away. He didn't look at his companions, stop and smile or make a joke. Jane watched as the weight she had lifted from Ed Logan's shoulders now rested on Monroe. He headed straight for the door.

Elizabeth broke the silence, 'You're a remarkable woman, Jane Blackburn. It is rare to find someone still prepared to get to the truth, regardless of the consequences.'

She gave the First Lady an irreverent grin. Elizabeth rose to her feet, 'I do hope we meet again, Jane. I would love to have a drink with you in a bar some time.'

Jane laughed and as she stood up, said, 'Yeah, just you, me and the thirty secret servicemen!'

Elizabeth turned to McIntyre, 'Dave, I believe we have a lunch to attend.'

The First Lady shook Jane's hand warmly then picked up the blue folder, 'I'll take this file and make sure it gets into the right hands. I would like to have met your FBI man, Logan.'

Jane smiled and turned toward the bar. She quickly found him. 'Look over there, the man at the end of the bar in the suit that's not expensive enough for this place.'

Elizabeth smiled at Logan and looked back at Jane. Logan felt distinctly uncomfortable as he sat under the gaze of the two women.

'You know,' said Elizabeth. 'I could get used to this.'

'Behave,' Jane told her. 'The White House couldn't cope with any more scandals.'

Elizabeth laughed.

Dave leaned over and hugged Jane, kissing her on the cheek.

'Well, you've won again,' he whispered.

'A hollow victory,' Jane sighed. 'We have to get West back first.'

Jane remained standing as Dave and Elizabeth left for their delayed lunch in the private dining room.

As she slumped back down in her seat, a blond-haired waiter appeared at the table.

'Another drink, ma'am?'

'Yes, thank you. I'd like another white wine and a Budweiser.'

She could barely believe what had just happened in such a short space of time, but it had seemed like hours. She had done everything she could and it was out of her hands now. All that fighting, all the frustration. She felt a sudden and overwhelming sense of release. Rest easy, Steve. We've got him, she thought. She also knew that once the Home Office got to hear of her interference, it would probably mean the end of her career at home. Either way, she had stepped on too many toes and could kiss goodbye to any hope of advancement, or perhaps even survival in the Cambridgeshire force.

Pursuing the truth had cost her everything.

CHAPTER SEVENTY-TWO

LOGAN JOINED Jane at the table. They were both silent, looking at each other as the waiter placed the drinks down. She stared intensely into his eyes. She almost felt light-headed.

'Are you going to tell me what's just happened? I don't understand,' Logan said.

'The FBI haven't understood what's gone on since I got off the plane at Dulles.'

'You didn't tell me you were coming here today.'

'I didn't need to. You followed me here anyway.'

'So, are you going to tell me what you're doing here?'

'One day, Logan. Just not today, not now.'

'You didn't tell me you were going to meet an old boyfriend. Why did you lie?'

'Why did I lie? That's rich coming from you. You and your men have been following me since I got off the plane and you accuse me of lying. You even put cameras in my room. You almost had me worried when you didn't stay on Friday night until I realised it was because of the cameras.' She paused, 'It was because of the cameras, wasn't it?'

Logan was momentarily floored. She knew. She'd known about the cameras all along. She was better than any of them had expected. Suddenly he broke into a big, broad smile.

'Performance anxiety,' he said with a laugh.

At last Jane relaxed. She told him the only part of the story that she hadn't admitted to him, his father's involvement in the case and the blue folder. Logan was past the point of knowing

314

what to think any more. She relented and told him how the First Lady had broken Monroe.

Logan let out a long sigh. 'Darling, you're nothing short of amazing,' he said. 'So, you've had drinks with the First Lady and ruined the career of a congressman. What have you got planned for the afternoon, I mean, in between the international peace talks?'

A suggestive grin appeared across her face.

He smiled, 'And after that?'

'After that, we're going to take a holiday. Denver I think,' Jane said.

'We?'

'You're still officially babysitting, aren't you?'

'Why Denver?'

'There's a man there with a private classic car collection I wouldn't mind seeing.'

'You can't just arrive there and expect this guy to greet you with open arms. How do you know he'll even let you see his cars?'

'Because, darling,' she said. That beautiful little grin was on her face again. God he loved those liquid brown eyes. 'Classic car collectors,' she continued, 'love nothing more than the chance to talk about their cars. Besides, anyone who can tell the First Lady of America that one of the country's best FBI agents is breathtaking in bed could pretty much talk her way into any situation.'

She watched his face as what she had just said sank in.

'You did what…?' but Jane was already walking towards the door.

EPILOGUE

A PORTABLE television played quietly in the kitchen. Ed Logan was preparing his evening meal as CNN broke in with a news flash from Jonathan Gale, their political correspondent at the White House.

'It has just been announced that Congressman Charles Monroe has stepped down from office...'

Ed turned, giving the television his full attention.

'...due to health problems. No further information is being released at this time. The President has been quoted as saying that Congressman Monroe's integrity will be a great loss to the House of Representatives. His long and distinguished career...'

The old man reached forward and turned off the TV.

*

Iain Robertson, Master of the *Star Supreme*, did a deal with the DEA which secured the convictions of the entire syndicate. He is now living in retirement in the Western Isles of Scotland. Having been found guilty in the USA of drug running, the four Italians are currently fighting extradition to the UK where they will stand trail for the murders of Detective Sergeant Steve Cheney and William Davies.

On June 16, Charles West pleaded guilty to murder. He is serving two life sentences. He is currently helping Cambridgeshire police with their investigations over the date rapes of three more victims...

The next day Superintendent Douglas Benson took a call from FBI Head of Operations, Senior Special Agent Chris Tenant.

'Mr Tenant,' said Benson, 'I'm sure you've already received my letter of apology over the unauthorised actions of Detective Inspector Blackburn. If there's anything else I can add...'

Tenant interrupted, 'I'm sorry Superintendent, you've quite clearly misunderstood the reason I'm phoning. This is a curtesy call to inform you I have put in a request to have Mrs Blackburn remain with us on a six-month attachment to the FBI. She was under the impression you wouldn't object. How did she put it, sort of getting the problem out of your hair.'

The line went silent.

'Are you still there Superintendent?'

'Yes, er... of course there are no objections. Anything to further the good relations between our two organisations.'

'Excellently put, Superintendent. Have a nice day.'

The line went dead.

Kenton Publishing hopes you have enjoyed
UNNATURAL JUSTICE,
and invites you to sample Su Ridley's
second DI Blackburn story,
ABSOLUTE JUSTICE,
due out in Autumn 2004.

ABSOLUTE JUSTICE

By Su Ridley

KENTON PUBLISHING

*Absolute justice is achieved
by the suppression of all contradiction:
therefore it destroys freedom.*

Albert Camus

PROLOGUE

Baltimore, Maryland, USA, October 1982

'I'M SORRY I haven't been to see you for over three months, Mama, but I've used the time well. I've found out his darkest secret. He is not the good man you thought, Mama.

'After all he said to us, after all his preaching, it's his fault you are here. Now I will get my revenge for all he has done to us. We were told so often in the past to just accept our lives. I know you're going to object but I have to do this, Mama, I will make him pay.'

The girl went to brush the hair out of her eyes but she had forgotten her recent trip to the hairdressers. It was now short, very short. She giggled, 'What do you think of my new hair style? You never say. I can see your eyes scolding me now that my lovely long brown hair has gone. Do you remember the countless hours you used to sit and brush it and tell me one day everything will be all right?

'I've waited a long time. At first I thought nobody would listen to me. I'm just poor little Sophie. That sweet little kid, isn't it a shame? I can hear them whispering it Mama, all day, every day.'

She could feel the warmth of her mother's smile, her tender touch, her loving embrace. She was the only person ever to show any affection towards the girl.

'Hold me now, Mama.'

She felt her breath on her neck.

'Hold me tighter, Mama.'

At last she said, 'I have to go now, Mama. I have to prepare for my new job. I was so scared when I first walked in. They said I looked too young but I have the right qualifications, so I start on Monday. You'd have been so proud of me, Mama, We'll be together again, I promise you. But first I have to do this. I have to make him see what pain really means.'

Nobody saw the girl looking down on her mother's grave, so beautifully kept, so neatly trimmed.

Expensive yellow roses lay next to her name. The girl took a clean handkerchief from her jacket pocket and wiped away the think blanket of snow partially covering the low stone plaque.

She bent over, gently kissed the brass nameplate and walked away for ever.

CHAPTER ONE

Monday October 6

THE GIRL was awake. She didn't know how long she had slept. Her throat was sore, her fists ached. Her normally well-manicured hands were bruised black. It came back to her. She had screamed until her voice gave out and no sound would come. Nobody had heard her.

She sat up on the makeshift bed and slowly looked around the room. It was no more than fifteen feet long and six feet wide. Aluminium bars, a foot apart, ran from floor to ceiling along one wall. A foul-smelling container in the far corner was obviously some kind of chemical toilet. Bottles of water were stacked in a line along the wall and a cardboard box in the corner by the door had been filled with canned food and packets of biscuits. Another two boxes were stuffed to overflowing with cheap paperback novels.

A forty-watt bulb glowed dimly behind a wire cage in the roof. She could hear the gentle hum of some kind of machine.

Her mind raced. Why me? She tried desperately hard to remember the first time she'd seen the woman. She looked odd, creepy. She had come straight up to her outside the red-brick entrance to the College of Notre Dame of Maryland. It was like she knew her, but didn't.

It wasn't until the woman called her name that she had realised who she was.

She remembered the shock. Thinking, what do I do?

The woman had taken her quite firmly by the arm and told

her, 'Come with me.'

She'd put up no protest. She hadn't even asked her where they were going.

Alysia had known this woman for most of her life. She had even given her birthday presents. The girl was still wearing the locket around her neck the woman had given her for her 20th birthday.

So why was she now doing this? Why did she look so different?

Alysia stared down at the piece of A4 paper the woman had given her. She hadn't read it until now. In her panic, she'd thrown it on the bed and started hammering and hollering.

Printed on it was a list of instructions. Tears welled as she read them:

*The light will stay on twenty-four hours a day.

*The container in the corner is your john.

*There is enough food and water to last one month. Don't pig out.

*Use the time to read. Enjoy your stay!

Why was the sick cow doing this to her? She remembered how when they got into the car that was when she first saw the gun. She wasn't to scream. She wasn't to do anything stupid. Just sit there. She recalled thinking, 'If I do as I'm told, she'll let me go'.

Now, here she was. She cursed herself for not shouting, not kicking, not screaming. She had lost track of time. She reached for one of the bottles of water. Cookies. She never ate cookies.

She always had to think of her figure. Her 21st birthday was soon. Mom and Dad were throwing a party for her. She remembered the soft-peach gown her mother had commissioned for her, no expense had been spared on the hand-made shoes and the beautiful dress. If she ate the food she'd been left, she would gain 15lbs and would never get to wear her beautiful dress.

Tears trickled down her cheeks. As she wiped the tears away, she could see her parents. She loved them so much. They would be out of their minds with worry. She would never start a row with them again. She'd never be headstrong again, if God would only let her hold them once more.

She said a prayer, 'Please God, let me see them again. I will never miss another confession. I will never miss another Mass. I will be the dutiful daughter you want me to be. Just let me see them again.'

The girl curled herself up in a tight ball and sobbed herself to sleep.

CHAPTER TWO

Monday October 26
The White House, Washington D.C.

THE TWO women greeted each other warmly.

'There's still no news, Lizzy. I think my heart is going to break,' the dark-haired one said, worry lines etched in her face.

They sat on a sofa upholstered in sapphire silk with a golden eagle motif on the back. Elizabeth Dacre was the First Lady of the United States but had never felt so powerless.

Her friend Rachel Hughes was living every parent's worst nightmare; the abduction of the most precious thing in her life. Her beautiful daughter. The women, who held hands in the Blue Room of the White House and looked out towards the flood-lit Washington Memorial, had been close since their college days. They had graduated together, gone into the law together, attended each other's weddings. Elizabeth was even Godmother to Rachel's missing daughter, Alysia.

The two women had such a strong relationship. They had been there for each other through everything life had thrown at them. It was Rachel who had held Elizabeth together through the long campaign running up to her husband's Presidency. Now it was her turn to be strong for her friend.

'It's the not knowing, Lizzy. We're being told so little. She's been gone three weeks.'

'I'm sure the FBI are telling you everything they know,' Elizabeth said softly looking into her friend's haunted eyes.

Life was being sucked slowly and painfully out of this

vibrant, witty, charming woman.

'There's nothing we can do, Lizzy. That's the hardest part. There are so many people working to find her and there's nothing any of them can do. All I have in my mind is every word of the kidnapper's note. She will die on her 21st birthday,' Rachel sobbed. 'That's this Sunday, Lizzy.'

Elizabeth wrapped her arms around Rachel and held her tightly. She could feel the angular bones under her blouse. She hadn't eaten or slept properly since Alysia disappeared. 'I know, darling. I know it's Alysia's birthday on Sunday.'

'They've got so many people working on this, we've talked to criminal psychologists, profilers...Nobody seems to get to the truth about why she has been kidnapped, why they want to kill her.'

Elizabeth gently pushed her friend away, and mopped her wet hair off Rachel's face. The First Lady's cool blue eyes lingered on her friend's tormented features.

At last she said, 'There's somebody I want you to meet, Rachel. Jane Blackburn can get to the truth. I want you to talk to her.'

Look out for details of the launch of

ABSOLUTE JUSTICE
on Su Ridley's website

www.suridley.com